Kate tuc

"Those were some dandy fish you caught," she said, planting a kiss on his head.

"Yeah." Tommy's eyelids drooped. "But two of 'em were Jason's. He's real cool."

"He sure is, kiddo."

"Are you going to marry him, Mom?"

Already at the door, Kate turned, shocked by Tommy's question. "It's not likely, Tommy. Why?"

"I just think he'd make a rad dad."

"Well, he makes a rad friend, too, doesn't he?"

"Yeah, but dad would be better. 'Night, Mom."

"Good night, Tommy." Kate closed Tommy's door behind her. *Rad dad.* The rhyming words rang in her head. Rad husband didn't have quite the same flair, but still, it had a certain charm....

ABOUT THE AUTHOR

"When I write, I always start with my characters' faults," says Casey Roberts.

"With Jason, the hero of *Walking on Air,* this was easy. I wanted to give this story a mythic, fairy-tale quality. *Beauty and the Beast* is the story I had in mind. Jason isn't an actual beast, of course, but he carries a beast inside himself that my heroine, Kate, has to bring out and chase away.

"Kate was easy to write, too, because she's a little like me. Her fault is that she wants to make people happy. That's good, of course, but Kate carries it so far that she forgets who she is and what she needs for herself."

Newly remarried, Casey makes her home in Scottsdale, Arizona. She has two grown children and three grandchildren, one of whom she used as the model for Kate's son, Tommy, in *Walking on Air.*

Books by Casey Roberts

HARLEQUIN SUPERROMANCE
429—HOMECOMING

Walking on Air

CASEY ROBERTS

Harlequin Books

TORONTO • NEW YORK • LONDON
AMSTERDAM • PARIS • SYDNEY • HAMBURG
STOCKHOLM • ATHENS • TOKYO • MILAN
MADRID • WARSAW • BUDAPEST • AUCKLAND

Published March 1992

ISBN 0-373-70493-3

WALKING ON AIR

To Bryan who,
in many ways,
is much like Tommy.
They both love baseball
and video games.

CHAPTER ONE

IT WASN'T as if he had never done this before.

The last time, over fifty pairs of eyes had stared at him this way, glassy-eyed, struggling to hide that combination of fear and hostility. This time there were no more than twenty.

So why were his palms clammy? His mouth dry? His throat tight?

"With the whys and wherefores over—" Randolf "Woody" Woodmanson, his new boss and general manager of the public broadcasting station, stood and gestured in his direction "—I'd like to introduce Jason Brock, our new operations manager."

Jason rose, struggling to compose his thoughts. They expected a statement—a statement no different from those he'd made a dozen times before: KZET-TV was solvent, their jobs were safe, although corners might need cutting.

All lies, of course. But necessary lies.

He allowed himself a moment to gaze around the room. A woman clutched her hands to her breasts, an age-old sign of fear. Another plucked at the neckline of her sweater. A man drummed his fingers against the table, lightly, silently, his anxiety carefully controlled.

"The first thing I want to do is reassure you," Jason began, then slipped into his slick spiel, the one written several years earlier by a first-class New York public relations agent.

But no one believed it anymore. His reputation preceded him. Even to this little station in a hick Arizona mountain town.

He rubbed the narrow diagonal ridge on his forehead. The scar ached. Stress reduced the blood flow, allowing pain to flow instead. Or so said his doctors. It had been over a year since his accident, but he had been told to expect this throb for several more. He lowered his hand. Rubbing just made the pain worse.

Concluding his brief talk, he let his audience know there would be more to come, then joined Woody to mill through the group for individual introductions.

"This is your assistant, Harry Bingham," Woody said upon reaching the nearest employee.

Jason thrust out a hand and felt it enclosed in a strong, almost brutal shake. "It's good to meet you, Mr. Bingham." Was there a flicker of amusement in the man's eyes? It passed so quickly it was hard to tell. Harry wasn't tall. He was several inches shorter than Jason. But he wore an easy confidence that made Jason realize that his own was very shaky. He tried to assess the man but felt he was being assessed instead.

Then Woody was leading him on to the next person. "A pleasure to meet you, Ms. Herrera." Then the next: "Nice to meet you, Mr. Rall." On and on until Jason wanted nothing more than to escape all those accusing eyes. They knew why he was here, and they didn't want him. There wasn't any question about that. The only question was: after years of doing this, why did it suddenly bother him?

"Now I'd like to introduce our crackerjack program manager, Kate Gregory." Woody spoke with obvious affection and took the hand of a slender woman wearing a bulky white sweater, the ribbing at the neck twisted out of shape. Jason recognized her as the one plucking at her neckline during Woody's opening remarks. Woody released Kate's hand into Jason's, and he shook it briefly. It was dry and warm. Her strawberry blond curls danced around her face as if they had life of their own. Blue eyes sparkled with interest. She looked kind...caring....

Kate felt gauche beneath Jason's gaze. Her sweater was already a mess. Why couldn't she break the habit that so blatantly betrayed her nervousness? In contrast his clothes were perfect. His crisply pressed white shirt and three-piece pin-striped suit looked as if he hadn't moved in them. Not a wrinkle anywhere.

She had anticipated someone quite different, someone short, possibly potbellied and balding, probably a cigar smoker. But this man was tall and lean. He made her feel petite in her five-foot-eight frame. His thick raven-black hair waved appealingly around his face.

"It's a pleasure to meet you, Ms. Gregory. I've heard good things about you." His stiff acknowledgment amused her. Harry Bingham had been mocking Jason during his trip around the room and was now ogling the ceiling, nodding in imitation of the formal gesture Jason used. Jason's back was turned to Harry, but Kate could see every clowning motion. Woody also caught Harry's act and shot a deadly glare.

"It's nice to meet you also, *Mr. Brock.*" She knew her intonation mimicked his, but she hadn't done it intentionally and her polite smile now widened into an amused grin. She chastened herself. There was no reason to make fun of this man just because he was so relentlessly formal. If only Harry would stop making those insane faces. Even Woody's glare hadn't squelched him much. She hoped she wouldn't break into a nervous giggle.

Forcing herself to ignore Harry, she met Jason's eyes directly. During the introduction, he'd flashed a fleeting smile, but now his mouth was a grave line, as rigid as his manners. As she looked into his large eyes, deep-set beneath straight black brows, she saw they matched the grim set of his mouth. Although a rich golden brown, they were opaque, shuttered. She wondered what made a person shut himself off that way.

Perhaps he saw the underlying question in her expression; Kate never knew. But without warning the shutter opened.

What she saw shocked her deeply, wiping the grin from her lips. Those eyes, now luminous instead of hard and cold, seemed to plead silently for her understanding.

And a vivid scar, which she hadn't noticed before, ran above them, from the middle of his left eyebrow to the hairline of his shock of black hair. It looked as if it still hurt, and she wondered if that narrow slash was somehow connected to the emotional pain she saw in his eyes.

Her heart went out to him, and she quashed an urge to reach out and caress his injury. Instead she murmured something about hoping he would like Lakeview. The shutters immediately snapped back in place. "We'll talk in-depth later," he said, then moved on to the next introduction.

Wondering if anyone else had noticed that strange encounter, Kate glanced around the room. Curiously she wanted to protect this vulnerable stranger from the antagonism of her co-workers. Then she immediately felt torn. These people were her friends, and Jason Brock might pose a threat to them all.

After circling the room, Jason again took his place at the head of the table. Conversations died down as he looked around with those cold amber eyes.

"I'm looking forward to working with everyone at Channel Seven and also to learning the ins and outs of public broadcasting." He glanced briefly at each employee. "I'll be meeting with my immediate staff and each of the division heads during this next week. I've taken the liberty of arranging a schedule." He ruffled a stack of papers, then passed it around the table.

When Kate looked at her copy, she stifled a moan. Two o'clock, Wednesday! The same time as her appointment with Tommy's teacher. "I apologize," she said, "but this time isn't very convenient. I have another commitment."

"Change it, Kate. This schedule is locked in stone."

Kate's head snapped toward Woody in surprise. In her five years with the station she couldn't remember her boss ever giving such a curt, direct order. Woody was always patient, almost fatherly, and she recognized immediately that even he feared Jason. It was common knowledge that the mayor and city council had hired Jason without consulting Woody. Woody had claimed he didn't mind, but his present action clearly showed he did. Kate felt an immediate urge to correct things, something she recognized she couldn't do. Her stomach churned helplessly.

"I'll see what I can do," she said, but she wasn't pleased.

Jason talked a little more about his plans for the station, but the restless group was shifting in their seats and ruffling through papers. Even Woody's warning stares had little effect.

Jason must have recognized that he was losing control, because he stopped after a few sentences. "Well, we have plenty of time to go over this later. Lakeview is a great community, and I plan to stay at KZET quite a while. It was good meeting everyone. I hope to get to know each of you better." He left the room, and Woody followed behind him.

Kate stood and tucked her notes into her briefcase, a nebulous dread in her chest. Apparently her co-workers felt the same. They were leaving the room like stampeding cattle, filing past Kate, heads down, talking to no one.

A disturbing mass fluttered in her stomach. She needed an antacid and began rummaging in her case, ultimately finding a tube stuffed deep inside a pocket. There were only three left. She popped two of them into her mouth, carefully rewrapping the last for future use.

Someone called her name, and she looked up to see Harry strolling around the conference table as though the meeting had been nothing more than a coffee break.

"What do you think?" Kate inclined her head toward the doorway, making it clear that she was referring to Jason.

"Sure is one mean-looking dude. His eyes make me think a new ice age is coming."

Kate nodded. Jason Brock had the eyes of a man with steel bands around his heart. Had she imagined that fleeting instant when they opened in agony?

Kate touched Harry's arm. "Are you okay?"

When the job of operations manager opened up, everyone at the station had assumed it would go to Harry and had been shocked when an outsider was brought in instead.

"No big deal. I didn't really want the job, anyway. It's too much responsibility, and I like tinkering with my toys."

"But you deserved it. Besides, it's bad enough they hired someone new ... but a known hatchet man." Kate's stomach took another nervous twist, and she hoped the antacid would start working soon. "And for the city council to bring him in over Woody's head that way..."

"Chop, chop." Harry ran his index finger across his throat, with a wry grin.

Kate didn't find Harry's banter funny. "Aren't you uneasy about the possibility of layoffs, Harry? I know I am."

"You know me. Easy come, easy go. I didn't have a job when I walked in here, so I won't be any worse off if I lose it." He made a dismissive gesture, then ran his hand through his fine sandy-colored hair. Kate couldn't help thinking the gesture betrayed a hidden apprehension.

"And that's the reason you aren't operations manager." Kate whirled toward the unexpected voice to find Carlton Spencer standing behind her. The man had an uncanny ability to sneak up without being heard. Something has changed, she thought. Carlton would have never dared insult Harry so directly before. His attack made Kate angry, and she started to rush to Harry's defense, but he beat her to the punch.

"Ah, the Tin Man speaketh. I notice you aren't operations manager, either."

"Not yet. But *I'm* going places at this station."

"Are you saying you aren't worried, Carlton?" Kate thought there was no use trying to hide her concern. Ever since learning about Brock's arrival, the employees had done nothing but talk about possible layoffs. The financial instability of their tiny public television station was common knowledge, as was Jason's reputation.

"Those who perform their functions well have nothing to fear, my dear Kate." Carlton peered down his long nose at Kate—a difficult feat, since their heights were nearly even—and she felt a surge of irritation, prompting yet another internal pep talk about getting along better with this pompous man.

"Besides, Brock really dressed with style," Carlton added as he ruefully looked down at his sport jacket and coordinated slacks. Already more formally attired than most of his co-workers, he apparently didn't think that was enough.

"Be still, my dancing feet," Harry drawled, relieving Kate of the need to respond to Carlton's inane remark. "His pin-striped slacks crease so sharply that they could stand up by themselves. If that's style, you can have it."

The late-morning sun streamed through the conference room windows, creating a hazy, uncomfortable fog, and Kate felt suddenly tired. She just wanted people to get along. Was that too much to ask?

"I have a telephone call to make." Kate snapped her briefcase shut loudly. "If you gentlemen will excuse me, I think I'll get back to 'performing my function.'" Despite her silent pep talk she succumbed to her impulse and shot Carlton a baleful look before leaving the room.

Plodding into her office, Kate stowed her briefcase and sat down at her desk, aimlessly sorting through the paperwork nearly covering its surface. She needed to make her phone calls, change her appointment and get on with her day.

The school's secretary informed Kate that Tommy's teacher was still in class, so she left a message and hung up. A pall engulfed her, and she willed it to go away. Why was everything happening at once?

And what was a network "golden boy" doing in Lakeview, Arizona? As operations vice president for a major network, Jason Brock had been written up in *Forbes,* *Newsweek* and several industry publications for the amazing way he'd turned around more than a dozen af-

filiates. Lots of jobs were cut during these magical res-
cues, earning him his "hatchet man" reputation, but the
final results had put him securely on the fast track. Industry experts had considered him a serious candidate for
future network presidency. Then he had disappeared from
the media, absent for over a year, only to pop up right in
Kate's backyard. What *was* he doing here?

The obvious answer created another twinge in Kate's
stomach. Deciding to halt this line of thought, she picked
up a tape from her desk and hefted it between her palms.
It was her first production, *Small-Town Women*, a half-
hour interview of successful women with small-town
backgrounds, and it needed reviewing. This would be her
first task of the day.

No. Her second. The first task was already accomplished. She'd just met the esteemed Mr. Jason Brock.
Cold, humorless Jason Brock, the hatchet man from New
York. What secret pain was he hiding behind those hard,
hard eyes?

"TRY LOSING the coat and tie." That was the first piece of
homespun advice Woody Woodmanson had given him,
followed by the opinion that the suit set him too far apart
from the other employees. Jason might come to like
dressing less formally, Woody had commented. But Jason didn't think so, although he kept his opinion to himself. How could he admit that the idea of shedding his
business uniform made him feel defenseless?

The tone of their conversation had surprised him.
Woody had been cooperative and friendly. Jason wasn't
sure he would have behaved so well if his superiors had
hired a subordinate behind his back.

As advised, Jason removed his tie and the pin-striped
coat and vest, hanging them carefully on a bent metal coat

tree near the room's only window. He looked around his cramped office without pleasure, wondering if he'd made a mistake in coming to Lakeview.

Ruefully he made a mental comparison between these threadbare quarters and the lushly decorated penthouse offices he'd used in prior years. He couldn't say he hadn't been warned.

The few friends who had stayed loyal after his automobile crash had advised him to stay in New York. Another network job would come up. There was no reason to rush to the sticks just because it was the first opening available. Those network bosses had been fools, anyway, not to wait for Jason's recovery. And surely, his friends had counseled, Beth was a veritable Judas to divorce him at such a time.

But all those assurances, no matter how true, didn't change the facts. Jason was a failure. Now he wasn't sure he'd make the grade even at this backwater station. How he feared those staring eyes with their unspoken recriminations. Eyes looking just like Beth's had looked when she told him their marriage was over. Eyes that looked like Stacey's when he held her in his arms for the last time. Eyes that stated that it was all his fault.

He'd only tried to do his job. That was all. It was a game. With high stakes, of course. And he'd done his best to win. Where was the crime in that?

The self-pitying thoughts disgusted Jason. He'd better pull himself together. There would be busy days ahead—employee files to review, ledgers to peruse, action plans to be put in place.

But he wondered if it was enough. *Idle hands are the devil's workshop,* or so his Aunt Phyllis used to say. And, in truth, what he had found most gratifying about his network job was the seventy-hour week. This job would never occupy more than forty or fifty. Too bad. Long, demanding hours didn't leave much time for a mind to dwell on unhappy thoughts.

Had he been unhappy before? He hadn't thought so. In fact, he had never even asked such a question. Dismissing the idea out of hand, he decided to sift through the personnel files that someone had so efficiently placed on his desk.

He opened his briefcase, running his hand absently over its slick leather surface, then released the latches. After pulling out several mechanical pencils, a yellow pad and an eye patch, he rolled up his sleeves and prepared to start working.

The new game had begun.

KATE SAT in the dimly lit previewing booth, examining her series pilot with a critical eye. Erika McCardy, a well-known television producer, was the first subject. In her early forties, Erika had been born and raised in a small California town, and her slender, stylish appearance and easy poise made her perfect for the kickoff of *Small-Town Women*.

A niggling doubt rippled through Kate's mind as she viewed the rough footage in front of her. Was it good enough? Harry and Woody thought so, and Kate hoped they were right. In a few weeks it would be ready to send to the city council for final approval. If the okay was given, it would then go to several banks in the Phoenix area, with requests for underwriting. She wanted everything to be perfect, and she studied the tape intently, looking for the smallest flaw.

A palm frond appeared to be jutting out of Erika's head, and Kate frowned. That would have to go. After making a quick note, she continued viewing, becoming so engrossed in her work that she barely heard her name being called. She looked up and saw Rhonda Weatherby. Kate glanced at her watch, wondering where the time had gone. It was nearly noon.

"Tommy's teacher is returning your call." Rhonda held the door open with a manicured hand and wore a sympathetic look. As station administrator, Rhonda did everything no one else had time to do—purchasing, payroll, phones, typing. She was also Kate's good friend. "Do you think you can work things out?"

"I hope so," Kate replied with a grimace. "I hate changing this meeting. Holly will think I don't care."

"That's preposterous. No one could ever think you don't care about Tommy!" Rhonda's indignation made Kate smile, although the woman's loyal defense was typical.

"Thanks for the vote of confidence. I'd better not keep her waiting, though. I'll take the call at my desk."

Kate stood and walked hurriedly to her office. After picking up the phone, she soon realized Holly Shortridge wasn't going to let her off the hook easily.

"Can't you work this meeting in, Kate?" Holly said, the slightly accusing tone in her voice pricking Kate's conscience. "Tommy's up to his old tricks."

"More pranks?" Kate sighed heavily, feeling pressured from all sides. What was getting into Tommy? He had always been imaginative and prone to joking but he had only recently started this disruptive mischief.

"It's just little-boy stuff at the moment." Holly spoke in that slow, distinct manner often used by grade-school teachers. "Like placing a live frog in my top desk drawer. Somehow the kids forget I grew up here catching polliwogs. This time he put a note on the blackboard, telling the kids to go to the music room. I knew it was him because he spelled music *musik,* and the *s* was backward. Of course, the kids took off in all directions. Took nearly half an hour to round them up.'' Holly paused, and Kate started to say something, but the teacher interrupted before she could begin. ''But that's not what worries me.''

''Then what does?'' Kate felt confused. Holly had barely disguised a chuckle when she mentioned Tommy's pranks; now she sounded deadly serious.

''It's not something we should go into over the phone. Is there any way you can keep that appointment? The district psychologist will be here Wednesday, and I want you to talk to him.''

''A psychologist?'' Tommy would scream bloody murder. So would Kate's father. He thought psychology and everything else to do with mental health was nothing but hogwash, and Tommy knew his feelings well. Kate hedged. ''You admitted his pranks are harmless. Why a psychologist?''

A noise drew Kate's attention to her doorway, and she looked up. Jason Brock was standing to one side of the door, pouring a cup of coffee. Kate cursed whoever placed that coffee maker there and herself for failing to close the door. ''Why a psychologist?'' she repeated, lowering her voice but doubting it would help. Sound carried a tremendous distance in the reconverted mobile home that housed the station.

''To evaluate him,'' the teacher answered. ''There are many reasons for behavior disorders. We can't help Tommy until we find out his reason.''

''But isn't that pretty drastic?'' Kate was certain Holly was wrong. Tommy was just a normal nine-year-old boy who didn't take school very seriously. ''Why haven't you told me about this before? It's already March. The school year is nearly over. Surely this didn't move from a few pranks to a behavior disorder overnight."

"I didn't get to it soon enough, Kate. The notes I sent weren't enough, I know, and I'm sorry." A defensive undertone appeared in Holly's voice. "But there are so many kids, and at first I just thought Tommy was . . . well, it's more than just his behavior, and we need to talk it over in person. Can't you find a way to make this meeting? The psychologist won't be back in Lakeview for another month, and this is important to Tommy."

What could Kate say? "I'll see what I can do." Her mind searched for a way out of this dilemma. She would just have to force Jason to change their appointment, no matter what Woody had said. "Can I call you at home tonight?"

"No problem. The sooner we get started, the better."

With a grudging thank-you Kate hung up. Jason no longer stood at her door, so she walked into the lobby where Rhonda, busily typing, looked up curiously.

"Is *Mr.* Brock in his office?" Kate asked. She was suddenly resenting his presence here at KZET. All this eastern formality, this mister, miss and miz stuff, irritated her. Normally an internal meeting wouldn't cause this kind of conflict, but now everything was changing. And he'd only been here half a day.

"He just went in. Judging from the way he hung around your office, I think he wants to talk to you." Rhonda patted her frosted hair and went back to typing. Kate sometimes thought her friend could use help updating her appearance, and that thought flitted through her mind now. But it wasn't important and she ignored it, walking resolutely to Jason Brock's door. Come what may, she had to change that meeting time.

She loved her job, but Tommy came first.

The door was slightly ajar, and Kate's light knock made it drift open with a groan. It swung slowly, revealing a large stack of files on one corner of his desk. Then, as her view increased, Kate saw Jason. He looked up.

Her breath caught in surprise.

She didn't know what she expected, but this wasn't it. Jason Brock sat at the big, beat-up desk surrounded by folders. A black patch covered one eye.

Afternoon light filtered through the window behind him and glinted blue-black off his hair. The slash on his forehead glowed red and angry. His tie was gone, his sleeves were rolled up, and his shirt was open at the throat, revealing a dark, curling thatch of hair. His uncovered eye narrowed slightly at her entrance, and he radiated a restrained masculinity, like a pirate ready to brandish a sword and steal her most valuable possessions. Even her virtue. The thought amused Kate, and she suddenly felt on a more even keel.

He removed the eye patch in one economical gesture and put it on the desk. "I'm glad you stopped in. I have questions about second-quarter programming."

Kate supposed she shouldn't expect him to explain—and he didn't—but she couldn't help wondering why he'd been wearing that patch. Since she didn't plan to ask, she waited as he produced the programming schedule from his stack of folders. He knew exactly where to look, impressing Kate with his organization. If that stack had been on her desk, she would have flipped through it several times before hitting on the right document.

They reviewed the schedule together, and she quickly answered his questions. Now and then as they talked she glanced covertly at the patch, hoping he'd satisfy her curiosity. But he seemed unaware that she might be interested.

Then, all points covered, she steeled herself for the confrontation.

"That's not why I stopped in, Jason. I need to re-schedule our meeting. I have another appointment at that time." She looked directly into his eyes, thinking, as she had earlier, that their lack of expression marred their luxurious hue. He had almost looked more appealing with one eye patched.

"You mentioned that." He spoke agreeably enough and plucked an appointment calendar from his desk. Flopping it open, he reviewed his week. "How about ten o'clock the same day?"

"Ten on Wednesday. That's fine. Thanks." Kate breathed an audible sigh of relief. Somehow she'd expected him to be difficult and rigid, unwilling to make even the slightest change in his plans. A smile flickered across his face at the sound, and just for that moment his mouth softened.

She returned his smile and added blithely, "If there's any way I can return the favor, let me know."

"How about a home-cooked meal?"

Before she had time to realize that Jason's reply had been as flippant as her offer, Kate felt the shock register on her face. In the same instant something flickered across Jason's face, informing her that he had noticed her response. The shutters over his eyes opened then, and instantly Kate knew she hadn't imagined that earlier incident. The ache she saw beneath that rich amber surface was real. Oh, so real.

Her first reaction was remorse for her uncharitable, unneighborly attitude. Then came a yearning, sweet and almost irresistible, to stroke the angular plane of his cheekbone, to ease the sorrow within him. Obviously he had lost something—or someone—dear to him, and she understood his pain. She had a loss of her own, and even after five years she still sometimes felt its effects. It seemed strange that a few moments earlier she'd disliked Jason Brock. Now she felt a compulsion to comfort him.

Their silence widened into a gaping chasm. Uncomfortable, yet somehow binding, as though a wordless conversation was passing between them.

"Why not?" she finally said, struggling to maintain a casual tone.

"What?" The shutters over his eyes snapped closed. The mood was broken.

"The home-cooked meal. Why not come to dinner tonight?"

"I was kidding, Kate." Jason flashed another fleeting smile, making Kate wonder why he didn't do it more often. "Although I am getting tired of restaurant food. Lakeview has a somewhat limited selection." He shook his head. "No. I couldn't ask you to fix me dinner, especially on such short notice."

"That's what microwaves are for." It occurred to Kate that getting to know Jason over a family dinner could only help her at the station. She didn't particularly like the calculating thought, or herself for having it. But it couldn't hurt to be on good terms with a hatchet man, and that, she decided, was her only reason to invite him. It had absolutely nothing to do with the strange moment they'd just shared.

"You're sure?"

"Yes, I'm sure," Kate bobbed her head definitely. "Come about six-thirty. That way Tommy and I can get his homework out of the way first."

"Tommy?"

"My son."

"Oh, I see." Although his words were noncommittal, Jason's expression made Kate think he found her answer significant. Remembering he had probably overheard her telephone conversation, she decided she didn't want to know why.

"So are we on?" she asked, returning to her original subject.

"We're on. Although the Mountain Café will accuse you of unfair competition."

"I'll take that chance." Kate laughed politely at Jason's comment and stood up. As she started to leave, she added, "I'll see you at six-thirty, then, Mr. Brock."

"Call me Jason. Mr. Brock is too formal for these parts, or so I've been told." Jason rose and moved to her side.

"All right...Jason." The name felt awkward on Kate's tongue. A surname, much as she hated them, seemed to fit this composed man. He walked beside her as they talked, and when they reached the door, he leaned forward and held it open. A sweet whisper of spicy aftershave filled the air.

As Kate passed through the door, her shoulder brushed his bare forearm. A fleeting shiver ran down her spine, and she looked again into his eyes. The sadness was there now, not as sharply defined as before, but still lingering. Again she felt a desire to erase it. Suppressing that impulse, she stepped through the door, anxious to leave Jason Brock and the uncomfortable feelings he stirred within her.

Hurrying back to her office, she picked up her notes and the *Small-Town Women* cassette and walked back into the lobby. At least Holly's timing had been good. Kate had just finished her review when Rhonda had announced the call.

She entered a doorway that exited on the right side of the lobby and led to the production wing. The hall was lined with windowed rooms, just like the operations wing on the other side of the lobby. Woody had ordered the windows installed several years ago, stating that closed-up rooms wasted time since a person had to go all the way into the wing just to see who was there.

Now Kate scanned the hall, searching for Harry Bingham. He usually arrived early for his shift, but today he had been forced to get up in the "wee hours" to attend the mandatory meeting with Jason. Kate thought he might have napped to make up for lost sleep, but apparently not. Harry sat at the newly acquired editing console, lost in his work.

She walked into the production studio, soothed by the familiar hum of the electronic equipment, and stood behind Harry. He jumped.

"I scared you. I'm sorry." Kate punctuated the apology with a short laugh.

"Nearly gave me a heart attack!" Harry feigned a swoon. "I guess I was concentrating too hard."

Kate glanced at one of the many video displays lining the studio wall. This one was directly overhead. A fuzzy, animated creature with a big fluffy tail bounded across the screen. The animal stopped and stared at them with huge black button eyes, two buck teeth protruding from his mouth.

"Chuck E. Squirrel!" Kate exclaimed in delight. "He used to be one of Tommy's favorites."

"Used to be?" Harry looked at her archly over his reading glasses. A strand of fine dusty-blond hair trailed over his forehead. "He's still one of mine. What happened to Tommy?"

"*He* grew up." Kate enjoyed kidding Harry. Although nearly fifty, his easy humor and eccentric clothing made him seem ageless. "He's into *Ghostbusters* now."

"I'm never growing up, Wendy! Never!" Harry slid into his Peter Pan parody, one he used frequently when criticized for his lack of decorum.

Kate chuckled. "So you keep telling me. What are you doing with Chuck E.? You don't usually work on *Candy Cane Road.*"

"The tape from the syndicator snapped while I was previewing it. I spliced it, but we lost a sequence, and now I'm trying to recreate it. Here, let me show you."

An image of the perky squirrel was freeze-framed on the video screen. Harry flipped a switch, turning on a computerized animator, which was part of the editing equipment. He pushed a few more buttons, and the image magically reappeared on the animator's in-line screen. With a few keystrokes Harry duplicated it, and a second Chuck E. appeared.

Fascinated, Kate peered over Harry's shoulders and watched as he manipulated the image into a different position, copied it, manipulated some more, eventually repeating the process half a dozen times. It was all done so quickly. Suddenly Chuck E. Squirrel was popping out of his familiar tree stump house and sashaying across the street, impossibly full tail swinging behind him.

"There. Now I can dub this on a new cassette and no one will ever know we had an accident." He looked up at Kate seriously. "It would have taken days to do this by hand the way we used to. I could never have finished in time for the broadcast. This new stuff is miraculous. Channel Seven is finally moving into the twentieth century."

"Yeah, and you're the only one who knows how to use it. Talk about job security." As she spoke, memories of Jason's hatchet-man reputation suddenly reappeared in Kate's head.

Harry shook his head. "I'm not the only one. Carlton got trained at the same time I did, and I've broken in a couple of technical directors. Rhonda's even played with it a few times. She wants to use it to embellish the patron's newsletter. Next week I'm going to show Jason, although he's already been exposed to animators at other stations."

"I bet no one else has your genius with it, though."

"Ah, you ain't seen nothing yet. Why, you should see what I can do with a little chewing gum and a hairpin."

"Probably build a rocket ship."

"Ah, yes. To explore the vast frontiers of space. But not now. First, I have to copy this so it'll be ready for the morning broadcast. Can't disappoint those kiddies. Or myself, for that matter."

"Can you wait a minute?" She handed Harry the cassette of *Small-Town Women* and a three-page list of edits.

Harry grimaced good-naturedly. "Kate, you'll be the death of me yet. From overwork."

"You love it, Harry. Admit it."

"True. True." Harry slipped Kate's cassette into a rack that stored all the tapes he was scheduled to work on that night. "I'll get to it later in my shift." With *Candy Cane Road* in his hand, he left the room.

Kate glanced at her watch. It was nearly five, and she'd better hurry or there wouldn't be enough time for Tommy's homework before Jason came. Not that Tommy would mind. She wondered if she should tell him what Holly had said, then decided to put it off until after

Wednesday's meeting. Holly was probably making too big a deal over a little mischief.

Between the early-morning meeting and her discussion with Holly, her day had been unbearably tense, and she wasn't looking forward to the evening ahead of her. Spending the remainder of this hectic day with a formidable co-worker didn't exactly thrill her to her toes.

Whatever would they talk about, she and this stuffy New Yorker?

CHAPTER TWO

KATE GREGORY'S PLACE was inviting, cozy. As he walked
from the dirt road up the winding path to the door—wind
softly rustling through overhead branches and the evening chill nipping at his face—Jason felt a glow of pleasure. The stillness of the majestic pine trees and the
random patches of snow over the frostbitten wild grass
created an aura of serenity. Kate Gregory hadn't attempted to tame this primitive landscape. It seemed that
no one in Lakeview did.

The idea of just leaving things alone was foreign to Jason. He never let things be. If this place had been his, he
would have built rock walls, installed flower beds and
tried to slick everything up. Surprisingly, though, he
rather liked it just the way it was. When the wildflowers
bloomed, he imagined the yard would become a per-
fumed garden, and he found himself wishing he would be
there to enjoy it.

But why was he here now?

His own shock at his brash request had matched the
expression on Kate's face. What had prompted him to
make such an uncharacteristic suggestion?

Was it curiosity about the son she'd been discussing on
the telephone? How many times had he overheard his
Aunt Phyllis having similar discussions? Of course, his
aunt's bored, disinterested tone of voice had been decid-

edly different. Kate had sounded deeply concerned, even hurt.

Still, he had no reason to care about a boy he didn't know. No, deep down, he had to admit it was the boy's mother who fascinated him. Maybe it was her eyes, the way they revealed everything she thought. He recalled how his pain had broken through—dizzying, that pain, almost overwhelming—and in Kate's blue eyes he'd seen immediate recognition. Or was it that eerie moment they'd shared in his office? That moment when empathy had flashed across her heart-shaped face.

With a sudden flash of insight he uttered a soft, cynical laugh, the enigma of that tugging attraction solved. She'd been the only person in that conference room who hadn't radiated hostility. Why shouldn't he like her? He supposed even a loner like himself needed one ally in a sea of antagonism.

He shook his head, knowing he couldn't afford allies. A friend today could be an ex-employee, an enemy, tomorrow. Besides, his luck with women wasn't all that good. No tugging attractions for him, thank you.

That decided, he shifted the package nestling in his arms, transferred it to one hand and knocked on the oak door now in front of him, confident that it wouldn't be answered by a man ready to introduce himself as Mr. Gregory. Woody had mentioned that Kate was a widow, so he knew the only man in her house would be her son.

A unpleasant tingle ran up his spine as he waited. Never again, he promised himself. He'd get through this evening and make sure it never happened again.

"Hi. You're right on time." Kate opened the door and greeted him with a friendly smile.

She wore tight, well-worn jeans and a peach sweatshirt. The color complemented her rosy-hued hair. Jason was immediately self-conscious about his business suit. He felt like a fish out of water in Lakeview and wondered if he'd ever breathe easily again.

Kate's eyes glittered above her smile. They were a startling color, those eyes. The irises seemed to have a million shades of blue dancing through them. He wondered if they lightened and darkened with her moods. "I hope pot roast is okay." Her tone was light and breezy.

"Sounds great." He thrust the package in her direction. "I brought chocolates for Tommy. Wine for you. Is zinfandel okay?"

"Zinfandel is perfect," she answered. "And Tommy will love the chocolates." She took the package from his hand and invited him inside.

The minute he entered the living room, he liked her house. A massive flagstone fireplace dominated one wall of the living room, its chimney reaching to the top of the high, exposed-beam ceiling. Family portraits covered the mantel, and a fire crackled as though inviting him to sit down and warm himself.

Running footsteps clattered on the wooden floor, and Jason turned. A young boy skidded to a stop, paused and then walked cautiously toward them. He wore a baseball mitt and carried a ball. "Are you Mr. Brock?" The boy transferred the ball to the mitt and stuck his hand out in greeting. This quick transition from wild roughneck to poised young man impressed Jason.

Most boys his age were all skinny limbs and knobby joints, but Tommy was solidly build. He was square and compact, with an early hint of the strong muscles that would develop later. "You must be Tommy."

"That's me." Tommy nodded earnestly as if everyone should know that. He plucked the ball from the mitt and began hefting it back and forth as he spoke. The ball made a sharp thud each time it struck the glove.

Jason felt a smile creep to his lips as the boy looked up at him engagingly. Then, remembering that Woody had said even children called adults by first name in this part of the country, he added, "Why don't you call me Jason."

"Okay, Jason." Tommy's sun-bleached tawny hair was still damp, carefully combed into place, although a cowlick at his crown threatened to break loose any moment. He wore painter's pants and an oversize designer sweatshirt, both very clean.

A moment of weighty silence fell over their small group and then Kate said, "Jason brought you chocolates, Tommy."

"Oh, boy!" Tommy reached for the box in his mother's hand, but she pulled it back with a small laugh.

"Not until after dinner."

"Can I have the ones with the cherries?" He looked up at his mother with impossibly round eyes, batting his lashes over their green-gray depths. Jason didn't know how Kate could resist such a pleading look.

It seemed she couldn't, at least not quite. "Yes, but after dinner, okay?"

Tommy seemed to know when he won one and lost one, because he dropped the puppy-dog look. "I suppose you want me to wash my hands, too?"

"You got it, kiddo. And dump that baseball and glove."

"Aw, Mom!"

Kate met Tommy's protest with an indulgent smile. "You can't eat dinner wearing a baseball glove, Tommy."

"Okay," Tommy said reluctantly, turning to leave the room, but Kate caught him before he disappeared into the hallway.

"Why don't you show Jason the bathroom so he can wash, too?"

Tommy ducked his head in a small, embarrassed gesture, appearing uncomfortable with the task his mother had assigned. "It's this way."

Jason followed, feeling awkward himself. What did a person say to a boy this age? An instant pang of loss punctured his transitory peace of mind as he thought of his daughter, Stacey. He hadn't quite known what to say to her, either, had always left that up to her mother, despite Beth's frequent complaints. He'd never understood how that woman expected him to support them in their grand style and still be available for all the activities she cooked up. Now it was too late. Anger and that hated pain bubbled up from somewhere deep inside him.

He looked intently around Kate's living room, a trick he'd learned to help chase away unpleasant thoughts. If he focused on the external, internal ghosts had a way of vanishing.

Homespun. That described the room best. An oval rug, braided in tones of beige, peach and blue, covered a gleaming wooden floor. The furniture—Early American, but without the cutesy ruffles Jason usually associated with that style—was covered in pleasantly faded chintz. The colors picked up the tones in the rug. Careless piles of magazines and books sat on natural pine tables.

Kate's tastes didn't resemble Beth's. Beth had been drawn to sleek chrome, glass and luxurious leathers. Surprisingly Jason felt more at home in this casual, lived-in room than he'd ever been in the expensively decorated house where he'd lived with Beth and Stacey.

"We'd better hurry," Tommy urged. "I'm starved! Aren't you? Mom won't let us eat until we wash our hands."

"Smart mom," Jason replied. "You don't eat any germs with your food that way."

"Aw...that's what she says, too. I don't believe it, but you know how moms are." Actually, Jason thought, he didn't know. His Aunt Phyllis had never seemed to worry too much about germs, at least not his germs.

Tommy headed for his bedroom to deposit the ball and glove, showing Jason the bathroom on the way. Jason turned on the water and punched the soap dispenser. The bathroom was spotlessly clean, not an easy task with a boy Tommy's age in the house. If he remembered correctly, young boys—and girls—constantly left socks, underwear and dirty T-shirts littering the floors.

Tommy returned, slumping lazily against the door while he waited.

"Are you my mom's new boss?" Tommy wore a suspicious expression. Jason supposed his reputation had preceded him all the way down to the junior Lakeview residents. Small towns kept few secrets.

"No. I work with her, though. Your mom and I are peers. Do you know what a peer is?"

"Sure." Tommy looked almost insulted that Jason would ask. "It's that wooden thing that leads out over the water. What does that have to do with my mom and you?"

"That's one definition." Jason suppressed the grin tugging at his mouth. "Another meaning is that people are equals. Like, you and your classmates are peers, but your teacher is sort of like your boss. Its spelling is different, too."

"Oh." Tommy nodded gravely. "I see what you mean." But Jason doubted that he did see. What did a kid care about peers? Maybe he should talk about things kids would relate to more easily.

"Do you like video games, Tommy?"

"Yeah! They're cool!" Tommy's face brightened, the suspicious cast vanishing. "I have a Nintendo in my room and I play all the time. Do you play?"

"No. But I've always wanted to learn." As he dried his hands, Jason stepped back from the sink to let Tommy in, surprised to realize he was speaking the truth. It seemed he'd worked all his life and there had never been time for games. Except for baseball and golf. A lot of business could be conducted on the golf course.

"I'll show you how, if you like." Tommy rinsed, then dried his hands briskly. When he began walking out of the room, Jason followed. "I've got the latest Mario Brothers, Double Dragon II and the new Wizards and Warriors, plus a bunch of other junk. Maybe we could play after dinner."

"Sounds good to me." The aroma of hot food drifted to Jason's nose, and his stomach growled.

Tommy laughed. "I'm hungry, too. Let's go eat."

Jason looked at Tommy's grinning face and smiled. He liked Tommy. A person could be prompted to smile just by looking at him. The boy's tanned, smooth face showed none of the freckles that so liberally sprinkled his mother's nose. Jason decided he must look like his father, and as he and Tommy entered the kitchen, he found himself curious about the man who had once been Kate's husband.

Kate had plainly gone to a lot of trouble. A pot roast nestled among gravy-coated potatoes and carrots, looking ready to fall apart. Two bowls of buttery vegetables, a fruit salad and a large basket of rolls flanked the steaming main dish. Jason's stomach grumbled again. He was now ravenous and glad he wasn't eating in a restaurant or out of a can tonight. He wondered if they always ate such heavy meals. Looking at Kate's trim figure, he couldn't believe they did.

Just then Tommy plopped into the chair next to Jason and said, "Wow! Sunday dinner. And on Monday, too!"

"You said you hadn't eaten home cooking in a while." Kate laughed nervously, taking her place next to Tommy while Jason fought another amused grin. "I thought it was the least I could do."

"How did you know I've been dying for pot roast?" He finally allowed the smile to flash across his face, thinking that Kate looked beautiful with that slightly embarrassed flush on her freckled cheeks.

"It was an easy guess. Most men are meat and potato eaters at heart," she said, returning his smile. Her eyes crinkled slightly at the corners, clear evidence she was no longer a girl, and Jason found those tiny wrinkles surprisingly sexy. "Dig in," she added, handing him a bowl of vegetables.

He ate with relish, checking his manners now and then. He felt as if he couldn't get the food in his mouth fast enough. Finally, taking a break to talk, he complimented Kate on the meal and asked Tommy how old he was. "Are you ten, maybe eleven?"

Tommy ducked his head the way he had earlier. The gesture reminded Jason of a swan tucking its head in its wing. "Nah. I'm only nine."

"Nine?" The boy came nearly to his armpit, and Jason didn't think nine-year-olds were that tall. "You're big for your age, aren't you?"

"Yeah. It helps a lot in baseball."

"I figured you were a baseball player." His deduction didn't take a lot of brains. After all, Tommy appeared glued to his mitt and ball. "Do you play Little League?"

"Yep. I'm already in the minors." A humble smile crossed Tommy's face, and he ducked his head again.

"The minor league. I'm impressed. I didn't make minors until I was nearly eleven."

"You played baseball, too? Were you any good?" As the words slipped off his tongue, Tommy shot his mother a questioning glance, apparently worried that he may have overstepped his bounds. Kate smiled and he went on. "Were you, Jason?"

"I played okay, Tommy. I pitched. But I wasn't any superstar. I wasn't that well coordinated." Tommy's open ways charmed Jason. The boy seemed almost totally without self-consciousness. He'd expected to feel a little ill at ease tonight, but Tommy made him feel accepted and admired.

"Wow! A pitcher. That's what I want to be. Do you think you could teach me to pitch? Our team's looking for a second coach since my Uncle Cory left town. He went to Australia to surf. I'm going to a surfer someday. Surfing's so cool." Then, returning to his original thought, Tommy added, "Maybe you could be our new assistant coach."

"I'm sure Jason doesn't have time to coach a kids' baseball team." Kate spoke with firm gentleness as though confident Tommy would see her point. "We wouldn't want to impose."

"Oh, yeah. I didn't mean to do anything like that. It's just that we need someone bad. Someone who knows how to pitch. Our coach is a great guy, but he doesn't pitch too good."

"I can't think of anything more important than base-ball." It was Tommy's open admiration that made Jason know he wanted to coach the team. At one time baseball had been the only thing he did well. Besides, hadn't he been worrying about too much time on his hands? Coaching a team would certainly fill up a lot of empty hours.

"Does that mean you'll do it? We have practice Wednesday at five-thirty. Could you come?"

Tommy spoke as if he were closing a deal. This kid would make quite a salesman, Jason thought, his grin broadening. Smiling was becoming a habit tonight. He could become addicted to it.

"Yes, Tommy," he said. It was clear he could grow to like Tommy, too, and as he watched Kate gaze lovingly at her son, curly hair swinging with her turning head, he thought he could grow fond of her also. He banished that idea immediately, just before realizing he'd already broken the promise he'd made to himself while knocking on Kate's door. But the die was cast. "Give me directions to the practice field before I leave."

"All right!" Tommy cheered.

Jason felt a curious mixture of fear and pleasure churn inside him. It felt good to be wanted, but what if it didn't work out?

"Can I show Jason my Nintendo after dinner, Mom?" Tommy's change of subject snapped Jason out of his thoughts. Kate didn't look thrilled by Tommy's sugges-tion.

"I thought we might play Scrabble," she said. "It's something we could all do."

"Scrabble? Oh, no, Mom! I'm no good at it."

"Then why do you always beat me?" Kate ruffled Tommy's hair, and his face grew a little pink.

"'Cause I know the best-scoring words. But half the time I don't even know those words you put down." Kate must have realized she was embarrassing Tommy, because she withdrew her hand, but she continued looking at him steadily and he glanced away. "Okay. Scrabble, then." He stared intently at his plate, then lifted a forkful of potatoes to his mouth, chewing with a sullen expression on his face.

Losing this minor battle had pricked Tommy's pride. It was something Jason understood. So long ago, but had he been as prideful at that age? He thought so.

"Maybe next time," Jason said, hoping to lift the boy's spirits. A small grin crossed Tommy's face, and he shot a sidelong glance at Jason as though he had found a kindred spirit.

His mood passing, Tommy began chatting again, and soon the meal was finished. Kate stood and picked up a few dishes, asking Tommy to set up the game, and before long they were gathered around an octagonal game table in a upstairs loft that served as a den.

"Can I have my chocolates now?" Tommy asked.

When Kate agreed, he dashed downstairs, returning with the box in his hands.

"Just four, Tommy."

Tommy looked at his mom, knowing argument would be useless. He ate greedily, wishing he could eat the whole box. But she'd set a limit, and he knew better than to push it with company around. Now he eyed the box longingly, his quota gone, and leaned against the edge of the table as he laid down his playing tiles. "Q-U-I-T. Triple word. Forty-two points, please." He grinned triumphantly. "Mark it down, Mom."

Tommy sometimes thought his mother let him win. But tonight he was ahead of Jason, too. Maybe he *was* good at this game.

Jason was kind of cool. Most grown-ups weren't at all interested in video games and couldn't pitch worth a darn. His Uncle Cory did. But he was gone now, and there wasn't anyone to have fun with anymore. Sure, Grandpa took him fishing now and then, and he did love to fish, but Grandpa was kind of cranky and, besides, Tommy was mad at him. If he hadn't yelled at Uncle Cory, his uncle would still be here.

"I think you're ready to graduate to real Scrabble, Tommy." Kate laughed as she wrote down his score. "You're beating the pants off us."

"That's 'cause you guys try to make big words. I know a bunch of words for the hard letters." The last thing Tommy wanted was for his mother to buy the harder game. Scrabble Junior was enough of a hassle, and he wouldn't play this stupid game at all if Mom didn't insist. She said it was educational.

Tommy cupped the tiles on his rack with his hand so that the letters would stop bouncing around. He wondered why words didn't bounce for his friends. One time, on the playground, he'd asked his playmates about it. When they started laughing, he learned a lesson he never forgot. He never asked again.

Jason put down a long word. "Eighteen points."

"See what I mean?" Tommy leaned back and preened. It felt good to be winning at something that was so hard. "You used all those letters and all you got was eighteen points."

"It was the best I could do." Jason pretended to have his feelings hurt. Tommy liked that. Most grown-ups couldn't pretend. "Besides, you took the last triple-word space. I had my eye on it, too."

"Some got it, some ain't." Tommy arrogantly rubbed his fingers against his shirt. His mother shot a disapproving glance. "I mean, some have got it, some haven't."

"Well, I'm one that ain't got it." Tommy saw his mother's gaze shift to Jason, but Jason didn't seem to notice. He just turned to Kate and asked her if she'd written the score down.

"Wouldn't forget for the world," Kate answered.

Tommy thought she sounded a little sarcastic but he knew she wasn't really mad. Most of the time his mom was a good sport.

Kate laid down her own play. "Only twelve points. It looks like you're going to be the winner, Tommy."

"Maybe..." All the tiles were gone from the box, and he had two letters left. If only the words on the board would stop squiggling. He leaned over and shaded the tiles with both hands. Zowie! There it was. The winning spot. "Z-I-T!" he cried, feeling like the King of the Mountain. "Thirty-six points, plus fifty for going out. I win!"

His mom laughed and Jason smiled, but Tommy noticed something else on Jason's face. It looked like worry. The way his mom looked when he did something bad in school. Maybe Jason didn't like to lose.

"I'm sorry, Jason. But you were close." He leaned over and looked at the score pad in front of his mother. "I only beat you by—" he looked up sheepishly "—a hundred and fifteen points."

Jason laughed then, his worried expression gone, and Tommy wondered if he had imagined it. "Right. A real close game." He reached over and ruffled Tommy's hair.

Tommy dipped his head. His face felt warm. But then so did Jason's friendly touch. He hoped his mom invited

Jason over again. He was thinking about that when she reminded him it was time to get ready for bed.

"Already?"

"It's past eight-thirty. You're not exactly a whiz kid when it comes to bedtime, you know."

"Awright, Mom." He got up reluctantly and walked over to Jason, sticking out his hand the way he saw the grown-ups do. "Nice to meet you, Jason."

Jason took his hand and shook it firmly. "It was nice to meet you, too, Tommy."

"I hope you come over again," Tommy added and, although he knew it was the polite thing to say because his mother had said so, he also meant it.

"Don't forget my good-night kiss." Compliantly Tommy went over and gave his mother a light peck on the cheek. But that wasn't enough for his mom. She hugged him and kissed his forehead. Aw, jeeze! In front of Jason, too! When she let go, Tommy nearly ran down the stairs to his room.

After changing into pajamas, he dutifully went to the bathroom and brushed his teeth. Finished, he returned to his bedroom and turned on the video game. The tinny music of Wizards and Warriors filled the room. He turned the volume of the television set real low, planning to play until his mom came and told him to turn out the lights. There was nothing he liked better than video games.

Unless it was baseball.

KATE COULD HEAR the low beat of Tommy's game through the floor of the loft but decided to ignore it for a moment. Jason would be leaving soon; she'd check on Tommy then.

She watched as Jason placed the Scrabble tiles back into the box. Nice hands, she thought. Long-fingered, strong.

The nails were meticulously clipped and clean—a thinker's hands, with no calluses to catch on a woman's skin.

Jason closed the box and handed it to her, and Kate nearly blushed, absurdly afraid he could read her mind. She didn't know where her train of thought was leading but was glad for the interruption.

She stood and carried the game to built-in bookshelves at the far end of the loft.

"I'll get the glasses," Jason said as he picked them up and followed Kate. He didn't need to do that. The game table was to the right of the stairs and he could have waited there, but he appeared reluctant to leave her side.

"Tired?" His voice was a soft, caressing whisper, making Kate want to move closer as, in actuality, she moved farther away.

"What?"

"Are you tired?" he repeated, more forcibly this time.

Kate felt foolish. After all, he'd only asked after her welfare. He hadn't made some sort of indecent proposition. She suddenly wished Tommy were back. She hadn't felt this way when he was around.

"Yes. A little," she finally answered. It wasn't such an unpleasant prospect, spending a little time alone with Jason. It was just unnerving.

She started down the stairs, and Jason came behind her, not commenting on her answer. When they reached the kitchen, he put the glasses in the sink. "Thanks for the evening, Kate. It was very pleasant. Tommy's a great kid."

"Thanks. I like him, too."

"I suspect you do." Then he laughed. It was a deep, pleasant sound, like the thunder of a welcome summer rain, but it also sounded like a release, as though laughter wasn't something he indulged in often. Kate found herself wishing she could make him do it again.

They had moved into the living area while they talked, and Kate went to the coat closet to get Jason's jacket. She watched him walk to the fireplace, thinking how trim and fit he looked. Not an ounce of extra flesh on that tall body. She carried the coat to where he stood, studying a brass-framed photograph on the mantel. "Is that your husband?"

"Yes. That's Lee." She picked up the portrait, running a lingering finger over the glass as green eyes, under sandy blond brows, stared out at her.

"I see where Tommy gets his looks."

"Yes, he's the spitting image, isn't he?" Kate continued gazing at the photograph, wondering how it was possible, after all that grief, to feel nothing but a warm fondness now. When the grim-faced doctor shattered her life with his unexpected announcement, she had thought she would never recover. Not that life with Lee was perfect, but surely it was better than most.

"His death was sudden, wasn't it?"

She looked up to see Jason gazing at her with sympathy and realized she didn't need it anymore. "Yes. How did you know?"

"Woody mentioned it."

It shouldn't have surprised Kate that they had discussed her—they probably reviewed the entire staff—but it did, and the knowledge vaguely unsettled her.

"Lee was a pilot and had flown to Philadelphia..." She didn't know why she was telling this to Jason. She hadn't talked about Lee in a long while, although she still missed him at times despite his irresponsible ways. "He slipped on a patch of ice and broke his leg. The airline flew me out right away, but I wasn't really worried. Who dies of a broken leg? But an embolism had formed. It broke loose and lodged in his brain. He was dead before I arrived. It's funny. After worrying about all those miles he spent in the air, it was the time he spent on the ground that killed him. It came as such a shock.''

''I know what you mean. My parents died suddenly, too.''

She wondered if that was the cause of the sorrow in his eyes. ''Recently?''

''No. I was just a kid. A little older than Tommy.''

He paused, and his mind seemed to drift off somewhere for a moment. It made Kate sad to think of a boy that young—as young as Tommy—being orphaned, alone. She started to say something, but Jason took the jacket from her hands.

''It was a long time ago,'' he said dismissively. ''Besides, I should be going and let you get some sleep. I'll see you at work and then again Wednesday night.''

''Wednesday night?''

''Tommy's Little League practice, remember? I'm taking him up on that offer. If the coach will have me, that is.''

''Oh, the coach will definitely have you.'' Kate was glad the conversation was moving into a lighter vein. ''Not many men are willing to take on those wild Indians. That's the team's name, by the way—the Indians.''

''Sounds appropriate. Will you be there?''

''You bet.''

''Good.''

They walked to the door. He smiled at her again, looking as if he wanted to say something. She opened the front door, and Jason moved onto the doorstep.

''I'm glad you came,'' she told him.

"Me, too." The wind tugged at his hair, pulling a few strands in gleeful abandon. His golden eyes shimmered in the reflected light from the living room. "Kate?"

She raised a quizzical eyebrow at the serious sound of his voice.

"I may be getting out of line here, but I overheard your conversation with Tommy's teacher this morning. It was almost impossible not to."

"And?" She was uncomfortable with the idea that this stranger knew things she hadn't told anyone but Rhonda.

"It's none of my business, but you might consider getting Tommy's eyes tested."

"His vision is twenty-twenty."

"Did you notice how he shaded his letters with his hands during the Scrabble game?"

"He always does that. What's the big deal?"

Jason sighed, running his hands across his face. "Please don't get upset, Kate. It's just...well, without pretending to be an expert, I spent a few years on the Literacy Council as a volunteer. When a kid does what Tommy did and doesn't have an eye problem, like farsightedness, it's often a sign of a learning disability."

Kate's mouth went dry. Cottony. She felt an edge of anger creep into her voice. With mama-bear intensity her mind denied what he was saying. How could Jason impose on their brief acquaintance this way? "A learning disability?" she repeated.

"Possibly..." He hesitated again. "I have some personal experiences that make me think Tommy could have such a problem."

For the first time in this tense exchange Kate noticed the tightness in Jason's face. He appeared genuinely concerned, something she hadn't considered even a moment before. She softened her tone. "A child?"

"Me." He shifted his stance self-consciously. "I have dyslexia. That's why I wear the eye patch you saw me in today."

Finally the reason behind the patch that she had been so curious about. But now she didn't want this information, piggybacked as it was onto his comments about Tommy. She remained silent for a long, uncomfortable moment. "How does that help?" she finally asked.

"It's hard to explain without getting technical, but it has to do with the way my eyes handle light. When I do intense reading, they get tired. Patching one eye off makes it easier for me to focus. It's really a minor handicap. I overcame it and anyone else can, too, especially if it's caught early enough. Mine wasn't discovered until I was nearly fifteen. It's a little harder then."

As she listened to his revelation, Kate noticed a small ring of pride in Jason's voice, as though he felt pleased that he'd succeeded in spite of his disability. She also understood what prompted his well-meaning intrusion. Still, Tommy didn't have the same problem. He'd never mentioned anything about tired eyes or words being hard to see.

She reached out and touched his arm. "I appreciate your interest, Jason. Really, I do. But there's nothing wrong with Tommy that a little hard work won't cure." She only wished she felt as confident as her words sounded. The only thing she knew for sure was that she didn't need Jason's help.

"I hope so." He looked defeated, his usually straight shoulders slightly slumped. His concern was touching, but also scary. He was undoubtedly a nice man. His offer to coach the team and his interest in Tommy proved that. But he was also a co-worker. Possibly a man to fear. She couldn't let him intrude on her life.

"Well, good night," he said softly. Then he turned and walked down the pathway to the street. Kate stepped back inside and shut the door, her emotions mixed.

As she walked to Tommy's room, the clinky-clink-clink of the video game growing louder, she searched her mind for what she knew of dyslexia. Very little.

She rapped softly before opening the door, smiling at her son's sheepish grin. This was a nightly ritual.

"Okay, Mom." He leaned over and shut off the game.

She moved to the bed and gave him a hug, which he returned warmly. *Now that Jason isn't here to see.* The thought amused Kate and saddened her at the same time. Her baby was getting older. "Good night, honey."

"Night, Mom."

He snuggled under the covers, and she could tell he was already sleepy. She tucked the blankets under his chin, then went to the door and shut out the light, watching him for a moment. He was so precious. Surely there wasn't anything wrong with him.

Jason must be mistaken. He obviously spoke from experience, but that didn't mean he was right. This was something she and Tommy could handle without Jason's well-meant intrusion.

It would be best for all concerned if she just kept her distance from that enigmatic man.

CHAPTER THREE

KATE WALKED AWAY from the school, head down, as fast as she could without running, hating herself for her primary concern. How would she tell her father? What would he say?

Tommy—Tommy's progress, Tommy's dismay—should be uppermost in her mind. Why wasn't it? And why, why, couldn't she simply wave her hand and make it all go away?

Not since Lee's death, since that shattering discovery of the financial ruin he'd left behind, had her mind suffered such turmoil, her stomach such turbulence. She suddenly ached to have Lee there, to lean on his shoulder and listen to him tell her everything would be all right.

She reached her car, not quickly enough, but finally, and as she opened the door, a bitter laugh erupted from her throat. Never in all their years together had Lee been present for a crisis. He hadn't even appeared for Tommy's birth.

But her mother had been there, had made excuses for him. A man had to do his work, she'd said, and a wife needed to understand. Kate had known better—known he had probably been lounging in an airport bar with his flying buddies. So why did she think his presence would make a difference now?

Turning the key in the ignition, she hit the accelerator hard and left gravel spewing behind her as she pulled from the school's parking lot. She drove fast, the roadside trees and buildings a mere blur in her peripheral vision, wanting nothing more than to keep driving until this problem disappeared. But she couldn't. She had a job to do, a child to raise, parents who loved her and wanted the best for her. But did they know what was best? And how could she do that and still keep everyone happy?

Those questions were still unanswered when she reached KZET. She pulled into the parking lot and drove to her designated space.

Kate Gregory, the concrete marker said, the lettering now gray with age. She remembered the day her name had been stenciled and the warm, secure feeling of permanency the act had produced. Finally, after the mess Lee had bequeathed, her life had come back under control with a secure foundation on which to rebuild.

Now, in the space of a few days, that foundation had become shaky, unstable. First, Jason Brock, with his threatening reputation, had appeared on the scene. Now the Lakeview School District was telling her that her son couldn't read.

Remedial reading classes! Tommy would have a fit. And psychological testing? My God, her father would explode at that idea.

She climbed out of the car and wearily walked into the station. Rhonda sat at the reception desk, and Kate noticed, as if seeing it for the first time, how shabby everything looked. The varnish on Rhonda's desk was peeling and it, too, looked shaky, unstable, echoing the way Kate felt inside. It was as though the room were a time capsule from an earlier era and Rhonda, with her French twist and overdone makeup, fitted the image as much as the faded floor and the antiquated furniture.

"How did it go?" Rhonda asked, looking up as Kate entered.

"Fine..." She felt vague, disoriented. "Just... fine."

"By the looks of your collar, I don't think so," Rhonda said gently.

"My collar?" Kate's hand moved to her shirt.

"It looks as if you caught it in a typewriter carriage." Rhonda got up from her desk, walked over to the coffee-pot and poured a cup of coffee. "A dead giveaway."

"Oh... that," Kate said with a wan smile. Rhonda crossed in front of the desk and handed Kate the cup, and she took a large swig. "I wish this were straight whiskey. My nerves are raw."

"That bad, huh?" Rhonda lifted her darkly penciled brows.

"Worse." She wanted to cry, and she batted her lashes furiously to ward off the stinging tears.

"Hey." Rhonda took Kate's arm and gently pushed her onto a metal framed side chair next to her desk. "Tell me about it." She placed a comforting hand on Kate's arm.

"I don't know where to begin." Kate searched her mind for some clue, something she should have done, could still do, to correct things. "They say Tommy can't read and they want to put him in a remedial class."

"Can't read? Why didn't anyone tell you this before? The year is almost over."

"Holly said she first thought he was just a little slower than the others. To be fair, she did send some notes that he wasn't doing well but never hinted it was this serious."

The flowery scent of Rhonda's perfume drifted to Kate's nose as she talked. It was a comforting smell, like talcum powder, and she wished such a small comfort was all it would take to soothe Tommy's pride. This was just going to kill him. Tommy liked to be the best at everything. Being placed in a class that so clearly announced he not only wasn't the best, but was far behind the others, would be a crushing blow.

"But that's not the worst of it. They want him to see the district psychologist . . . to see if he has some underlying problem."

"Would that be so terrible?"

"Maybe not . . ." Kate didn't want to admit her real concern—that a thirty-two-year-old woman was still bothered by what her parents thought—so she skirted the issue. "It's just—he *can* read, Rhonda. He plays Scrabble. Can a kid who can't read play Scrabble? It doesn't come easy to him, that's all.

"I help with his homework every night. I thought if we worked hard he would improve. Now Holly says all I do is teach him to memorize the stuff. They said his reading difficulties are the reason he is getting into so much mischief. Oh, Rhonda, my dad will hit the ceiling when he hears about the psychologist." There. It was out.

To Kate's surprise Rhonda didn't tell her she was being silly. She simply patted her hands. "Honey, I can't speak from experience because I don't have kids, but I do know that even the best parents have problems. You're a good mom, Kate. It's just that you can't live Tommy's life for him. Neither can your dad. You and Tommy have to do that yourselves. You have to make the decisions you think are right."

Even through her pain it occurred to Kate that it was unfortunate that her friend didn't have children, because she would have made a great mother.

She thought, then, of how different Rhonda was from her own mother. As far as anyone knew, Rhonda had never married and was her own person—competent, outspoken and sure of herself. Kate's mother, by contrast, hovered around her husband and brood, forever pleasing, forever serving.

It frightened Kate sometimes to think she might become like that, and now she knew why she was seeking Rhonda's advice instead of her mother's. "Do you think the remedial reading class is a good idea?" she asked, needing confirmation for her decision.

"It can't hurt, can it?"

"No, it can't hurt." Still, Kate felt uneasy. "I'm just not sure it will help. They say he could have a learning disability. And I don't know what to do about the psychologist."

"What did you tell the school?"

"I agreed to the remedial classes but said I wanted to think about the testing."

"Then why don't you leave it there for a while, Kate? Time will give you the answers."

"Yeah. Time." Everything took time, Kate thought. She leaned into the chair and sighed. She was so tired. She should have gone home after the school meeting. But there were still a few last-minute corrections to be done on *Small-Town Women,* and she might as well get started. The sooner she did, the sooner she could leave. She withdrew her hand from Rhonda's grasp. "Thanks," she said as she rose.

"There's nothing to thank me for. What are friends for?"

"Just let me know if I can ever return the favor."

Telling Kate not to give it a thought, Rhonda returned to her work and Kate entered her office.

After sitting at her desk, Kate searched her drawer for her ever-present antacid tablets. Finding them, she popped several in her mouth, then pulled out a file folder. Only five weeks left until *Small-Town Women* went to the city council for review. Her excitement about the series was already returning, replacing her anxiety. She decided she would deal with the future one day at a time and stop trying to solve everything all at once.

As her work began absorbing her, the turbulence in her stomach reduced to a rolling marble instead of a thundering boulder. After all, a child could have worse problems than poor reading skills.

JASON ENTERED the lobby just in time to hear the latch click on Kate's door. He had heard the soft murmurs of the two women through his own door and suspected they were discussing Kate's meeting. He wanted to ask Kate how it went. In fact, he'd stepped into the lobby for just that purpose.

Somehow Tommy had crawled into his mind and lodged himself firmly there. No matter how hard he tried, Jason couldn't erase him. He wanted everything to be all right—to offer the help he knew he could give—although he doubted Kate would accept it readily.

He knew he should just back off and stay away from Kate. The future of the station was unstable, jobs hung in the balance. It wasn't a good idea to get involved with other employees.

He started to return to his office, then thought of Tommy's practice that night. He could verify the time with Kate, which would give him a reasonable excuse to visit her office. She might volunteer something about her meeting with the school, although given her previous reaction to his observations about Tommy, he doubted it.

But it was worth a try and, the decision made, he walked toward Kate's office, passing Rhonda Weatherby who sat at her desk studiously ignoring him.

"Hello," he said, deliberately forcing her to acknowledge his presence. Of all the employees, Rhonda was the most blatant in her animosity. She looked up slowly, nodded, then returned to her work. Jason shrugged and went to Kate's door. It was closed and he rapped softly.

"Come in."

He opened the door.

"Hi," he said, wishing he had a wittier opening.

Kate looked up from her notes and wondered why she felt instantly happier. "Hi."

His eyes were open, sympathetic, their rich hue bringing to mind the whiskey she had yearned for earlier. That morning, when they met as previously planned, he had worn his usual guarded expression, all business, not overstepping the bounds of their acquaintance as he had done the evening of their dinner. Kate had been grateful for that. Whiskey eyes or not, she planned to keep her distance.

"The day is almost over and I realized I wasn't sure what time Tommy's team starts practice."

"So you're really going to do it?" she asked, wondering what Jason could possibly hope to get out of coaching that team. Somehow he didn't seem to be the type to wrangle small boys. He still wore the pin-striped suit, although he'd left the vest at home, and she wondered if he planned to attend practice in it.

"Actually, I'm looking forward to it."

The sincerity in his tone made Kate smile. "I'll check back with you after practice. You might be getting more than you bargained for."

"I don't think so." He smiled in return, wrinkled his nose, then shook his head. Kate found the out-of-character, almost boyish gesture appealing. She began to think there might be several sides to Jason Brock, and a little of the distrust she felt for him melted.

"Like I said, I'll check with you after." Her smile widened. "They meet at five-thirty."

"Are you going to be there?"

He seemed hesitant, as though restraining his eagerness, and Kate wondered if he was anxious for her company. The possibility made her pulse quicken. "Wouldn't miss it. But I have to get this tape to Harry first."

"Then I won't keep you. See you later." He smiled again and left the office.

Kate stared at the door he'd shut behind him. Something had been very odd about that exchange. She couldn't figure out exactly what it was. Then realization dawned. Jason had been smiling practically the whole time.

That brought a smile to her own face, and as she bent back over her work, she suddenly felt better equipped to deal with Tommy. Why something that simple should make a difference, she didn't know. She only knew it did.

"SO IS THE TEAM getting in shape?"

Kate, sitting on the bottom row of the school's wooden bleachers, turned to the sound of the voice and saw her father standing above her. Normally she would be pleased to see him, but not right now. She had enough on her mind and didn't feel like facing her father's reaction at the same time she would be dealing with Tommy's.

"Hi, Daddy." She forced enthusiasm into her voice.

"Sorry to be so late." Sam Springer eased down beside her. "A guy came in at the last minute with a rush printing job."

Kate planted a kiss on her father's forehead and patted his thick reddish hair. "I thought you retired. You aren't supposed to work like a slave anymore.'' The whole purpose of her parent's move from Phoenix to the mountains was to allow Sam to slow down. But less than a year later he'd bought a small quick-copy shop and now worked nearly as hard as ever.

''A man's got to feel like he's doing something useful, hon. Besides the guy practically got on his knees and begged. Said he had to get his résumés in the mail this week.''

Kate knew darn well the man hadn't begged. Her father was a sucker for the challenge of a deadline. It was what had made him so successful.

''Sure, Daddy.'' Her dry tone made him smile before he leaned forward, resting his elbows on his knees.

''Who's the guy in the suit helping Charlie coach?''

''Jason Brock, the new operating manager I told you about.''

''Does he always dress like that?''

''I suppose he does. I've never seen him any other way.'' Kate laughed out loud, glad that Jason's clothing gave them something to discuss.

''Anything going on between you two?''

''Daddy! Would you quit!'' Lately her father had been nagging her mercilessly about dating again, telling her she was too young to live like a nun. But he was stretching it this time. ''He just offered to help coach Tommy's team.''

Sam shot a playful punch at her arm. ''So you want me to butt out, right?''

''Right.'' Kate punched him back. Hard. He gave a mock flinch. ''Is Mom coming?''

''Not tonight. She asked me to invite you and Tommy for dinner.''

A tremendous yell interrupted them. Practice was over, and now the boys clustered around their coaches. Kate's hand flew to the collar of her jacket. It was time to talk to Tommy.

"What?" She'd already forgotten her father's question.

"Dinner. Do you want to come to dinner?"

"Oh, yeah, sure, Daddy. But I have to talk to Tommy first." Her stomach knotted into a fist when she looked at Tommy's flushed face. He was listening to instructions from Charlie and Jason. "Can we come by in a little bit?" She stood and so did Sam.

"What do you have to talk to Tommy about?" her father asked.

Kate vaguely noticed the frown on his face. Her mind felt slow, unprepared to evade his question. But she wasn't interested in hearing his opinions, which she knew so well. He didn't value education much, and if it hadn't been for Kate's mother, neither she nor her brother would have gone to college. It was one of the few battles her mother had won. Rather than attempt to sidestep, Kate decided to give him half the story.

"Oh, more mischief. This time he sent the entire class to the music room. Holly spent half an hour tracking them down."

Sam slapped his knee with a guffaw. "Kid's a regular chip off the Springer block."

"Don't encourage him, Daddy."

"Don't you worry, hon. Tommy'll turn out just fine. A little spunk never hurt a boy."

Sam's attitude bothered Kate. Yet she wasn't certain he didn't have a point. Maybe she mothered Tommy too much. After all, boys had to be boys, didn't they?

"Well, don't let him think it's all right to do these things, okay?"

"Okeydokey," Sam said, winking.

Despite her inner turmoil, Kate had to smile a bit. It wasn't that her dad didn't have Tommy's interests at heart. They just saw things differently, that was all. They had crossed the field while they talked, and now Tommy came running up.

"Grandpa! Give me five!" He slapped his grandfather's hand in that jock greeting men used with each other.

"You gonna knock 'em dead this season, Tommy?"

"You bet. I'm gonna pitch."

"Good boy." Sam lifted Tommy's baseball cap, then set it back on his head.

Kate knew that would end their conversation. Tommy and his grandfather never had much to say to each other. As much as Kate wanted them to be close, as much as she was sure her father wanted it, it just didn't happen. Tommy's noisy ways always ended up causing Sam to ask him to quiet down.

"Jason's a cool coach, Mom. He's teaching me how to throw a curveball."

Jason had approached while they were talking, and Kate called him over and introduced him to her father. Sam immediately asked about the curveball, and Kate excused herself, saying she had to talk to Tommy.

"What do we have to talk about, Mom?"

Tommy strolled beside her, baseball glove on one hand, looking worried. Kate supposed he was afraid Holly had called about what he'd written on the blackboard. "I met with the school today." She had led them back to the bleachers and now sat down. "Sit here with me." She patted a spot beside her.

Tommy, face glum, settled obediently and Kate began. "There's no easy way to tell you this, Tommy. They say you have trouble reading." His gray-green eyes stared at her seriously, but he didn't say anything. Kate almost wished he would. "They want to put you in a remedial reading class and I agreed."

The eyes turned dark, the green nearly vanishing, and instantly glistened. He blinked furiously, fighting back the tears that threatened to roll out at any moment. "Please, please, Mom. Don't make me do it."

"Kiddo, there's nothing I can do about it. This is real serious stuff. You're going to fail fourth grade if something isn't done soon." Kate's chest throbbed painfully at Tommy's anguish.

"Miss Shortridge is going to flunk me?" A lone tear escaped his eye, creating a crooked streak on his dust-covered face. "That ugly old witch."

Normally Kate wouldn't have permitted such outright disrespect, but this time she allowed it. Tommy had enough to deal with. She put an arm around him and tried to draw him near.

"Don't!" He testily brushed her arm away and wiped his eyes with a grimy fist. When he looked back, his tears were gone, replaced by a streak of dirt on his face and an angry glint in his eye. "Why didn't you just say no, Mom? Why are you letting them do this? The other guys'll make fun of me."

"I want you to pass, Tommy. I want you to learn to read well." Kate looked away. The intense emotion on Tommy's face was more than she could bear.

The sun was dipping behind the mountains now and the night lights had come on. Across the field a team of older boys practiced. Jason and Sam stood at the edge of the parking lot, talking. So her father had waited. Apparently he and Jason had hit it off.

Kate wished they weren't so far away. She needed help, the kind only a man could give. But she knew her father couldn't do it, and Jason was merely a stranger, a co-worker.

Well, she had handled Lee's death and the crippling debt he'd left behind. That proved she could handle anything. She returned her attention to Tommy. "It won't be forever. Just until you catch up."

"Yeah. That'll be forever. I'll never learn."

"Sure you will." She ran her fingers through his hair, gratified he didn't push her hand away this time. He seemed ready now for a little comfort and, as if reading her thoughts, he moved over and leaned his head on her shoulder. "It's going to take you a little longer, that's all. You'll just have to try harder."

"But I already do." His child's voice had lost its angry edge and sounded so piteously plaintive that Kate wanted to cry. She knew he tried. They both tried. "I don't know if I can do any better. Am I stupid, Mom?"

Stupid! There. He'd asked it. The question she had been afraid to hear. She rushed to reassure him. "No, honey. You're very smart. Look how well you do in math. And baseball. But some people are smart in some subjects while others are smart in a different way."

"You're sure I'm not stupid? You're not ashamed of me?" He spoke with a small, suppressed hitch.

"I could never be ashamed of you, kiddo." She stroked his head, smarting at his words. Yet she knew she *was* ashamed. Not of Tommy. No, not of Tommy, but of his difficulty. Everyone could read. It pained her to admit Tommy couldn't. "Never!" she added more fervently, trying to banish her real thoughts.

She straightened, pulled a tissue from her purse and helped Tommy wipe the streaks off his face. It would embarrass him if the men could tell he'd been crying. Satisfied, she forced a smile. "There. You look good as new. Let's go now. Grandpa invited us to dinner."

"Oh, swell. Now I'll have to be quiet all night."

Kate knew it was hard on him, being at her parents with nothing to do, not even able to watch his favorite television shows. "We won't stay long, okay?"

He looked up at her, lips compressed, and nodded. Kate decided to make sure she kept her promise.

They crossed the field silently and joined the men who were still standing by Jason's car. Sam was animatedly telling Jason about a recent rush printing job, and Jason looked appropriately attentive, but Kate noted a glimmer of relief in his eyes when he saw them drawing near.

Sam saw them, too, and gave Jason a manly slap on the shoulders. "This is a helluva guy, Kate. Like him so much, I invited him to dinner.'

Oh, swell, Kate thought silently, echoing Tommy's earlier words.

"Cool!" Tommy said, his woebegone face suddenly coming back to life. "Are you coming, Jason? Are you?"

If Jason had wanted to say no, it was too late now. And Kate noticed how pleased he seemed to learn that Tommy wanted his company. It hadn't occurred to Kate until then now starved Tommy was for masculine attention. Cory's departure from Lakeview had left a big hole in her son's life. Maybe Jason would be good for him.

"If it's no imposition." Jason looked at Kate as though it was she he didn't wish to impose upon.

"No imposition at all," Sam said.

"We'd love to have you," Kate said in tandem with her father.

"Cool!" Tommy repeated immediately after.

A short time later they pulled into the Springer driveway, where Kate's mother was standing at the door. Sam had beaten them home and must have alerted her that Jason was coming. She met him with typical cordiality.

"Thanks for the invitation, Rita," Jason said, his voice unusually warm.

Rita shot an approving glance toward Kate, who responded by raising her eyebrows. She sensed there was a scheme brewing. Since moving to the mountains, Sam had developed a "ya'll come" attitude toward strangers, and the invitation wasn't out of character, but there seemed to be a matchmaking motive behind this one. Surprisingly she didn't mind, although she wondered how the reserved Jason would fare with her outspoken, noisy father. He seemed to be getting along well and looked cheerful enough as Tommy led him into the living room.

"Need some help, Mom?"

Kate followed Rita into the kitchen. The aroma of the steam puffing from a pot told her chicken and dumplings were on the menu.

"Everything's under control," Rita replied, looking pleased. But then she furrowed her brow. "But you look tired, dear." She reached over and stroked Kate's forehead.

The gesture was like a balm, and for a moment Kate let her cheek rest against her mother's warm hand. "I met with Tommy's teacher and the district psychologist today. Tommy's in deep trouble." She hadn't meant to tell, but it just slipped out. She had to ease the ache in her heart some way.

"Oh?" Rita tilted her head.

Kate immediately regretted her admission. Her mother's lone word was so typical, leaving all the burden of talking on Kate. No "What happened?" or "What did they say?" Just "Oh?"

Well, she had started it, she might as well get it out. "Don't tell Daddy, okay?" When Rita nodded, she began talking about the remedial class, the psychological testing the school advised and the suspicion of a learning disability.

"What kind of disability?" Rita finally asked, her first words since Kate had started.

"They aren't sure. That's why they want to do the testing."

"Well, the worst is over for now, and I'm sure you can handle whatever comes up."

The lid of the chicken pot rattled. Rita wiped her hands on her apron and turned toward the stove. "It's time to put the dumplings in. Why don't you join that good-looking man of yours?"

"He's not my man, Mom." Kate tried to keep her voice even. She cringed inside from the comment about her ability to handle things. Her mother always said things like that, never recognizing that Kate might be uncertain or worried, virtually shutting the door on any desire Kate might have for feedback about her problem. It left her feeling very alone. "He's Tommy's baseball coach and my new co-worker, that's all."

"Uh-huh." Rita dipped a spoon in a bowl of batter and dropped a dab into the pot. Her mouth pursed and she seemed suddenly preoccupied. With a resigned sigh Kate planted a kiss on her cheek and went to join the men. These were her parents, she loved them, and she might as well accept them the way they were.

The television blared as she entered the room. It was tuned to Channel Seven, and Kate smiled, wondering whom her parents thought they were kidding. They seldom watched KZET and, without question, her father had no interest in *The Frugal Gourmet,* the program now playing. She joined the guys at a table where they were working a jigsaw puzzle. Tommy, his anger apparently forgotten, had just triumphantly found another piece. Jason was sifting through a pile on the table.

"Never was any good at this," he muttered as Kate sat down beside him. She winked conspiratorially and began helping him sort through the pile.

A few moments later Rita appeared at the door and asked Sam for help in the kitchen. When Kate offered instead, Rita refused, saying she needed a tall man to get down a bowl. As Sam left the room, Tommy successfully placed a puzzle piece and cheered loudly.

"You're a lot better at this than I am, Tommy." Jason still struggled with his original piece. Tommy's pleased smile warmed Kate, and she found herself liking Jason for making her son feel good.

Soon Rita called them into dinner, and Kate excused herself to wash her hands first, something the men had already done. When she entered the dining room, the others were already seated.

"An elephant with a bunch of bananas on its head," her father was saying, laughing loudly at his own punch line. Jason responded politely but, as Kate sat down, she felt mildly embarrassed. She wished her father would stop telling those dumb elephant jokes. No one had told those since she was in grade school.

The meal should have smelled wonderful—rich, creamy gravy, butter-laden vegetables, steaming rolls—but the odors mingled unpleasantly and Kate found she wasn't very hungry, so she took small servings from each bowl.

"Is that all you're having, dear?" Her mother glanced disapprovingly at her plate. "You should really eat more. You're much too thin."

Kate thought of the small roll of excess flesh on her hips and realized her mother wasn't seeing her the way she was. She still saw the scrawny adolescent who used to live here. "A woman can never be too thin or too rich, Mom," Kate said, quoting a famous socialite.

"Men like women with a little meat on their bones, Kate." Sam patted Rita's round thigh and grinned devilishly. Rita giggled. "Eat up."

"I'll have seconds if I'm still hungry." Kate dipped a fork into the chicken and dumplings and raised it to her mouth.

"I got a postcard." Tommy stuffed a dumpling in his mouth, chewed some, then continued. "From Uncle Cory. He's in Australia for a surfing contest."

The table became silent, and the silence stretched uncomfortably. Sam, mouth full of food, stared at his grandson as he chewed. Finished, he lowered his fork. "We don't talk about Cory here, Tommy. He's a bum."

A flash of pain and anger leaped into Tommy's eyes. He lifted his chin and met his grandfather's stare. "He's not a bum, Grandpa. He won ten thousand dollars."

"It's not right. A thirty-year-old man getting paid to play. Don't be thinking that it is. A man needs to work hard, settle down. Your uncle is a bum, Tommy. Nothing more."

Jason put down his own fork, watching the interchange between Tommy and his grandfather. He found the scene intriguing. Rita, dark hair pulled behind her ears, looked at her husband helplessly with wide blue eyes much like Kate's. Kate looked suddenly sick, a mottled flush covering her cheeks. How different Kate's family was from the home in which he'd been reared. His uncle would never have dared say an angry word in his wife's presence. Aunt Phyllis had dominated the entire household.

Beth's parents had been so sublimely well-bred that such an outburst wouldn't have occurred at their table. And their own rare family meals had been filled with meaningless chitchat.

Families. They were a mystery to Jason, and he suddenly recognized that each one was different.

"Tommy," Kate asked, one hand clutching her collar, "would you get my purse from the living room? I need something from it."

Tommy, seeming to realize he had jumped in over his head, leaped up and bounded out of the room.

Sam turned his gaze to Kate. "Why did you send him away like that? The boy needs to learn the facts."

"Daddy, please." Kate glanced covertly at Jason, hoping to remind her father he was there.

"Look, the kid has to grow up, Kate. Like this business Rita told me about the school. If Tommy works hard, he can get over all this, but he'll never do it if he hero-worships a deadbeat like your brother. By the way, I think you made the right decision about the psychologist."

Kate saw her mother's horrified expression as the words came out of her father's mouth. He didn't appear to notice.

"Don't want those white-coated eggheads poking around in his mind," Sam continued. "He'll end up like Cory for sure, with all that sensitivity training and stuff. Shrinks are for nutcases, not normal kids like Tommy. We don't need that mumbo jumbo. A man works hard, a man gets what he works for."

Oh, God, Kate knew she should never have confided in her mother. The chicken suddenly felt like lead in her stomach.

So that's what happened, Jason thought, and he knew the school probably wanted to test for a learning disability. Jason had thought about Tommy a lot—the way he shaded his letters when they played Scrabble, his mischievous disruptions—and felt certain the boy was dyslexic like himself. Now he understood Kate's resistance to his suggestion.

"Okay, Daddy, okay." Kate jabbed at her food with her fork. She could hear Tommy approaching. "But could we just drop it. Tommy's coming back and he'll be embarrassed."

His following harrumph told Kate he wasn't pleased but would comply. He must have realized that his behavior in front of Jason was out of line. As Tommy entered the room, gave Kate her purse and sat back down, Sam turned to his guest. "Hey, Jason, did you hear the one about the guy with the duck?"

Kate suppressed a sigh. She supposed these corny jokes were preferable to their previous topics of conversation.

While they finished eating, Rita jumped up continually, getting this, getting that, studiously avoiding Kate's eyes. As betrayed as she felt, Kate knew her mom felt the same. It was clear her father wasn't supposed to have let on that he knew about the meeting with the school.

It was a relief when dinner was over. Kate left her plate virtually untouched and, for once, her mother didn't fuss or make a comment when Kate reached into her purse to get an antacid tablet.

She offered to help clean up but, thankfully, her mother demurred. Soon she, Jason and Tommy stood at the door to the living room, their coats on, ready to leave. Sam was telling Jason yet another deadline story, and Kate couldn't quite understand why Jason appeared to be enjoying himself.

Finally Sam completed his anecdote and opened the door, allowing a cool breeze to enter. The television blared from the corner, their departing pleasantries blending with the noise. Then the room became strangely quiet, their voices the only sound. Kate glanced over, wondering what had happened.

"My God, Jason, we're off the air!"

She stared in horror at the soundless snow filling the television screen. Dead time! The nightmare of the television industry, and the result of human or technical error. Kate helplessly wondered which it was as she saw Jason swivel his head to stare also. Only a few seconds passed, although it seemed an eternity.

Suddenly, unannounced, Chuck E. Squirrel filled the peppered screen. The fuzzy creature weaved drunkenly above his tree stump home, then sank slowly inside, wailing, "Hey! Who turned out the lights?"

CHAPTER FOUR

"THAT'S WAY OUT OF LINE," Kate heard the sharpness in her voice as the words tumbled out but was unable to control it. While Jason and Carlton continued to give her their full attention as though nothing had happened, Kate could tell by Woody's questioning glance that he'd noticed her unusual tone.

But these were unusual circumstances. Never, in her five years at the station, had firing been suggested as the solution to a simple error.

"He put in the wrong cassette," Kate continued without apologizing for her lapse. "It was an honest mistake, that's all."

Jason rubbed his forehead and looked at her calmly. "Mistake or not, Channel Seven cannot tolerate this kind of carelessness and still be a serious contender in the PBS network."

His voice, in contrast to hers, was unemotional, inflectionless. If Jason had noted her irritation, he was choosing to ignore it, and that made Kate even angrier. How could he so coolly discuss taking away a man's livelihood?

"Besides, Kate, operations is my department, which makes this my decision."

"It was an accident." Kate repeated, beginning to think that Jason was very dense. "Steve Karako has been with the station for many years. He has three children and his wife is expecting another. How is he going to support his family if we fire him?''

"Has he been an outstanding employee? Or just average?''

"He does his job,'' Kate snapped. "Does a man suddenly have to be a superstar to earn job security around here?'' She looked around at the others for support, but Woody remained impassive, while Carlton nodded at Jason's every word, his colorless, close-set eyes sparkling with interest.

"For heaven's sake, you can't just fire someone the minute things go wrong. There has to be an alternative.'' Kate took a deep breath, trying to control her anger. Her hand flew to her collar, and she rubbed the silk fabric for comfort. If she didn't get a grip on herself soon, she might find herself saying some very unprofessional things.

She knew she was pushing more than she should. Normally she wasn't even asked to attend operations meetings, and this *was* an operations problem. But Woody had said he wanted her input, so she turned and fixed an imploring glance on him. "Don't you think so, Woody?''

"To answer Jason's question, Steve is about average,'' Woody responded. "But I'm not sure firing is the answer. Especially here in Lakeview. We're the only game in town, and firing someone almost amounts to running them out of town on a rail. Also, I think this could have happened to anyone. The possibility of loading the wrong cassette is one of the risks you take with automated equipment.''

"Only through carelessness.'' Jason punctuated his remark by slapping a fist on his hand, his first display of emotion, and Kate suddenly realized that Jason felt very strongly about this. It didn't seem just a business decision to him but a kind of personal vendetta against sloppy work. "You and I were up half of last night, Woody. We both know he could have prevented this by checking the labels before loading the jukebox," Jason concluded, referring to the multitowered bank of videotape players by its nickname.

"It's still new to us, Jason," Kate said, jumping in before Woody could respond. It looked as if he was vacillating toward Jason's point of view, and that just couldn't happen. A man's life was being decided here. "Our technicians don't have much experience with jukeboxes, and we don't really have procedures in place."

"It's no easy trick to balance what's good for the station with what's good for its employees," Woody commented, still apparently uncommitted to a point of view. "Ideally they should be the same thing." Kate allowed her hopes to rise. "I understand your concern for Steve, Kate, but we can't just let this pass. Jason's made some valid points. Something has to be done, and you haven't offered any workable alternatives."

Kate's hopes deflated as she realized that her earlier intuition might, indeed, have been correct. She had expected more of Woody, but it wasn't as if she hadn't seen this coming.

A dull headache behind her eyes muddled her thinking, and she felt very tired. After Chuck E. Squirrel's unscheduled appearance, Jason had left for the station immediately. He hadn't seemed upset, merely purposeful and intent on resolving the problem.

Kate had returned with Tommy and slipped into a restless sleep, only to be awakened around midnight by a phone call from Woody. He'd said that Jason thought they should discuss the incident before the day shift arrived. From Woody's tone Kate had suspected that Jason was running the whole show. The implications behind that suspicion had disturbed her, and she hadn't been able to fall back asleep.

But after the meeting started, Woody had demonstrated his usual objectivity, and she'd felt a little better about things. Now Woody seemed to be sliding into Jason's camp. Judging by his intermittent nods, Kate assumed that Carlton was already there. Three against one. She didn't like those odds.

Still, Woody didn't seem totally convinced. She simply had to come up with an alternative. Fuzzy-minded or not, she needed to devise something quick. But what?

No procedures. What had she said about no procedures? Suddenly an idea formed. "What if we develop a discipline policy? We've discussed it in staff meetings before."

She was pleased when she noticed Jason's eyebrow rise, but she didn't want to let him talk yet, so she continued quickly. "For instance, on a first occurrence like this one we could suspend the employee without pay for one day. A second offense or a deliberate violation of policy could carry a one-week suspension. That way employees would be given a chance to correct their behavior."

Carlton's lip curled in a thinly veiled sneer, and Kate wanted to punch him. But since Jason and Woody were the ones she had to convince, she ignored him.

"It could work," Woody said.

"I'm not sure it's enough," Jason commented thoughtfully. "But under the circumstances, with the absence of thorough training, it might be the best action. Steve is an experienced employee, and breaking in someone new would be costly."

Jason's logic offended Kate. Did this man base all his decisions on a balance sheet? What about people? But she kept her opinion to herself because she saw Carlton's sneer vanish, replaced by a brief flash of defensiveness. Kate recognized the source of Carlton's reaction. He had spearheaded the installation of the automated equipment and was ultimately responsible for proper training. Jason's comment had implied that he'd been less than successful.

He recovered quickly, and when he said, "It has possibilities," Kate knew the wind had changed.

She suppressed a triumphant smile and plunged in with the others to develop a viable policy. The negotiations didn't proceed smoothly since Jason and Carlton pressed for longer suspension periods, while Kate pressed for shorter.

But eventually the policy was hammered out. A three-day suspension for a first offense, two weeks for the second offense and termination of employment for the third. Deliberate violations of policy would incur termination of employment on the first occurrence. They then worked on a checklist for loading the automated tape player.

It was nearly eleven o'clock before Woody dropped his pen and said, "Well, folks, I think we got it."

Everyone smiled, and Kate leaned back in her chair, relieved. Steve might have to endure a three-day suspension, but he still had a job.

Then Woody's smile slowly faded. "There's only one thing that bothers me."

Kate looked at him curiously. She thought they had covered everything.

"I talked to Steve for a long time last night. He admits he was the only person loading the tape deck for the evening broadcasts."

"Which he was," Jason said.

Woody nodded. "I know. But Steve still claimed he didn't load the Chuck E. outtakes. He says he would have remembered the scratches on the top side of the cassette. He insists he never saw that tape before.''

"Which just proves my point," Jason countered. "The man was careless. So careless he didn't even look at the tape."

It was clear to Kate that Jason didn't see what Woody was getting at. But she did, and was certain her boss wasn't convinced Chuck E. Squirrel's appearance was an accident. *But that's silly,* she thought. She had to agree with Jason this time. Steve had been the only one working in the master control room last night.

Woody nodded, not pressing the issue, and Kate dismissed the idea entirely. After all, why would anyone do such a thing intentionally?

KATE RUBBED her collar vigorously, thinking, thinking. Through compromise she had won the battle, but she could still lose the war. As the meeting was breaking up, Jason had agreed to inform Steve Karako of his three-day suspension, almost cheerfully, or so it had seemed to her.

She thought of the rumors about layoffs that had surged through the station after Jason was hired. Since his arrival she had come to think the rumors were simply the result of all the sudden changes. After all, automation had just come to KZET. The staff had barely adjusted when the previous operations manager had resigned, amid vague speculation that he'd done so under duress, and then Jason arrived on the scene. No wonder her co-workers were uneasy.

But now she knew Jason, and he didn't seem to be the heartless monster he'd been made out to be. He'd been very good to Tommy, and Kate could tell her son already admired him greatly, as did her parents. Undeniably he had a likable human side.

But this morning he'd seemed so cold, remote, almost robotlike in his dedication to business. It suddenly wasn't hard to believe he could orchestrate a layoff and be unconcerned that such an act would shatter people's lives. Profits—only profits—mattered, and Kate was afraid. One of the best things about working at Channel Seven was that upper management—in truth, Woody—had always been concerned about employee welfare. Was it possible that this attitude was about to end?

As she thought, she battled an impulse totally foreign to her nature. She hated confrontations, always had, and she fought the impulse once more as it pushed at her unmercifully.

She gave in.

Getting up from her chair, she marched out of her office and into Jason's without waiting for an invitation. Shutting the door behind her, she noted that Jason had started to smile.

Seeing the expression on Kate's face, Jason aborted his tentative smile, his quick surge of joy vanishing. "Is there a problem?" he asked politely.

He wondered what caused the barely concealed rage on her face. It couldn't be the meeting, could it? Disagreements of this kind were common in business. Surely Kate understood that.

"It's about the meeting."

Jason nodded, disappointment flooding him as he realized for the first time how much he wanted Kate as an ally—or even more. He suppressed an urge to walk over to her and stroke her smooth, freckled face, to ease the lines of tension around her eyes and turn them into smile lines. But it was clearly not to be. They viewed their jobs from totally different angles, and he doubted either one of them would change. He gestured to a chair, but she ignored him.

"You don't care about people at all, do you, Jason?" She frowned and almost spit the words. He hadn't thought this sweet-tempered woman could feel the intense anger her face revealed. Obviously he was wrong, and normally he would have tried to calm her.

But she should have chosen different words. Her question hit him hard and brought ugly echoes of the past. Her words sounded familiar, because they were. Beth had asked that very question many, many times.

A responding anger bubbled up from someplace deep within him, jolting him with its intensity. How had she done this to him? At first he couldn't remember the last time he'd felt such intense emotion, but then the memories returned and he tried to shove them back.

Forcing himself to remain silent, he fought the angry waves now threatening to cloud his judgment and listened as Kate went on about how easily he had suspended Steve and how he held people's lives in his hand but only cared about profits.

Control came back. Rigid control. He raised his hand, palm out, with such jerky force that Kate stopped talking in midsentence. "Listen up, Kate."

His interruption fueled her outrage, but his soft, deadly tone made her wary of continuing, so she simply stared at him, refusing to back down from that stony face and hard glare.

"This is a business, Kate, not somebody's hobby. The station may be a nonprofit organization, but that doesn't mean no profit. If we fail to make money, no one will have a job, because there won't be any more station. My job is to make sure that doesn't happen. That's not a crime, and I refuse to be treated as if it were."

Kate shifted uncomfortably, recognizing an unpleasant truth in Jason's words. "But that has nothing to do with suspending Steve," she protested, beginning to think Jason was changing the subject.

"It has everything to do with Steve." Jason slapped his hands on his desk, the only sign Kate had seen that his control might be shaken. "In commercial broadcasting sloppy stations don't get sponsors. The same holds true in public broadcasting. Too many mistakes like this and we'll lose underwriters. We can't afford to let that happen, and your do-gooder attitude isn't helping a bit."

"You make *that* sound like a crime." She was finding it hard to stay firm in the face of Jason's logic. But caring about people *wasn't* wrong.

Jason's expression softened and so did some of Kate's resolve. She remembered, then, the way he lit up when he smiled and the resonance of his infrequent laughs. She was trying to place him in an enemy camp, trying hard, but it just wasn't working. She couldn't ignore that he had many wonderful qualities, couldn't ignore the sadness in those golden eyes or her desire to kiss it away.

"No, caring isn't a crime, Kate. It just has to be tempered with business sense. You can't keep people just because they need their jobs. They have to do their jobs, too. The installation of the automated controls has cut the work loads by more than half. The plain fact is, we have too many employees."

"So it's true. You were brought in to organize a layoff." Kate's shoulders slumped, and she felt suddenly tired and helpless. "You have a reputation, you know."

"I know I do." Jason sighed and looked down idly at his hands for a moment, then raised his head. "But, rumor aside, I don't automatically start laying people off. There may be other options, like transferring personnel into other departments and not replacing people who quit. I'm not sure yet because I haven't finished reviewing the financial records. But I promise I'm doing the best I can do to avoid any drastic actions." He paused for a moment, as if waiting for her to comment. When she didn't, he went on. "Just leave it be for a while, Kate. Don't add to the rumors."

She suddenly felt his burden. But if the burden was so heavy, why did he do it? "Why...?"

"It's what I do," he replied, as if reading her thoughts. "Now, if we're done, I have unfinished work here."

His request was mildly curt, but considering the way she had barged into his office, Kate supposed it wasn't unwarranted. She backed out of his office and into the hall, her mind whirling with confusion.

She no longer knew what to think. She wanted to stay angry at Jason and hold tightly to her belief that people were more important than profits. But Jason had given that belief a sharp blow. It wasn't that she didn't still have faith in her belief, but she couldn't ignore the harsh reality that, without profits, there might be no more Channel Seven. Besides, his words suggested that there wouldn't be layoffs. True, he seemed more than able to let people go without a second thought, but he didn't seem to be the hatchet man everyone thought he was.

And she didn't want to oppose Jason. To do so would endanger their friendship and, suddenly, she realized she was beginning to value that very much.

JASON WAITED until he heard Kate enter her office before getting up. He should have gotten his supplies on his first day here, but he hadn't, and now was as good a time as any. Besides, he needed a break, some time to recover. He still felt wobbly inside from their argument and was puzzled by his reaction. Where were all these unfamiliar feelings coming from?

He heard a soft, throaty laugh as he entered the lobby and saw Harry leaning over Rhonda's desk, looking down at her. Her head was tilted coquettishly, and she was obviously amused by something he'd just said. They both looked at him. Harry straightened up.

"I'll catch you later," Harry said, then went through the door to the production wing.

Rhonda fixed her attention on Jason, her expression hardening. "Can I do something for you?" she asked.

"I need lead and eraser refills for my mechanical pencil and some notepads and file folders," Jason replied.

"Certainly." Rhonda's gaze was as cool as her voice, contradicting her rather tartish looks. With her frosted dark hair in its lacquered French twist and the heavy makeup that gave her face a porcelain doll appearance, she reminded Jason of a fifties glamour girl. She wasn't unattractive, Jason realized, just overdone and maddeningly chilly.

She took a key from her desk and walked over to the supply cabinet, opening it with a proprietary air to reveal a tidy interior. "Fill this out, please," Rhonda said, handing Jason a form.

He propped it against the cabinet surface and obligingly completed the form. What had he done to offend her? He knew by observing her with the other employees that she was normally outgoing and friendly, so he finally decided she must be reacting to his reputation. Her attitude made him feel shut out and stirred a vague ache buried deep in his memory.

Another day he might have attempted to win her over, but today he had other things on his mind, so when

Rhonda gave him the supplies in exchange for the properly filled out requisition, he returned to his office.

As usual his cranky chair complained dolefully when he sat down, as if to remind him of KZET's dour financial situation. He glanced around the room with mild dismay and grimaced at the yellow accumulated wax on the dingy vinyl floor.

Pebble-grained walls glared unpleasantly from the light of the curtainless window, reminding him that he should do something about the glare. He was leaving the office each day with a headache.

He laid his supplies on his desk, opened several drawers and placed each item meticulously in its assigned place. As he closed the drawers, he ran his hand over the battered wood, finding it hard to begin working. The desk reminded him of the old-fashioned library tables he'd laboriously studied at as a child. It had been hard to start working then, too.

You don't care about people, do you? Kate's accusations rewound in his head like an unending instant replay. Of course, the words had been recorded there already; all it took was repetition to bring them back.

Why did everyone else have such difficulty seeing things the way he did? He simply saw what needed to be done and did it, just as he'd done today. If there was ever a place where something needed to be done, Channel Seven was it. He scanned the room, looking for evidence to confirm his opinion, and was gratified to see that it was all around him.

Every inch of this makeshift building screamed lack of funds. If the problem wasn't solved soon, programming hours would need cutting. Cuts would reduce the station's already weak rating, and while Jason knew that ratings weren't as important in public broadcasting as in the commercial sector, underwriters usually pulled funding if they felt a station had no audience. It was a vicious circle, and it was Jason's job to find a way out of it.

He slipped on his eye patch, then bent over a ledger pad and returned to his work. An hour later he sighed loudly and threw his mechanical pencil onto the desk.

No matter how he juggled the figures, the answer was the same. There were too many employees in operations. Before automation had taken over, these people had had functions. Now they stood around half the day while the equipment did most of the work they used to do.

He flipped through the personnel files one more time. By now he knew each person's history nearly by heart. Length of service, skill levels, performance—all committed to memory. Every department was overstaffed by at least one person. Some would have to go. The realization sickened him at a deeper level than he wanted to admit.

One of those people might be Kate.

During his first meeting with Woody, Jason had asked if Kate knew how important her interview series was and had learned that Woody hadn't told her because he felt she didn't need the additional pressure during her first production. At the time Jason had wondered if Woody might be making a mistake, but after getting to know Kate, he was certain she would pour her whole being into producing *Small-Town Women*, even though she didn't know how important it was to her own future.

She was safe for now. No one else had the skill to carry this project off. If it was successful, Jason would be able to kiss these money problems goodbye because the syndication revenues alone would be enough to put Channel Seven into the black. But if she failed...well, Carlton would be more than happy to take over Kate's programming duties.

He didn't know when his hands started trembling, but now he clenched his fists and willed them to stop. He had always hated this moment when the numbers on the ledger sheet became flesh-and-blood people with names and faces, so this wasn't an unfamiliar reaction. But it was much stronger this time than it had ever been before.

Of course, there were major differences between this job and his network assignments. KZET seemed almost like a large family. Letting even one person go would be like pushing a bird out of the nest.

Also, his current employers wouldn't greet the news of layoffs with the same complacency that network management did. Woody would feel he was abandoning his children, while the mayor and the city council wouldn't forget that their employees were also voters.

But that wasn't the only reason for his trembling hands, and he knew it. He had failed to follow his own advice. He had allowed himself to get close. That mistake might prove very costly.

Costly or not, this was his job. He had an obligation, and no one could ever say that Jason Brock didn't fulfill his obligations. He picked up the phone to buzz Woody, anxious to get this nasty business behind him.

Finger poised to punch the numbers, he stopped and glanced at the ledger sheet once more, then slowly lowered the receiver back into the cradle. What if he reviewed the budget figures one more time?

Maybe... just maybe.

CHAPTER FIVE

"HAVE YOU SEEN Carlton today?" Harry Bingham asked. He leaned against the wall next to the lobby coffee station and watched as Kate filled her cup.

"No. Why?" The tone of Harry's voice made Kate smile in anticipation.

"He showed up in a three-piece suit, looking like a miniature clone of Jason. Pinstripes, red on blue tie, wing tip shoes—the works." Harry laughed, and the lusty sound was contagious, making Kate laugh, too. "But the best part is that Jason is wearing cord jeans and a sweater today," Harry continued, then dissolved into more laughter. When he caught his breath he added, "Wait until Carlton sees that."

"Carlton always was a jerk, and clothes won't make Brock one of us," Rhonda testily commented. She sat at her desk, pen poised over her paperwork, looking decidedly unamused.

The laughter died on Kate's lips, and she looked at Rhonda in amazement, stunned by her bitter tone.

"Why don't you cut him some slack, Rhonda?" Harry asked. Her comment had obviously dampened his good humor also, because he sounded very serious. "He seems like a nice enough guy."

"We were all doing fine until he got here." Rhonda twirled her pen between her fingers, scowling as though

Jason had single-handedly destroyed the entire station. "You should have gotten that job, Harry. You earned it."

"I have better things to do than push paper all day." Harry crossed over to Rhonda's desk and chucked her under the chin. "Don't you get in an uproar, hear, because I'm sure not going to."

Rhonda brushed his hand away. "You don't have to, because if we have layoffs, you'll be the last person to go."

So that was it, Kate thought. Rhonda was concerned about her job. Kate rushed to reassure her. "And you'll be the second last, Rhonda," she said. "Without you everything would fall apart. Besides, Jason and I talked, and he's doing everything he can to prevent laying people off. There's nothing to worry about."

Kate remembered Jason's reassurances during their heated discussion a few days ago, as well as his warning not to add to the rumors. She was trying her best to follow his advice, but even as she spoke she hoped the reassurances weren't false.

"I'll bet that's what Steve Karako thought just before he got suspended," Rhonda shot back, her face forming into hard lines of disapproval. "Besides, who can believe you? He's only been here two weeks, and I hear you've had several hot dates."

"Rhonda!" Kate whirled and planted her fists on her hips. She understood Rhonda's apprehension, but this was going too far. A flush crept to her face, and she knew it wasn't entirely from annoyance. Rhonda had touched a little too closely to something Kate wanted to deny. Of course Kate wasn't dating Jason, but didn't she wish they were? "I'd hardly call two family dinners and a Little League game hot dates. Besides, even if it were true, it's none of your business."

"This is a small town. Everybody's business is everybody else's."

"Then let's just correct the record." Kate knew Rhonda was right. It was one of the more annoying aspects of small-town life, but it had never before mattered to Kate because she had never done anything to elicit even the slightest interest from others. She still hadn't, but Rhonda's innuendo made her realize how much she wished she were. "Jason helps coach Tommy's baseball team. That's all."

Rhonda's heavily penciled eyebrow arched. "Oh? Now he's an expert on baseball?"

"For heaven's sake, Rhonda!" Kate's patience reached its limit, and she struggled to keep her voice level. "What on earth is going on with you? I've never seen you act this way. A man doesn't have to be a pro to coach a Little League team. Tommy likes him a lot and, with Cory gone, he needs someone in his life right now."

Rhonda's face softened somewhat, and she looked down for a moment. From the corner of her eye Kate could see Harry watching them with interest, a faint hint of amusement on his face. For once Kate didn't appreciate Harry's sense of the ridiculous. This wasn't funny. It was important to her that Rhonda accept Jason. She hated it when people she liked didn't get along.

"You don't even know him, Rhonda," Kate concluded softly, not wanting her friend to get angry again. "Give him a chance."

"Yeah," Harry said. "Give him a chance."

"Maybe I should have kept my opinions to myself," Rhonda replied. Her voice was more even now and her combative posture had relaxed. "But I still don't like it. He was Mr. Brock, the hatchet man, when he walked in here, and you guys are welcome to your own opinions but, to me, he's still Mr. Brock, the hatchet man.''

Kate knew this was the closest to an apology she was going to get from Rhonda, and she wasn't even sure an apology was in order, so she decided to drop the subject. "I do see your concern, Rhonda," she said in a conciliatory tone. "But Steve was only suspended for three days. Not fired. And he's already back to work. Maybe a little wiser. You can't deny he was pretty careless. Trust me, you have nothing to fear from Jason.''

Rhonda nodded, then lowered her head and went back to posting numbers in a ledger as though Kate and Harry were no longer there. Kate walked away, shaking her head, feeling very bad about this encounter. She and Rhonda had been friends for five years. Now there was a rift between them.

Throughout the day she was troubled by thoughts of their argument. As she walked to the production studio that afternoon, it occurred to her that Jason's arrival at the station had been like a rock falling in a pond, causing ripples to spread far and wide. She wondered how many parts of her life were going to change because of those ripples.

Lost in thought, she was startled when she entered the studio and saw Carlton Spencer hunched over the animator. The studio was alive with activity. The wall of monitors was all turned on, although the sound was muted. Some of the screens displayed the program now airing, while others showed the various dissolves and fades that would be coming up. But the monitor over the animator was blank.

"Well, hello," she said.

Her greeting caused Carlton to swivel his chair toward her. He looked momentarily alarmed, then recovered and smiled insincerely.

"Hello," he replied, reaching back to the animator and casually pushing a key before giving her his full attention. He brushed back his expensively cut brown hair and crossed his legs, carefully arranging the legs of his pinstriped slacks. He didn't wear the suit as well as Jason, Kate thought, but somehow he, too, had managed to stay unwrinkled. Irreverently she wondered if those suits came with instruction manuals.

"What brings you in here?" Kate forced herself to ask politely, not relishing having to make small talk with Carlton. She looked around as she spoke. "Where's Amy?" she continued before Carlton could answer.

"She went to get some blank cassettes. She's helping me do some promos for the fund-raising telethon and realized her stock of tapes was low. I'm learning some nifty stuff."

"Oh?" Kate hoped Amy wouldn't be too long. She didn't have the time or the interest for a long discussion of Carlton's annual telethon, but she asked the expected question, anyway. "How's your campaign coming along?"

"A lot smoother now that we've become automated. With the animator I can do some dynamite spots." He then launched into a description of the various advertisements he planned to develop. Kate was trying to come up with a graceful exit line when Amy Herrera walked into the room. Relieved that she was no longer alone with Carlton, Kate quickly turned toward the young technical director.

"Have the tapes for the wildlife special come in yet, Amy? I need the identification numbers for the programming schedule."

"In the storage rack, I think." Amy walked toward the rack, appearing distressed that she didn't know for sure, then looked up with an apologetic smile. "Yes, they're right here." The girl rummaged through the rack, then frowned. "That's funny. One of them seems to be missing." She made a big show of tapping each tape, obviously counting.

She looked up at Kate, nervously running her hands through her dark curly hair. "I'm sure there were four, but now I only have three."

"Let me look," Kate said as she moved to the rack. She ran her hand across all the tapes, checking the labels, but none of them was the missing tape. She shrugged. "You're right. There are only three."

"I'm sorry, Kate. It's got to be here somewhere. I'll have to look around. I don't know what I could have done with it."

"It's all right," Kate reassured, wanting to alleviate Amy's anxiety. The girl was practically wringing her hands with worry. "It'll show up. Let me know when you find it, okay?"

Amy smiled gratefully, agreeing to give Kate the information she needed as soon as she found the cassette, and Kate returned to her office. Although she hadn't let it show, she was annoyed over the delay because she had wanted to finish the programming schedule before she left for the day. But it wasn't as if the information about the special was the only thing left to do, so she decided to work on her other tasks until Amy got back to her.

A few hours later Kate's intercom buzzed.

"I've got all the cassettes now," Amy Herrera informed her, then went on to provide the identification numbers.

Kate wrote down the information. Finished, she asked, "Where did you find the missing tape?"

Amy hesitated a moment, then began speaking in a rapid, agitated voice. "It's the darnedest thing, Kate. I looked all over for it and couldn't find it anywhere. Finally I decided to check the rack again, wondering if I'd overlooked it. I didn't have much hope, but there it was. I'm really embarrassed and I apologize. You must think I'm an idiot. And blind, besides."

"No, no. These things happen. Besides, I must be blind, too, because I didn't see it, either. Don't worry about it. It's no big deal."

Kate hung up, feeling a little foolish herself. It didn't seem possible that two people could both search for and pass over a cassette label. But finally concluding that people overlooked things all the time, she dismissed the thought and went back to her work. As she had told Amy, it was no big deal.

When she left the station that evening, she found herself still troubled by her quarrel with Rhonda. During the course of the day, they had run into each other several times and both had acted as if nothing had happened. But Kate could sense the subtle change in their relationship.

Kate was torn. She felt as if Rhonda had challenged her to choose between her and Jason, and the thought disturbed her. It wasn't only unfair, there was no reason Kate should have to make such a choice.

Still mulling over the ramifications of that argument, she pulled into the parking lot of Lakeview Elementary School, knowing she'd better hurry. It was nearly five-thirty, the game was about to begin, and she was the official scorekeeper.

She slipped her feet out of her high heels and into sensible flats, grabbed her down jacket and the scoreboard, then rushed to the field. The teams were just taking position as she slid into her seat in the bleachers. She smiled when she saw the team mother give her a relieved glance.

Tommy's team was in the field, and he was on the pitcher's mound. Watching, Kate saw he could now put a definite curve on his pitches, something he'd strived for throughout the previous season without success. She knew that his improvement was a result of Jason's coaching and was only one example of the positive influence he had on Tommy. How could she cut Jason out of their lives just because Rhonda disapproved of him?

The slap of the ball against the bat pulled her back to the present. The runner was put out on first, and several similar plays followed. Pretty soon Tommy's team was up, their opponents having failed to score any runs.

The Indians were batting well. The first three players got hits and now the bases were loaded. Tommy came up to bat. He walked to the plate, hefted the bat above his shoulders and took his stance with a look of fierce concentration on his face.

"Hey, batter, hey, batter, hey, batter, hey," voices chanted from the outfield.

Jason walked behind the batter's cage and watched Tommy through the chain-link fencing. He could almost hear the boy silently commanding himself to block out those taunts.

"Strike two," the umpire called.

"That ball's history, Tommy. Forget about it and concentrate on the next one," Jason advised softly.

Tommy grimaced, wriggled his body, then reassumed the batting position. The pitcher threw again.

Crack! The impact of the bat against the ball was ear-splitting.

"Run, Tommy!" Jason cheered. "Go! Go! Go! Go!" Uninhibitedly Jason joined the chants of the small boys in the dugout beside him. He looked up. The ball zoomed beyond the school yard into a small stand of trees. A home run. Jason's heart soared with the ball and nearly burst with pride.

Tommy trotted home, following the three runners he'd batted in. Then he ran to the dugout where the other players greeted him with cheers.

Jason turned with a grin on his face and saw that it matched the one Kate wore. "Did you get that?"

"You bet," Kate responded, making an okay sign with her fingers. The wind played in her curly hair, and Jason thought she looked very pretty sitting there wrapped in her down jacket, her face flushed with pleasure. "It feels good to be the mother of a superstar."

"And not so bad to be his coach," he replied, wanting to reach over and smooth down a strand of her hair that the wind had displaced. He wondered how her hair would feel against his fingers. Was it as fine and silky as it looked?

A small tug on his sleeve interrupted that thought, and he turned to see Tommy standing there with a triumphant grin nearly splitting his face. "It looks like we're winning."

"Thanks to you." With a victorious whoop Jason swung Tommy into the air, and the boy squealed happily. "Keep up the good work!"

"It's your doing, you know," Tommy said, then scampered back to the dugout.

A warm glow seeped into Jason's limbs. But before he had a chance to enjoy it, an ugly feeling of betrayal crept in—a niggling thought that he should have paid this kind of attention to his daughter. He dismissed that thought angrily. These boys were jubilant, as they had every right to be. He wasn't going to let his memories destroy that for them.

Kate had looked up at the sound of Jason's whoop. Tommy seemed happier than he'd been in a long time. Not that he had ever been moody. But there had been a wistful quality about him ever since Cory had left town. Now it was gone.

Kate came back from her reverie to mark down another run. The whole team had improved since Jason had begun coaching. They had ended the last season near the bottom of the standings and had attended practices with glum faces and defeatist attitudes. Now the boys were all high morale and confidence. The ripples Jason created were having a mixed effect—bringing both improvement and conflict in their wake.

She found herself increasingly drawn to him as a man. Like right now, looking at him bent over, talking earnestly to one of his players. She saw the alluring way his cord jeans defined his buttocks. Firm, muscular. She pictured her hand stroking—

Another hit. It looked like another homer, and she watched the ball fly across the ground into the next diamond, then marked down two more runs.

Kate's feelings for Jason disconcerted her. At night she ached with vague longing and struggled to sleep as she fought wispy images of Jason's lips smothering her own while his long, smooth fingers stroked her fevered body. Although this need had become familiar during the many lonely nights when Lee had been away, it had seemed to die when he did. Now it was back with an overwhelming intensity she had never felt before, and she didn't know how to deal with it.

A raucous yell erupted on the field. The game was over, the Indians were victorious, and now all the players clustered around their respective coaches. Kate jumped up excitedly, nearly dropping the score pad from her lap, and ran onto the field.

"Who do we appreciate?" Fifteen crimson baseball caps flew into the air in unison as the Indians gave the customary tribute to their battered opponents. "The Beavers!"

"We won! We won!" Tommy ran toward her, waving his cap, and nearly leaped into Kate's arms. She struggled for balance beneath his enthusiastic embrace.

"Way to go, kiddo." She stepped back to arm's length. Lord, he was growing tall—already nearly to her shoulders. In a few years she'd be looking up at him instead of the other way around. Soon he'd go off to college, leaving her all alone.

She mentally chided herself for the dismal thoughts. That day wasn't here yet and wouldn't be for quite a while.

Jason and the head coach, Charlie Simpson, were surrounded by bouncing, yelling boys, and Tommy left her side to join them. Jason stood among the throng with his hand outstretched, commanding, "Give me five." As each boy delivered his high-spirited whack, Jason tousled his hair and said a few words of praise.

Kate waited, and soon he spotted her and nodded an invitation to join him, so she threaded through the excited boys and stood next to him. As the last boy slapped his palm, he turned to Kate and gave her a big hug, planting a noisy kiss on her lips.

The enthusiastic frenzy must be contagious, Kate thought. But the kiss, coming so close behind her erotic daydreaming, left her a little dazed. He also seemed dazed and looked slightly sheepish. "Sorry," he mumbled. "I got carried away. I just had to kiss someone."

"That's not very flattering," Kate said with a laugh. Was that an embarrassed flush she saw creeping up Jason's neck, or just the results of fending off sixteen miniature ball players?

"Why don't you start packing the bats, Tommy?" she suggested to relieve Jason of the need to respond to her remark.

"Can Jason eat with us, Mom?"

Kate hesitated. The question forced her right back into her quandary, making her recall Rhonda's comment about "Hot dates." As long as she kept her association with Jason limited to work hours and ball games, nobody could speculate about a possible relationship.

Then, as loud as the slap of a boy's hands on Jason's palm, realization dawned. She was no longer sure she didn't want a relationship. That admission caused a shiver of apprehension to race down her spine.

"Your mom's had a long day, Tommy," Jason said, apparently trying to get Kate off the hook. "Maybe some other time."

"No, no," Kate found herself saying hastily. "We'd be happy to have you. But it's just hot dogs and beans tonight. Then Tommy and I were going to watch the AIDS special Channel Seven's been promoting."

"Nothing like hot dogs, ball games and sexually transmitted diseases to whet a man's appetite. Sure you don't mind?"

She nodded, smiling, and thought Jason seemed pleased that she'd stood behind Tommy's invitation.

"Aw, Mom, do we have to watch that program? What does AIDS have to do with me? I'm only nine."

Jason joined in with Kate's laugh. Tommy had a point, but Kate thought that responsible sex education was a vital part of parenting, and she wanted to give Tommy the opportunity to ask the right kinds of questions while he was still young. On the other hand, there was no reason to shove it down his throat.

"Let's watch for a little while, Tommy. If you aren't interested, we can do something else. Okay?"

"Okay," he answered, green eyes doubtful. "But I bet it'll be real boring."

To a nine-year-old probably, Kate thought, but kept her opinion to herself. "Now let's help Jason. Those bats still need packing."

While Tommy ran off to gather the bats, Kate walked to the water jug and bent to lift it. It was still almost full and much heavier than she'd expected.

"That's too heavy for you." Jason took it gently from her hands and emptied it onto the ground.

"Why didn't I think of that?"

"Men have to be good at something, don't they? If women thought of everything, we wouldn't have any purpose."

"I don't know about that." Aghast, Kate wished she could take the words back. Their double meaning, suddenly all too evident, at least to her, had been unintentional.

Jason just smiled, not seeming to notice Kate's embarrassment. He hefted the water jug on his shoulder just as Tommy appeared. She hadn't known what to say next and breathed a sigh of relief at her son's timely appearance.

Tommy had carefully placed the bats in their storage bag and now struggled with his heavy burden.

"Thanks." Jason grabbed the handle of the bag and gave the jug to Tommy. "I'll trade you loads."

Tommy shot Jason a grateful look. He'd seemed reluctant to complain about the weight, and Jason had made the trade so smoothly that Tommy didn't even realize the two adults knew the load was too much for him. That small, perceptive gesture touched Kate.

Charlie and the team mother had also been picking up, and now Kate, Jason and Tommy walked to Charlie's car to deposit their cargo. As they walked, Kate saw Tommy trying to mimic Jason's long strides. Suddenly she felt left out. There was something about the way a boy related to a father that a mother could never share, and she was witnessing it now. But then she reminded herself that Jason wasn't Tommy's father, merely a friend.

The thought caused her to wonder about his past. She knew so little. He was in his middle thirties and divorced. That much was common knowledge. But did he have children? If so, they must have suffered a terrible loss when their parents split up, because Kate could tell that Jason had been a wonderful father.

She tried to picture what his children might look like. Did he have a daughter? If so, did she have Jason's dark, intense coloring?

Kate had wanted a daughter, and she and Lee had planned to have another child. Considering his untimely death, it was fortunate that she hadn't become pregnant, but she still often yearned for a little girl to round out her family.

A picture flashed through her head—a small girl, blue-black hair curling softly around her face, blue eyes widening in delighted surprise. Another image followed, one that hinted at the ecstasy she might feel while creating such a child. The images shocked Kate out of her musings.

Behind those images came a conviction that somehow she would have to persuade Rhonda to see Jason's finer points. For if she failed, the day would come when she would have to choose between friendship and... And what?

Kate didn't have an answer.

THE EVENING WAS BEAUTIFUL, Kate thought as she and Tommy entered the house. One of those mountain nights when the air carried only a hint of chill and promised that summer was just around the corner. After dark the sky would fill with stars, and when the television show was over, maybe she and Jason would sit outside and enjoy the rest of the evening alone.

Tommy went to his room to change from his baseball uniform, and Kate headed for the kitchen to start dinner. When the doorbell rang, she started for the front door, but Tommy beat her to it, and by the time she got there, he was excitedly rehashing the baseball game with Jason.

Jason looked up from Tommy's animated face as Kate entered. He felt unaccountably awkward. For some reason she looked exceptionally beautiful, even though he'd seen her several times that day dressed exactly as she was right now. He wanted to stroke the curve of her neck, to pull that soft body next to his and melt right into her.

"Thanks for inviting me," he said formally, then cursed himself for falling back on his eastern manners. "You look wonderful," he added, feeling shier with each word. Why was he behaving like a schoolboy? It wasn't as though he didn't see Kate every day. But his casual invitation to dinner, even though initiated by Tommy, would move their relationship onto a new level. He didn't know why that was, but he knew it nonetheless, and that knowledge both excited and unnerved him.

"Thank you," Kate mumbled. She couldn't help but notice the new sparkle of appreciation in Jason's eyes and wasn't sure what had brought it on. All she knew was that she wanted that reaction, even as she told herself she didn't. Her gaze drifted to his lips. Lips that could sometimes be tight and cold. But now they were soft, as if a smile was about to burst through. She ached to touch his mouth with her fingers, to cover his lips with her own.

Tommy seemed to sense the change between them, because he grew silent, then, to Kate's astonishment, offered to set the table, leaving the two adults alone in the living room.

"Can I do something?" Jason asked, aimlessly walking to the center of the living room.

Yes. Oh, yes, Kate thought, then quickly reminded herself that her nine-year-old was in the next room. "How about lighting a fire?" Keeping them both busy was the best way to avoid all these uncomfortable feelings. "I'll finish dinner. It won't take long."

Jason nodded, and Kate hastened to the kitchen, patting Tommy on the head as she made her way to the counters. She heaved a sigh of relief on escaping the indefinable tension that Jason's presence provoked and buried herself in preparing the simple meal.

After dinner Kate fixed popcorn and sodas, and they all settled in the living room in front of the television set. With Tommy there the uneasiness she'd felt earlier vanished. Her son's easy chatter relieved them both of the necessity to fill empty space with manufactured conversation.

As the special began, Kate told Tommy to be sure to ask questions if he had any, fervently hoping they wouldn't be too embarrassing.

The first segment covered children with AIDS, and at first Tommy showed some interest but soon got restless, frequently popping up from his place for more popcorn.

When the next segment began, a truly tragic depiction of a young homosexual who'd been tried for murder after ending the life of his AIDS-stricken lover, Tommy's restlessness increased. "This is boring, Mom. Can I go play my Nintendo?"

Kate grinned. "Sure." A part of her was relieved. She wasn't certain how she would have answered his questions with Jason present and, fortunately, he hadn't asked any. Well, there would be other times. "Remember, though, lights out in an hour."

"Uh-huh," Tommy replied absently, then dashed out of the room, leaving the popcorn bowl on the table. Jason, who'd been sitting on the opposite end of the sofa, moved closer and reached for a handful just as Kate did the same. Their hands met in midgrasp.

A shock, like a high-voltage charge of electricity, shot through her body. She drew her hand away quickly, trying to avoid Jason's eyes. But she couldn't. Her gaze was pulled upward, and she found herself staring into his eyes. They had no cold veneer now. They were deep, warm and luminous.

Her mouth parted in expectation as she watched Jason's lips soften. When his head moved slowly toward hers, she knew what she wanted . . . and how much she wanted it. Her heart quickened, thudding inside her chest with insistent little throbs, sending exquisite vibrations through every inch of her body.

In those few short seconds of anticipation it seemed as if an eternity passed, and when his mouth finally brushed hers, she shuddered, driven to close the distance between their bodies. Her hands lifted involuntarily, and she buried her fingers in Jason's hair.

Jason slid his arms behind her, pulling her against his chest. He increased the pressure of his kiss, and Kate darted her tongue in and out of his mouth as his tongue touched, withdrew and teased. She savored the taste of him, the musky scent of him, the texture of his dark hair beneath her insistent hands. She wanted to melt into him as hot, sweet need raced through her body, and her mind seemed to have slipped away, floating above them, heedless of anything but her desire that this kiss should never end.

"Free love is dead!" The voice, shrill and loud, came from far away.

Kate slid her hand down Jason's neck, stroking the corded muscles. Then, through the fog of urgency now enveloping her, the oddness of that announcement intruded.

Free love is dead?

Simultaneously Kate and Jason ended the kiss, their heads snapping toward the television.

Chuck E. Squirrel!

Strutting across the screen, he jumped into his tree stump home and vanished. The program continued as though he had never appeared.

"Damn!" Jason muttered, then leaped from the couch and ran to the phone without saying another word.

Damn! Kate thought, clutching at her collar and wondering what was going on. Struggling to shift gears, she focused her mind on what had just happened. How?

Why? Even more important, why now, while Jason was kissing her?

"What do you mean it wasn't there when you previewed it?" Jason snapped into the telephone receiver. His impatient voice surprised Kate. Until now his greatest show of irritation had been to slap his fist against his hand.

"I'll be there in a few minutes. We only have the closing credits left on this show, so we'll preview the next one while it's airing." Jason's usual composure was returning, and Kate thought he must be feeling more in control. The special was nearing its end. Surely there couldn't be any more unwelcome intrusions.

He hung up and turned back to Kate, head slightly bent, rubbing his scar. As he lifted his head, Kate saw that the softness had left his eyes, replaced by those familiar steel shutters.

"This was no accident, was it?" Kate spoke softly, almost afraid Jason would erupt if she was too forceful.

"It would be the world's biggest coincidence if it were." Not waiting for Kate to get up, he walked to the coat closet and pulled out his jacket. "I just can't fathom why someone would do this. It's got to be a practical joke."

"Well, I guess I haven't got a sense of humor," Kate replied, feeling a twinge of loss as she thought of their kiss. She wasn't sure what upset her most, the squirrel's unscheduled appearance or the interrupted embrace. "I don't think it's very funny."

"You aren't alone. Neither do I," he said, slipping into his jacket and opening the door without giving the slightest indication that he might also have regrets.

His all-business attitude disturbed Kate. She supposed she should understand. The burden of this unexpected occurrence would fall upon him. Still, she wished he would say something. Anything.

"It's going to be a long night," he said. "I'll see you tomorrow." The door closed behind him, and he was gone.

Kate walked back to the couch and sat down, elbows on her knees, face in her hands. Her workday clothing felt confining and uncomfortable, and she wanted to get up, slip into some sloppy nightclothes, watch a mindless sitcom and forget the conflicts emerging in all aspects of her life. First, the structure of her workplace changed. Then she learned that Tommy couldn't read. Next her best friend at work had become critical and edgy.

Now a closed-off, overly controlled man had kissed her. What was worse, she had kissed him back. Where was the peace of mind she thought she had found?

The television still hummed in monotonous counterpoint to the turmoil in her mind. She should probably leave it tuned on Channel Seven in case Chuck E. popped up again, although it seemed rather pointless. There wasn't anything she could do even if he did.

Leaving that minor decision unsettled, she got up, walked to her bedroom to change, then peeked into Tommy's room, reminding him that it was time to get ready for bed.

The television still murmured comfortingly as Kate returned to the living room. She began picking up the clutter left from Jason's visit when the murmur stopped.

"Stay around. I'll be back," a squeaky voice commanded.

Oh, no! Kate stared at the television as her onetime favorite cartoon character wagged a warning finger at her. All hell would break loose. She knew Jason would be furious. If the previewing had been started right away, as he'd instructed, this second episode wouldn't have happened. Tomorrow would be full of finger-pointing and speculation, and everyone would be expected to choose sides. It would be a struggle to remain neutral, which was the only position Kate wanted to take.

A lingering thought, previously nebulous, solidified in her mind. The timing of that first incident had coincided with Jason's appearance in Lakeview. Was it a coincidence, or were they somehow connected? The idea seemed absurd. What possible connection could there be? Clearly Jason wouldn't do something like this, and what would anyone gain by creating silly interruptions just because of him? Chuck E. Squirrel's impromptu performances were merely a nuisance, not an act of terrorism.

She was learning to hate that squirrel and his disruptive appearances. Then again, maybe she should thank him. That kiss could have thrust her relationship with Jason into a new dimension. Considering the irresistible need the touch of his lips had provoked, she was certain they wouldn't have stopped there. It was probably best that they hadn't made that leap.

She wasn't yet ready to make a choice.

CHAPTER SIX

WHEN KATE ARRIVED at work early the next morning, the phones were ringing nonstop. As she entered the dingy KZET lobby, she saw a girl from the file room assisting with the calls. The poor thing already looked harassed, and the call director continued blinking relentlessly.

Rhonda was in also and shook her head in dismay as Kate said, "Good morning," then gestured to Woody's office in a silent message that she was wanted there.

Woody was glued to his phone, silent on his end but obviously listening, and Kate could hear an irate voice coming through the receiver. "Yes, George, I read the morning paper," he said, finally getting a space in the conversation, waving Kate into a chair as he spoke.

Kate cringed at Woody's remark. She had also picked up the Phoenix newspaper on the way to work. She had planned to get one, anyway, because she'd wanted to check out the entertainment editor's opinion of the AIDS special. But today's column covered an entirely different topic.

Strange Doings in the Boonies, screamed the headline, and the columnist had devoted the entire space to sarcasm and puns regarding Chuck E. Squirrel, with considerable pondering on the purpose of his sudden debut. After comparing him unfavorably with Max Headroom, the writer had infuriated Kate with his final conclusion that the whole thing was a tasteless publicity stunt.

Thinking about that accusatory column, she had lost the train of Woody's conversation but now heard him say, "I'll talk to Jason about it right away. We'll get a handle on this, George. Keep calm." Kate almost smiled at Woody's reassurance. Mayor George Creighton's excitability was legendary, and few people could handle him as well as the imperturbable Woody.

But this morning even Woody looked perturbed. As he hung up and looked wearily at Kate, he asked, "Have you read the column?"

"Yes. Pretty ugly, isn't it?"

Woody nodded. "But the worst part is the attention it brought to these episodes. Now people will be tuning in just hoping to see a Chuck E. commentary. Although, judging by the volume of phone calls, there isn't a soul in this state who missed it."

"What's the reaction?"

"Mixed. Some think it's funny, but most people were offended because he appeared during that special. People don't find AIDS amusing."

"It isn't." Kate responded, then turned to the sound of footsteps. Jason smiled at her wanly and sat in the chair beside her. Dark circles surrounded his eyes, making Kate suspect he had slept very little the night before.

"It will be even less amusing if it keeps on happening," Jason said.

"Yes, I wanted to talk to you about that, Jason." Woody leaned on the desk and clasped his hands in front of him. His thick gray-tinged hair looked disheveled, as though he'd been running his fingers through it. "George and I agree that security has to be tightened and I understand you have experience with broadcasting security systems. Kate and I were scheduled to attend a public broadcasting conference in Seattle week after next. I'd like you to go in my place and look into a system for Channel Seven. Can you arrange it?''

Kate frowned. ''But you and I promised to have dinner with Erika McCardy, Woody. Can't we all go?'' The idea of traveling alone with Jason made her uneasy, yet her body tingled at the thought of what they could do with the hours they would spend away from the prying eyes of their co-workers.

''Can't afford it. The station's budget is already stretched to the limit. At this point I would cancel your reservations if we hadn't made that commitment to Erika.''

''It's fine with me, Woody,'' Jason said. The surge of happiness he'd felt at Woody's request was unexpected. Self-reproach immediately followed. These episodes were very serious, and he doubted that Kate, or even Woody for that matter, completely understood how much damage this practical joke could do. He and Woody had spent half the night trying to determine who might be responsible. This was what he should be concentrating on.

Instead, he found himself picturing walks with Kate along the Seattle waterfront under silvery moonlight. Silvery moonlight? Where had that come from? He didn't even talk, much less think, that way.

Well, that was that, Kate thought. Two weeks from today she and Jason would get on a plane, check into a hotel and attend the conference's social functions together. The idea sent a full-fledged shiver down her spine and, unwillingly, she glanced at Jason. He met her gaze for a brief instant, then looked away.

She wondered what he was thinking as memories of their kiss flickered through her mind. Well, it wouldn't happen again in Seattle. She'd made her decision the night before. A personal relationship with Jason would unquestionably disturb her friendships at work, and she didn't plan to let that come to pass. Besides, for all she knew, Jason shared her relief that their kiss hadn't been carried through to its natural conclusion.

"Who do you think did this?" Kate fiddled with the neckline of her knit pullover, trying to contain her discomfort, and asked the question of no one in particular.

"Jason and I narrowed down the possibilities simply by ability." Woody answered. "The only people who know how to use the animator are Harry, Steve Karako and Amy Herrera. Rhonda also knows how but not well enough to do something like this."

"Well, Harry wouldn't do it," Kate shot back. "Steve might have a motive. I'm sure he wasn't pleased about the suspension. But why would he have caused the first occurrence while he was on duty and sure to be blamed? And Amy has no reason. Besides, they aren't the only ones who can operate the animator. So can Carlton and Jason."

"Are you suggesting I did it?" Jason laughed, the rare, deep laugh that Kate loved.

"Of course not." Kate had to laugh, too. Her protective instincts were getting way too strong if they brought that much indignation to her voice. Then she remembered the brief thought she'd had the night before. "But, you know, it might indirectly have something to do with you."

"How?" Woody asked.

"This only started happening after Jason got here. It might sound silly, but could this be some kind of revenge?"

"For what?"

"I don't know." Kate's voice faded as she realized where this line of thinking was taking her. If means, opportunity and motive were the way to eliminate suspects, then she was clearly narrowing the field.

"Harry Bingham has a reason," Jason said. Kate stiffened, kicking herself for bringing them down this path. "But I don't think he did it," he added quickly.

"Neither do I," Woody agreed.

"Well," Kate said, glad that both men had rejected the idea she'd unwittingly introduced. "The rumors about layoffs have been spreading like crazy. Maybe it has something to do with that."

"It's a possibility," Jason replied. "But if that were the case, we can eliminate Harry. His technical knowledge makes him too valuable to lose, and he knows it. Carlton's out, too. His annual telethon brings in so much money, we'd be crazy to let him go."

"All this supposition is getting us nowhere," Woody interjected. "I still think it's a joke. Could be that this joker doesn't realize the consequences. A memo about how serious this is might end it right there. Still, until we install a security system we'll be double-manning the control booth so one technician can preview what's been loaded while the other one monitors the switching."

"What happened last night, anyway, Jason?" Kate asked. "I'm sure you know that Chuck E. came on while you were on your way to the station."

Jason nodded before answering. "Steve reviewed the next segment, just like I asked, and nothing was on the tape. He was flabbergasted when the squirrel appeared, anyway. After I got here, we printed out the switching sequence. It seems the switcher had been programmed to go to another slot in the jukebox where the outtake cassette had been placed. The squirrel wasn't even on the tape for the AIDS special. Never was."

"You mean that someone actually inserted a switching command in the master control unit? How could they do that?" Kate asked. She had naturally assumed that the cassettes had been switched just like the first time.

"It's not that hard. He or she would just have to wait until the technical director left the room for something. If you know what you're doing, it just takes a few seconds to key in new commands. It could have been done anytime night or day." Jason massaged his forehead while he talked, as though his scar ached. "It's clear to me now that the first incident wasn't Steve's fault, and I've put in a request that he be compensated for the days he lost during his suspension."

Jason introduced his offhand apology so casually that, for a moment, Kate wasn't sure what she'd heard. This immediate acknowledgement of his mistake told her he was a fair man. Before she could comment, Jason added, "It never occurred to me to have the switching sequences checked. That's something we'll have to do from now on."

"The employees are really going to be busy for a while, aren't they?" Kate said, losing her thoughts about Steve in the flash of the proverbial light bulb that had just gone off in her head. The motive behind all this was becoming quite clear, at least to her. "You know," she said thoughtfully, "revenge may not be the motive. If someone wanted to squelch the layoffs, they couldn't have picked a better way."

Jason and Woody both stared at her, their expressions clearly showing that they wondered why they hadn't thought of that before she did. For a long moment neither spoke. Then Woody let out a deep breath. "If we were looking for a reason, folks, I think Kate just found it."

JASON TRUDGED UP the steps to the station door, his shoes clanking on the metal surface, dreading the greeting he knew awaited him. Rhonda would fix that unfriendly stare on him, then look away as if he didn't exist.

Under normal circumstances it was unpleasant enough, but today he could barely face the prospect. He opened the door and steeled himself, feeling immediate relief when he saw that Rhonda's desk was empty. Quickly he walked to his office, as though he'd just eluded the dragon in her lair.

How had he come to this—intimidated by an administrator? He used to eat her kind for breakfast, just like Mayor Creighton had eaten him this morning during their meal at the local country club.

George had been quite unhappy. Chuck E. Squirrel had shown up three times during the past week and a half, and the mayor was getting some heavy flak from the network executives. This morning he had apparently decided to pass some of that flak on to Jason.

"Don't forget, Brock, that you were hired on my recommendation and I can withdraw that recommendation at any time," the mayor had reminded him in his booming voice. "This squirrel thing has to be fixed. It's making me look bad with the city council and my constituents."

"I don't like it any better than you do, George," Jason replied, choosing to ignore the implied threat, which he considered nothing more than hot air. If the incidents continued, though, he was well aware that it would be a different story. "And I understand your problem, but we're doing everything we can. The programs are being reviewed just before airing, and the switching commands are printed out hourly.''

''I'm not interested in what you're doing, because it obviously isn't working.'' George was pulling no punches, and Jason shifted uneasily in his chair, not quite knowing why. The dining room was nearly empty, and he and the mayor were seated next to a large windowed wall that overlooked a golf course. Several golfers moved across the immaculate greens.

''What I want are results,'' George continued, pushing back his ever-present painter's cap. ''Quick results. End these episodes, Brock, and end them fast.''

Jason picked up a tumbler of orange juice and sipped, trying to buy time. He knew he was slipping. Before the accident he had batted back confrontations like this one without a second thought. Now he didn't know what approach to take. The only things he was sure of were that George wanted reassurances—not hard truths—and that the man was very susceptible to flattery.

He decided to flatter. ''To tell the truth, George, I was hoping you had some ideas. You've got a reputation for being shrewd. What do you think?''

George's half smile told Jason his comment had worked. He just hoped George wouldn't suggest something outrageous. The mayor frowned and seemed about to speak but, just then, the waitress appeared with their breakfasts and both men remained silent until she left.

''Frankly, I don't know what to think.'' George's voice was calmer, telling Jason his tactic had succeeded. The man was now working with him instead of against him. But the conversation was taking its toll. He felt jittery, uncertain, and the omelet sitting in front of him looked decidedly unappetizing. He took a bite, anyway, waiting for George to go on.

"If I had my druthers, I'd suspend everyone who knows how to use that animator."

Jason nearly choked on his food before swallowing his urge to tell George what a stupid idea that was. "We'd really cripple our production ability if we did that," he said smoothly, as though George had made a viable suggestion.

"I know, I know." The mayor gazed out the window as if looking for answers somewhere on the golf green. The pause gave Jason an opportunity to direct the conversation, and he took it.

"Let's review my suggestions for the security system, George." Jason leaned over and unsnapped his briefcase. Originally the mayor had told him that the purpose of the meeting was to discuss the system. Wanting to be prepared, Jason had brought the plans with him. "I think this will end our problem for good and maybe even catch our practical joker."

George's eyebrow lifted in interest as Jason placed the plans on the table, and for the following two hours Jason explained the system, listening attentively to the mayor's suggestions, making notes and nodding a lot.

By the time they had left the country club, George was beaming approvingly and Jason had felt he was off the hook. At least for the time being.

Now, as he sank into his creaking chair, he blew out his breath in relief, glad to be back in his shabby little office and away from the mayor's scowling face. He wished he were as confident that the proposed security system would solve the problem as he'd implied to George. But the truth was, if the current security measures weren't stopping this sabotage, Jason wasn't certain that a more sophisticated system would.

These last three times were different than the others. The squirrel had appeared and left no tracks, no changed programming commands, no maverick tape in the jukebox. Nothing. Chuck E. Squirrel had simply popped up from nowhere with his zany remarks, then disappeared without a trace.

Jason was totally baffled about the method. Obviously the tapes were being aired as the result of a command to go to an off-line, remote location. But where were the commands coming from and how could he stop them?

There was only one way—limit access to the equipment. Because that was the only way, Jason hadn't changed his recommendation about the system. It was very expensive and, under normal circumstances, would be much more than the station needed. But these were abnormal times. How many television stations had a madcap cartoon squirrel romping through its airwaves?

None that he knew of.

He thought about George's threat to fire him, and a sudden shiver shook his body. Not that he took the threat seriously. Yet.

The idea humiliated him. He had never let his earlier successes go to his head, but he *had* been a well-respected national network executive, and the possibility of being canned by a second-rate PBS station was so ludicrous that he could laugh.

Almost. Because deep down he knew he was wondering what his aunt would say if such a thing ever happened.

Suddenly unwelcome memories answered his question, memories of an afternoon a few weeks after his parents' death. An afternoon he had almost forgotten.

He was still trying to understand why his parents had died, as he struggled to adjust to a new household and a new school. So much had happened so quickly, and he no longer had the encouragement that had been such a part of his life. His old school and his parents had understood him. Now everything was different.

By the second day in his new class, he knew his new teacher was flustered by his difficulties. She set him off by himself to study, without help, earmarking him from the beginning as a slow learner. Then, that morning, she called on him to read aloud.

He stuttered the words out, missing again and again, his mortification keeping him from concentrating. He only had to read two paragraphs but it seemed like an entire book. He could hear the other children whispering as he read despite the teacher's warnings to hush.

But that was only the beginning. The worst happened on the playground after lunch. The other kids began clustering around him, forming a circle.

"Moron," they taunted, laughing among themselves. "Can't read. Dummy, dummy, dummy."

They held hands and circled him, as if playing ring-around-the-rosy, but chanting the terrible words over and over, their jubilant faces like leering gargoyles. Tears rushed to Jason's eyes, and a crushing, suffocating sensation filled his chest. Humiliation and the pain of fighting back his tears robbed his strength as he unsuccessfully tried to beat his way out of the circle. One little girl giggled gleefully each time the others shoved him back.

All the while they chanted and chanted until, in desperation, Jason sank to the ground, wanting to bury himself in the loamy smell of the earth. He scrunched into a tiny ball, covering his ears, trying to block out the taunts, but the words beat relentlessly on his eardrums. Inescapable. Irrefutable.

Finally a voice shouted, "Stop that!" The children scattered in all directions, leaving Jason still huddled on the ground. An older boy helped Jason to his feet and asked what had happened, but Jason didn't answer. Instead, he turned and ran to hide in the boys' bathroom and swallow his tears.

He endured the rest of the day glumly, fighting off the frequent urge to cry until finally, at home, he sank onto the front porch step and allowed the suppressed tears to spill over with chest-wrenching sobs.

He didn't hear the door open and didn't notice his Aunt Phyllis until she sat down beside him. "Tears again?" she asked. "You're really too old to cry, you know."

She patted his shoulder absently, but even that casual touch filled an emptiness that until then Jason hadn't known he'd had, and he threw himself into her arms, despite her reprimanding words, frantically clutching her neck. He needed a mother's touch, a mother's reassurances, and this was now the only mother he had.

"I couldn't...see the words," he wailed. "I...I... couldn't see." His sobs became so violent that he couldn't speak anymore. Then, with a big gulp of air, he bellowed, "They called me a moron."

She held him. Sort of. Kind of a loose embrace, as though she had a wild animal in her arms and was afraid to move. He sensed her tension, but still he needed...he needed.

"I'm not a stupid...not a moron. Mom and Dad said," he added with an angry little sniffle, wiping his nose as he spoke.

Aunt Phyllis disengaged his remaining hand and gently moved him away from her. "Don't get me all messy," she said, her tone uncustomarily kind, although the words weren't.

He nodded and scrunched up on the step, head on his knees, arms around his legs. His aunt patted him again and, while her gesture wasn't truly tender, it was more attention than Jason had received since the funeral. It was better than nothing.

"They shouldn't have filled your head with ideas. It was wrong of them," his aunt said.

At first Jason didn't know what she meant. Then a realization dawned. She thought his parents were wrong. A white-hot surge of anger gobbled up his pain, and he lifted his head and glared his disapproval.

"Don't look at me that way, young man." The kindness in her voice vanished, and she shot him a responding glare. "Your parents *were* wrong. They should have taught you to be realistic about your abilities. Look at you. Ten years old and you still read like a first-grader. How they could have given you the idea you could do great things is beyond me."

With an impatient gesture she stood, then reached down and took Jason's hand and tugged. "Come in now. You have chores to do, and you're too old to be crying about this. Those kids shouldn't have said those mean things to you, but you better face facts, Jason. You're no genius, and the sooner you accept your lot in life, the better off you'll be. A person is born the way they are born, and there's no changing it."

She stood over him, blocking out the sun like a huge monolith, and Jason looked up at her, a chilling shudder consuming his body as he rose to his feet. She'd just told him he *was* a moron. That he was born to fail. He squared his small shoulders, and his anger melded into something cold and hard, a wall that blocked out his pain. It gave him a strength he hadn't had a moment earlier, and he held on to it tightly as he realized that she was right about one thing—he was too old to cry. In that instant, standing in his aunt's oppressive shadow, Jason vowed she would never see him cry again.

And she hadn't.

But over the years that hadn't stopped her from repeating the same prediction: he was born to fail.

Now that niggling question he'd so successfully buried in his subconscious since childhood resurfaced with a sickening thud.

What if she was right?

"I STILL HAVEN'T DECIDED, Holly," Kate said as she gripped the telephone receiver between her neck and shoulder and searched for a notepad.

"The psychologist will be back the last week in April," Tommy's teacher informed her. "While the remedial class is helping, I still think there's a lot more we could do for Tommy if we could pinpoint his exact problem."

Kate's stomach tumbled, and she searched for the words to tell this persistent woman that she didn't think Tommy needed a psychologist or, at least, Tommy didn't think he needed one. "Holly," she said, then stopped as she noticed Jason standing in her doorway. She wondered how long he'd been there. "Holly, Tommy doesn't want to be evaluated, and I'm not sure I want it, either."

"Just think about it, please," Holly implored.

Kate motioned for Jason to come in before answering. She would have preferred that he didn't hear this conversation, but it was too late now. Besides, he already knew Tommy had difficulty with reading, and because of his own problem he should understand better than most. "I'll mark down the date and talk it over with Tommy. Maybe he'll change his mind."

"He's only nine, Kate. That isn't old enough to make this kind of decision. Ultimately you have to decide."

Kate agreed, but the idea of overriding Tommy's and her father's objections nearly undid her. The tears, the recriminations, the disapproval that such an act would provoke were almost beyond facing. "How soon do I have to let you know?"

"Anytime. I'm going to schedule Tommy in tentatively. Just let me know and I'll firm up the appointment." There was a long pause during which Kate didn't speak. Then Holly added, "I know you'll do the right thing, Kate."

Jason moved into Kate's tiny quarters and stood, looking around. The room was much smaller than his office, really not much more than a closet, and she didn't have a window. But somehow she'd made it homey. Colorful posters advertising various PBS specials covered the smudged walls, and a grouping of plants concealed the top of the chipped filing cabinet. How well she managed to bring beauty to her surroundings, he thought.

He'd come in here on the pretext of discussing programming, but in truth he just wanted to see her, to allow her presence to soothe the agitation he'd felt since his meeting with George. But now he listened to her end of the telephone conversation, vitally interest in the subject.

He heard her grunt a thank-you as she jotted something down before saying goodbye. She hung up the phone and looked at Jason, a small frustrated sigh escaping her lips.

"Was that Tommy's teacher?"

"Yes." Kate's hand absently went to her collar. Jason thought she looked as frazzled as he felt and considered letting her pass over this issue, since she obviously wanted to. After starting his day as fodder for George Creighton, he didn't relish upsetting Kate also.

He understood her reluctance. That spur-of-the-moment dinner at her parents' had revealed a lot about Kate and about her attitude toward Tommy's problems. But he had intimate knowledge of the boy's struggles and couldn't allow Kate to ignore it any longer. That wasn't fair to Tommy.

"It sounds like she wants Tommy to be evaluated," Jason said, deliberately pressing the issue.

"Yes," Kate repeated.

"You don't sound too enthusiastic."

"Would you be?" He saw anger flash in Kate's eyes before she quickly suppressed it. "How would you like having someone poke around in your kid's mind?"

Jason sat down, hoping he could be gentle. This blind spot of hers irritated him, and he struggled with impatience as he delivered his next line. "That sounds like your father talking, not you."

Her blue eyes flashed again, fiery, challenging. "You hardly know us, Jason. What gives you the right to say something like that?"

He had kept her voice low and even, but Jason realized he had gone too far. "Because it's the truth," he shot back. " I don't think you share your father's belief, yet you let him poison Tommy's mind against something that could help him a lot."

"He has a reading problem, not a behaviorial—" She stopped in midsentence and changed direction. "Please, Jason. I know you mean well, especially after what you told me about your own problem. But this is a family thing. I have to handle it myself."

The fire had left her eyes, and she looked sad as she spoke. Jason's irritation vanished, immediately replaced by the wish that he hadn't interfered. In less than five days they would be traveling together, and he wanted that trip to be pleasant. He was looking forward to spending that time with her, away from everyday demands. He preferred not admitting this to himself, because beneath that anticipation was the hope of developing something deeper, something he didn't think would work. But not admitting to the truth wasn't his way.

Now, as he saw her, once again, putting off a problem for fear of upsetting someone, he squarely faced the unwelcome fact that they approached life differently.

From his perspective, when something was wrong, it should be fixed as quickly as possible. What she saw was entirely different. To her the only good solution was one that made everyone happy.

He should apologize, walk out of here and forget the possibility of any relationship with her. But as he looked at the little worry lines around her eyes and saw her clutch at her already-wrinkled collar, he only wanted to pull her into his arms and comfort her.

He reached out, gently pulled her hand away from her neckline and squeezed it. "I'm sorry, Kate. I'll stay out of this from now on."

"Okay," she said, smiling weakly.

Only then did he realize how close she had been to tears. A pang of remorse wrenched his heart, and he patted her hand, then stood, suddenly anxious to escape for a moment and deal with his unexpected feelings.

"Did you come in for a special reason?" she asked as he started for the door.

"Nothing that can't wait."

Jason hurriedly left her office and returned to his own, his agitation now greater than before. Not only had he not persuaded Kate to deal with her problem, he now found himself more concerned with her feelings than with finding a solution.

This sudden weakness disturbed him very much.

CHAPTER SEVEN

"BILLY WEKED. No, Billy worked...no, walked." Tommy looked up from his page, emerald eyes filled with frustration. "It's so hard, Mom. I just can't get it." They'd been working for over an hour, and Tommy's eyes were red-rimmed and watery. He rubbed them vigorously before trying again to decipher the words.

"Just keep trying, kiddo." A pang of compassion pricked at Kate. She felt heartless, pushing him this way, but he needed to finish his homework—or at least be close to finishing—before going to stay with her parents while she was in Seattle. She referred Tommy to the colorful letter chart the school had provided to remind him which way the letters went.

Why wasn't it helping? Kate knew she was no expert, but Tommy had been in the special classes for nearly a month now and showed no improvement. Shouldn't his reading be just a little better? Maybe Holly was right about the testing. Maybe they weren't doing the right things. Then again, a month was a very short time for a miracle.

"Walked dawn, no, done...no, down..." Tommy continued, then stopped as they heard Kate's father climbing the stairs.

"Well, your bags are loaded, hon," Sam said as he reached the top and walked to the game table, pulling out a chair for himself. "We can leave for the airport anytime you want."

"We've got over an hour." Kate smiled at his restlessness. Her father was always one to get going, unhappy unless he was on the move and doing something. "I need to pack my flight bag and check to see that I've got all my paperwork in my briefcase."

Sam grimaced and said, "You should've done that before. How come you're never prepared?"

"I could hardly pack it last night, Daddy. I needed to use my makeup this morning." She made an impatient noise against her teeth. She was a grown, capable woman, so why did her father always make her feel so incompetent?

"Don't get in a huff now." Sam reached over and patted her shoulder. "I'm used to your flighty ways and I love you, anyway."

Kate smiled in spite of her annoyance. To him she was still his flighty little girl. He was comfortable seeing her in that light and he did love her. Why couldn't she just accept his skewed perception and brush it off?

Tommy watched them with interest. Stuff like this always went on between his mom and grandpa, and he wondered why his mother acted so different when Grandpa was around. She acted, sorta, well...scared. Of course, Grandpa was often grumpy and, at times, Tommy was scared of him, too. But he didn't think grown-ups were afraid of anything. Especially not Mom.

"Will you help Tommy with his reading while I finish packing and change clothes? You and Mom will have to do it while I'm in Seattle, so you might as well get some practice." Kate turned to her son. "Why don't you read for Grandpa, Tommy?"

Tommy stared at his mom for a moment, not sure what to say. He knew he had to say yes, but he didn't want Grandpa to help. It was bad enough with Mom, but at least she had a little patience. Grandpa didn't seem to know what the word meant. "Okay," he finally responded without enthusiasm.

His mom shot him a questioning glance, then headed downstairs, leaving him feeling as if he'd just fallen into the wizard's trap.

"Get humping, champ. Let's see your stuff." Grandpa had already pulled up his chair and now placed an affectionate arm around Tommy's shoulder. It was a Grandpa kind of thing, the stuff he knew his grandfather thought he should do, but somehow Tommy always felt he just went through the motions and didn't mean it.

"I'm not very good at it," Tommy said, hunting for the sentence where he'd left off.

"That's what your mother tells me. But women worry too much. Us men know what's important and we don't sweat the small stuff, do we?"

"I s'pose not," Tommy agreed, and with a deep, silent gulp of air he began to read. "Billy walked down the red to the story."

"Down the red to the story?" Grandpa peered over Tommy's shoulder at the words. "What kinda book is this?"

He took it from Tommy's hands and turned it over, studying the spine. "This is for first-graders, Tommy." He pointed to the number one printed in large type on the spine. "What are you doing reading a first-grade book?"

"It's what my teacher gave me to read." Tommy shrank down in his chair, mortified. What would he do if Grandpa told everyone he could only read baby-grade stuff? "I told you, Grandpa. I'm not very good at reading."

"Yes...but..." Grandpa frowned, appearing to have lost his thoughts somewhere. "But you go to school. Don't they teach you anything?"

Tommy buried his head in his hands. "They try," he muttered into his fingers, wanting Grandpa just to go away and stop asking all these questions.

He expected a lecture about working harder. Surprisingly Grandpa just patted him on the shoulder. "Just hang in there, champ. You'll catch on. Your mom and uncle had trouble reading at first, too."

Tommy looked up. "They did?" he asked skeptically.

"Sure. Sure. All kids have trouble at first."

But not like this, Tommy thought, and hearing his mother's footsteps on the stairs, he leaned back in his chair, relieved. Now he wouldn't have to hide what he was thinking. Because he knew with absolute certainty that Mom and Uncle Cory had never had this much trouble reading, and he wondered why his grandfather had lied.

"I'm ready, Daddy. Tommy just has to get his things together and we can go." Kate stepped up into the loft as she spoke, ready to help Tommy gather up his books. But then, noticing the glum, heavy mood, she stopped, wondering what had happened during her absence.

"How did the reading go?" She pulled out a chair and sat down. Tommy made a big show of closing his books, then intently began folding his chart. No one answered her question.

"Well?" She uttered a short laugh. "It couldn't have been that bad."

"It was fine," Sam mumbled. He seemed uncustomarily lost in thought, but neither of them seemed angry, so Kate surmised it couldn't have been an argument.

"Yeah, it went great," Tommy said without conviction.

"Good," Kate replied, not believing a word of it. "Why don't you get your suitcase, Tommy? We've got to get going. Don't forget to take your books."

Tommy jumped up and scooped his things from the table, appearing eager to get out of there. "Okay. But do I have to do my homework while I'm at Grandpa's house?"

"Of course you do. He'll help you."

Tommy looked doubtful and Sam coughed.

"I think I'll let your grandmother take care of that," he said. "She'll be a lot better at it."

Tommy brightened at that. "I'll hurry," he said, then clattered down the stairs.

As soon as she was certain Tommy was out of earshot, Kate turned to her father.

"What went on between you two?"

"I don't follow," Sam replied.

"Yes, you do, Daddy. Enough of this male bonding. Out with it." Kate had lived in her father's house too long not to recognize the signs that he was hiding something.

"Tommy would probably rather I didn't talk about it...." A plate of cookies sat on the table. In an obvious delaying tactic Sam picked one up, took a bite and seemed determined to achieve twenty-two chews before continuing the conversation. Kate waited.

"It's just... I hadn't realized Tommy's reading was so bad." He looked so upset that Kate reached over and patted his hand.

"We'll get through it, Dad. Don't worry." She wasn't sure she believed her own words, but she didn't want her father getting incensed over this. When he picked up a cause, he was like a raging bull. Besides, his worry seemed to be very real and deep. She felt suddenly close to him in a way she hadn't in a long time. They used to have such a special bond when she was little, and she wondered what had happened to it. She was about to bring up the subject of Tommy's testing when he spoke.

"You did the right thing about that testing stuff. You must have seen what those people did to Cory's head," Sam said, dashing Kate's momentary hope that she might get him to change his mind. Resigning herself to her father's inflexible viewpoint, she was totally unprepared for his next words. "Just don't ignore this like you did that thing with Lee."

Bile rushed to Kate's stomach, along with a spurt of anger. He said the words so carelessly, as if they were undeniably true, unaware he had just shattered what she considered a tender moment between them. She had never ignored the financial mess Lee had created. She just hadn't known about it. Why did her father blame her, especially after all these years?

Hadn't she returned home and pulled herself out without his help? One thing was certain. If she had, even for a moment, considered asking her dad for help with Tommy's problem, she would discard that idea right now.

"Yeah, Daddy," she replied evenly, suppressing her anger with disastrous consequences to her stomach. "How are things at the print shop?"

"Busy, busy," Sam answered, then launched into a tale about his latest rush job. Kate listened dutifully for a short while before standing and picking up the plate of cookies.

"We'd better go now. The plane leaves in forty-five minutes."

"Right." Sam stood also, and they walked down the stairs. Tommy was coming into the living room, hauling his duffel bag behind him, and Sam helped him take his things to the car while Kate did a last-minute sweep through the house, checking for lights and misplaced objects, still seething over her father's thoughtless remark.

A few minutes later they were in Sam's car on their way to Lakeview's little commuter airport. As Sam continued his print shop story as though he'd never left off, Kate listened with half an ear, glad for the diversion, because her mind was consumed with what she should have said in response to her father's unfair accusation. But she knew she'd never say it, because Sam wouldn't have accepted it, anyway.

Soon they pulled up in front of the small terminal. Sam parked and got out of the car to unload her luggage, leaving Kate alone with Tommy.

Kate opened her door and set her flight bag and briefcase on the blacktop, then turned to her son. "You behave for Grandma and Grandpa, okay?"

Tommy nodded, his green eyes looking large and sad.

She lifted a hand and stroked his cheek. "It's only four days, kiddo."

"I know, Mom," he said, throwing himself into her arms and giving her a fierce hug.

Kate hugged him back, realizing that these moments were getting rarer and rarer. Tears rushed to her eyes. Suddenly she felt as if she were leaving her little lamb to the wolves. But that was ridiculous. He was staying with her parents. She rushed to reassure him . . . or was it herself? "Grandma will make you chocolate chip cookies, and I'll bring back a present. What would you like?"

He released his frantic grip on her and settled back in his seat before answering with a forced smile. "How about a T-shirt?"

"Big and baggy?" Kate forced a smile of her own, trying to push away her silly feelings.

"Big and baggy," Tommy repeated.

"Everything's unloaded," Sam now stood by her door, having placed her luggage beside the flight bag and briefcase. "You brought enough for a month," he added grumpily.

Normally Kate would have smiled at his typical comment, but not now. She'd had just about enough from him today. Instead, she simply stepped out of the car and began picking up her bags.

"I'll get you checked in," her father said.

"Don't bother, Daddy. I'll do it myself."

She saw a puzzled frown cross his face and wondered how he could be so oblivious to the pain he caused her. He looked as if he were about to say something but, instead, planted a goodbye kiss on her cheek, then said, "Okay. I'll see you Thursday night."

"Thursday," she repeated, picking up her final suitcase and turning back to Tommy. "See you Thursday, kiddo. With a T-shirt."

Tommy gave her a sad little wave, and as Kate walked toward the terminal, it occurred to her that Tommy didn't seem to like her father very much. But then sometimes she didn't like him, either. The thought made her feel guilty.

A SALTY, SEAWEED SCENT hung in the air and filled Kate's lungs with new energy. The sun nestled like a golden medallion, low in the sky, preparing to disappear. Overhead, sea gulls cried. The sound refreshed her, making her realize how much she missed Los Angeles. She had always loved the coast, and as she and Jason waited for the limousine driver to unload their luggage, she was filled with a sudden restlessness, a desire to leave Lakeview and settle somewhere else.

She wondered where this uncharacteristic wanderlust came from, then thought about her father and his insensitivity and realized she wanted to run away. His remarks had haunted her throughout the flight, and if Jason hadn't been such wonderful company, she would have succumbed to a deep depression.

They had talked a lot during the trip, and Jason had told her a little about his childhood with a few veiled references to his aunt's indifferent and demeaning treatment of him. As she listened, Kate realized how little Jason revealed about himself. When she pressed for more information, he smoothly changed the subject.

Soon he was telling her about plays he'd seen in New York, celebrities he'd met. Often Kate had squelched an impulse to reach out and touch him...his arm...his face. Once, their shoulders had brushed, jolting Kate, and she had pulled away quickly, denying her desire to get closer. The impulse to run her hands through his thick dark hair, to kiss his wonderful mouth with its full, almost pouty lower lip, had threatened at times to consume her.

Now, as Jason tipped the driver and turned toward her with a smile, she smiled in response and tried to banish those insistent thoughts one more time.

"Shall we check in?" he asked, and when she agreed, they entered the high-ceilinged lobby of the hotel. Lush tropical plants filled the room. They walked around a massive marble planter, approaching the check-in counter where a long line was waiting.

Seeing the line, Kate groaned. The trip had been long and uncomfortable, what with the change of flights in Phoenix, and the last thing she wanted was to wait again. Incredibly Jason didn't look the least bit tired. "Why don't you sit down? I'll take care of this," he said.

"That's not fair." She appreciated his thoughtfulness but couldn't leave him standing in line by himself. "I'll wait with you."

Jason smiled again and nodded. Then there seemed nothing more to say. They both shifted uncomfortably and looked in different directions. Three days of product shows and workshops loomed ahead. So did three nights. Kate wondered how they would fill those nights.

Would they take leisurely walks along the wharf, enjoying the beauty of the ocean together? Or share romantic dinners at candle-lit tables? A shiver raced down her spine, and she looked back toward Jason to find him staring at her with a strange, uncertain expression.

"Nice lobby," Jason commented, glancing around.

"Very nice."

"I wonder who takes care of the plants."

"I don't know. Probably a plant service," Kate answered.

Then Jason brought his gaze back and their eyes connected. Simultaneously they broke into laughter.

"We sound like two nodding acquaintances meeting in an elevator," Jason remarked, his face creasing as he laughed.

"Yes," Kate agreed. "What is it about being out of town that turns co-workers into strangers?"

"I don't know about other people, but our situation has nothing to do with being co-workers." The smile vanished from Jason's face. "Does it, Kate?" he asked softly.

His remark caught Kate off guard. It instantly ended their pretenses about the nature of their relationship. "Are we ready for this conversation, Jason?"

"The time is right, the place is wrong." An enigmatic smile crossed Jason's face. "But we need to talk."

Her heart skipped a beat, then caught in her throat. She found herself unable to speak as anticipation and fear warred within her. Her moment of decision was getting dangerously close.

"Okay?" he asked.

The counter in front of them became vacant. It was their turn. Jason looked steadily into her eyes, obviously expecting an answer.

"Okay," she whispered hoarsely.

Jason nodded and, together, they moved to the registration desk.

KATE LOVED HER ROOM. It was tastefully decorated in subdued earth tones and high enough so that she could glimpse the ocean from her window. But what she liked best was that it adjoined Jason's, and that relentless image of kissing him invaded her mind once more. But now it was joined by other images, images of hot, hungry bodies entwined among tangled sheets, of urgent, whispered words. Her body. Jason's body. She glanced at the locked door separating the rooms, knowing another locked door lay behind it. It seemed symbolic, like their fledgling relationship. They both had to turn their locks before they could be together. Was she willing to turn hers?

Her mind wasn't sure. But her body had no doubts.

In the next room Jason dropped his suitcase onto the bed and began methodically unpacking. If it weren't for Kate, he would resent this trip. He'd lived out of suitcases too long and found himself glad that his present job allowed him to settle in one place for a change.

He wondered what Kate was doing. Was she showering? He pictured her under the shower, water beads glistening on her lightly freckled skin. He suddenly ached to touch that skin, to kiss every last freckle, to hear her moan with longing. A dark heat emerged in his solar plexus and radiated through his body. God, he wanted her. Wanted to follow his desire. But it wasn't just her body he desired. He wanted to laugh with her as they had already done so often. He wanted to talk with her, tell her about Beth and Stacey, about his Aunt Phyllis.

Kate was different from other women he'd met. She had her life in balance and juggled the demands of her job and raising Tommy with apparent ease. Her cheerfulness amazed him. Such a contrast to Beth. Not until Kate had entered his life had he realized how much Beth had whined. About her wardrobe. It had never contained the perfect outfit. About the furniture. That six-month-old chair was getting shabby. And endlessly about the long hours he'd worked to provide all those things. She'd blamed him for all of it and ultimately had blamed him for the greatest tragedy of their lives.

The memory made Jason feel dull and empty, and to escape those feelings he turned his thoughts back to Kate. He wanted to know her, not just biblically but in all ways. Wanted to know what pleased her, what frightened her, what her dreams and regrets were. Now he had the opportunity. Would he take it?

He had surprised himself this afternoon when he broke their unspoken agreement not to talk about their attraction. Why had he done it?

Certainly he was more than ready to make love with her. How long had it been since he'd held a woman? Longer than he wanted to admit. But he couldn't kid himself—any woman would do for that. With Kate the merely physical wouldn't be enough. Lovemaking would just make him want her more, and soon he would need her, want to possess her totally, leaving him open for betrayal and the possibility that he would, once again, he prodded into feeling those dangerous emotions.

Was he ready for that?

Reassuring himself that Kate was unlike Beth in every way and that such a thing could never happen, he dismissed his worry. The wheels were already in motion; he'd be prepared for whatever might happen.

He placed his underwear into a dresser drawer, then picked up his two-suiter and carried it to the closet. As he placed the hook over the rail, he noticed the door between their two rooms. Just two simple locks keeping them apart.

He would turn his. He knew that now.

Now only one question remained. Would Kate turn hers?

KATE AND JASON stopped at the hospitality suite entrance for name tags. As they waited, Kate scanned the room for Erika McCardy, the first subject of her series, while Jason looked for security system representatives.

As they entered, Kate noticed several people glance in their direction. She knew they made a good-looking couple. She'd worn a kelly green, wide-strapped camisole of clingy satin over a crepe skirt in a deeper shade of the same green and had taken extra care with her makeup. She felt good about the way she looked tonight, but when she glanced at Jason she felt delightfully eclipsed.

His three-piece suit, undoubtedly taken out of careful storage, fitted him flawlessly, the subtle stripe emphasizing his lean height. It was as completely appropriate at this convention as it had been out of place in Lakeview, and he looked elegant and confident. His appearance took Kate's breath away and made her remember their cryptic conversation in the registration line.

She'd felt strangely shy with Jason since then. But it wasn't an uncomfortable feeling, mixed as it was with tingling anticipation. Occasionally their eyes would meet and soften as a half smile crossed their lips.

"There's Erika." Kate pointed across the room, trying to dismiss the erotic bent of her thoughts, or at least push them away until later. Although she had agreed to discuss this attraction with Jason, she was still wary of moving forward. "I'm going to reconfirm our dinner engagement."

"I'll get drinks," Jason said, idly searching for his own contacts. He didn't seem to want to leave Kate's side, and his obvious reluctance gave Kate a heady feeling. "White wine for you?"

Kate nodded and headed across the room, her eyes following Jason as he walked toward the bar. He covered the room in long-legged strides. His shoulder appeared endlessly broad, and his coat tapered down to narrow hips. Several women turned their heads as he passed, but he didn't seem to notice as he kept his eyes glued on her. Kate smiled. She couldn't blame those other women for looking at him so longingly.

Kate caught up with Erika, and they immediately began discussing Kate's series, setting up a time to view a rough copy of the tape Kate had brought.

Jason approached with the wine. Kate introduced him to Erika, then Jason excused himself, saying he'd found the manufacturer he'd been wanting to meet. After he left, Erika turned to Kate with an arched eyebrow.

"Nice," Erika said.

She was a tall, slender woman in her early forties. Her clothes clung to her like a manikin's, and she was undeniably lovely. Kate felt an unexpected pang of jealousy, a primeval territorialism, as the woman's smoky gray eyes glinted appreciatively.

Stiffly Kate agreed with Erika's appraisal and was about to turn the conversation back to business when Erika asked, "Yours?"

Kate emitted a nervous laugh, not quite knowing what to say. "Not exactly" was her witty response.

"Well, don't let that one get away," Erika said, smiling broadly.

Kate laughed again, but this time the nervousness was gone and her laugh tinkled with pure relief. Relief at Erika's unspoken message that she would respect Kate's claim and relief that someone had finally echoed her hidden thoughts. She nodded and then said pointedly, "Now about those camera angles."

The tall woman arched her eyebrow again, then began filling Kate in on how to use the camera for the most emotional impact. They didn't discuss Jason again, but even as Kate focused on the considerable knowledge Erika so generously shared, her gaze roamed the room until she found him.

He was standing near the door talking to a small group but, like herself, he looked restless. Their eyes caught for a moment, and an exquisite tremor rushed through Kate's body. Suddenly the room seemed empty. The chattering voices and clinking stemware dropped away. The only sound remaining was the throbbing pulse in her temples. Just she and Jason existed, standing miles apart in a large room.

At that moment something invisible but unquestionably tangible sprang forth and connected then. A thin, silken thread—seemingly fragile and yet unbreakable—bound them, and Kate had a feeling the bond would last throughout eternity.

"What do you think, Kate?"

The sounds of the room returned, and with a painful tug Kate brought her attention back to Erika. When she saw the woman's knowing smile, she attempted to respond intelligently to the half-heard comment. Erika's indulgent expression told her she wasn't succeeding very well.

Throughout their conversation Kate glanced in Jason's direction, often finding that he was also looking at her. Her legs grew weak as a pervasive languor spread throughout her body, flushing her face with a carnal heat. The thread grew unbearably taut, creating pressure that demanded she close that gap between them.

As the evening stretched on forever, Kate began thinking she might die from the tension. As much as she enjoyed Erika, all Kate wanted was to leave that room with Jason and—

And make sweet, hot love. That was exactly what she wanted, and she was going to be honest enough to admit it. She wanted to stroke his abundant black hair and trace the curve of his lips, feel those slim hips grind against hers. The heat deep inside her flared with nearly intolerable intensity, and when she heard Erika say it was time to call it a night, her heart leaped in anticipation.

"It's been a long day," Erika said. "Besides, I think you have something more important on your mind."

The comment flustered Kate. "Was I that obvious?" she mumbled uncomfortably.

"What's going on with you two is vibrating this whole room. It's just that most of these people are too absorbed in their own business to notice." Erika grinned teasingly. "If I were nice, I wouldn't have mentioned it. But I'm not known for being nice. Just honest. And my honest opinion is that when two people have something like this, they mustn't let it get away. It doesn't come along that often.'' Before Kate could answer Erika patted her arm and disappeared with a good-night and a wink.

A little dazed by such frankness, Kate stood for a moment and reflected on the woman's words. Erika was obviously an honest, sharing woman. Honest in business, honest with herself and honest about her sexuality. Kate realized now that she'd buried her own sexuality along with Lee and had been dishonest about her needs, dishonest with herself. She needed Jason. She wanted him. And nothing stood in her way. She would take Erika's advice.

With long, purposeful steps she crossed the room. Jason was there, and she wasn't waiting a minute longer.

Jason watched her approach, feeling as if the distance between them was a matter of miles instead of mere feet. He wanted to break into a run, encircle her tiny waist and lift her into the air with a roar of delight. Instead, he studiously contained himself, and when she reached his side, he placed a restrained hand on her waist.

''Are you ready to talk?'' he whispered into the sweet fragrance of her hair.

His touch sent shivers through Kate's hypersensitive body, and she struggled against the impulse to melt against his body. Tilting her head, she stared directly into Jason's warm, shining eyes, certain now that their glow came from his desire for her.

''Yes,'' she replied in a low, throaty voice, steeling herself to go beyond boldness. With a wicked smile she said, ''I hope you're a man of few words.''

THEY WERE IN THE ELEVATOR. Alone. But this wasn't the behavior of two nodding acquaintances meeting by chance, and Kate thought she'd lost her mind. What if they stopped on another floor before they reached their own?

But she didn't care. The maddening pressure of Jason's insistent hands exploring beneath her camisole, along with the tantalizing intrusion of his tongue, pushed all practical thoughts from her mind.

She ran her own tongue across the delicious underside of his lower lip and squeezed her arms between their bodies, tugging at his tie. It came loose easily, and she began working wildly on the buttons of his shirt.

Jason released her mouth and moved his lips to her ear. "Are you going to undress me right here?" he asked, his voice thick, his soft breath caressing her ear.

Recklessly she pushed aside his warning question. "Would you resist if I did?" She arched her neck to accept the frantic kisses he now bestowed along the sensitive curve of her jaw.

"How could I?" He sighed softly and brought his mouth back to hers.

The elevator door opened with an explosive whoosh. Kate and Jason sprang apart. An elegantly dressed couple stepped inside and exchanged wise glances as they took their places. An embarrassed flush crept up Kate's neck, rushing to cheeks she knew were already reddened. She looked sideways at Jason, afraid of what she might see. He caught her glance and grinned sheepishly, discreetly trying to button his shirt.

Kate carefully avoided looking at their new companions during what seemed to be an interminably long ride. Finally they reached their floor and, mortified, Kate stepped out with Jason, certain that the couple would start snickering as soon as the door closed. What she hadn't anticipated was Jason's robust laugh the moment the elevator was gone.

For an instant she was offended, but Jason's laugh boomed off the walls of the vestibule and infected her. A small giggle erupted in her throat and she fell, laughing, into Jason's open arms.

"I wonder what they'll make of that?" he asked as soon as he was able to control his laughter.

"Whatever they want." She wrapped an arm around his waist and pulled him toward their rooms. "But you and I—that's another story. What are we going to make of it?" A small inner voice protested her brazenness, but she ignored it. Instead, she placed a kiss on his cheek and giggled with him as though they were two small children as they walked down the hallway.

Jason quickly unlocked his door, opened it and pulled her inside, smothering her with a deep, slow kiss.

"You're good at this," she whispered when he released her lips. "Looks like you've had practice."

"Not in a long time." With an uninhibited whoop he lifted her into his arms and closed the door. "Much too long," he murmured into her hair. "And ever since I met this dynamite strawberry blonde I haven't thought of anything else."

"Tell me more."

Jason placed her gently on the bed, then knelt down beside her. "I love everything about her." He drew Kate into a sitting position and deftly lifted her camisole top over her head. A quick, uncomfortable feeling overcame her but then disappeared. It seemed right to have him gaze at her near-naked torso, her breasts covered only by a lacy bra.

"I love this redhead's bouncy curls, her creamy skin and its dusting of freckles. I want to count those freckles one by one."

"I've had the same problem. It's about this man I met." Kate lifted her arms to Jason's shoulders and slowly removed his jacket as she huskily whispered into his ear. The texture of the fine wool caressed her sensitive fingertips, sending delicious tingles throughout her.

"Tell me more," Jason said, his breath grazing her ear.

Kate's tingling intensified. She removed his tie and began unbuttoning his sleeves. "I love everything about him. His golden eyes that seem to shut everyone out but open up for me. His broad shoulders and long legs."

Jason shrugged out of his shirt as Kate traced free-form patterns across his chest. The sprinkling of hair on his chest tangled in her fingers, and she bent her head to kiss the hollow where her hand rested.

She ran her hands up his chest and behind his head, entwining her fingers into his thick hair. "I love his thick black hair and the way it feels under my hands." She leaned back, pulling Jason with her, bestowing kisses along the angle of his cheekbone as they sank into the softness of the bed.

"Uh-huh," Jason murmured, falling on top of her. She could feel him growing erect against her, and she gloried in her power. He quickly opened the zipper of her skirt, then pulled it slowly down her hips, allowing his fingers to trail seductively across her skin. His cool touch against her burning skin caused her to shiver.

She brought a finger to the scar on his forehead and said, "I even love his scar and sometimes wonder how he got it."

Jason's hand stilled, and suddenly something changed. Kate could feel his desire slacken, then disappear altogether, the sensuous, playful mood evaporating. Jason released her and sat up, throwing his legs over the side of the bed.

Kate touched his back tentatively. She'd never played this teasing game before, not even with Lee, and realizing how easily she'd fallen into it embarrassed her. She must have gone too far.

"Jason?" Her questioning word hung in the air, joining the sudden tension between them. "Did I say something wrong?"

He didn't answer at first. He simply lowered his head into his hands, and the silence tore into Kate's gut. She should have known better. She still wasn't ready for a relationship. But as she looked at Jason's bent back she somehow knew better. Something was hurting him deeply, and whatever her own fears were they couldn't be as important as his need.

He lifted his head and turned to look at her. "No. You couldn't have known." He picked up one of her curls and stroked it absently with his thumb.

"There are things you don't know about me, Kate." In the dim light of the room Kate saw the pain that had flashed in his eyes the first time they'd met, only stronger now. They were huge pools of agony, the eyes of the tormented.

"I know the important things. You're kind and loving."

"No one's ever told me that before." He laughed bitterly.

She brought his hand to her breasts, and he shuddered, then forcefully drew back his hand and turned away again. His sudden withdrawal caused an immediate stab of pain in Kate's chest, a pain that felt as real as a knife. She was about to grab her clothing and scramble out of the room as fast as possible when she heard his rasping sob.

"I've never talked about it, Kate."

Her searching hand stopped hunting for her clothes. The honest misery in his toneless message erased all her self-concern.

"Not even to the doctors. They kept trying to get me to open up, but I couldn't bring myself to say the words."

"What?" She spoke in a breathy whisper, somehow feeling that normal speech would shatter him. "What?" she repeated when her only answer was silence.

"She's dead." His voice was raspy.

"Who?"

"My daughter. She was just a baby." His back quivered with uneven spasms. Suddenly he snapped and broke into heaving sobs. "Oh, God, Kate," he cried, his words gushing out convulsively as if a dam had broken. "She was just a baby."

CHAPTER EIGHT

ALL KATE COULD SEE was Jason's quivering back turned away from her, blocking her out. He had shared the words, yet he was still experiencing his pain alone.

She didn't know what to do. She'd only seen a man cry once before. When Lee's father died, she'd held him one night as he'd wept out his loss. But Lee's tears had been sparse, while Jason was unleashing a torrent of grief.

Uncertainly Kate rose on her knees and wrapped her arms around Jason's body, resting her head on his shuddering back. What he needed now was comfort. No questions. No platitudes.

He turned to her then, as though realizing he wasn't alone, and rested his head on her chest. His sobs subsided some and his trembling stopped. Kate slowly reclined on the bed, bringing Jason with her, and he clung to her while she ran her fingers over his hair with soothing strokes.

Jason submitted gratefully, shamefully, to Kate's consolation. She smelled as sweet as springtime, but he knew that she would never hold him again, not after he'd broken down in this disgraceful way. But, for the moment, he wanted the comfort her closeness brought and wasn't willing to let it go.

The pain was unbelievable, wrenching him as though his whole body was shattering into millions of agonized pieces. He had always known it would be. That was why he'd never put those thoughts into words. He had believed that if he held his emotions tightly, smothered them, they'd go away without hurting. But now the promise of love and a simple, unknowing question from this woman who held him had broken through all his defenses. Suddenly he wanted to tell her about it.

"I always believed in Beth—my wife," he began. "She was the only person I ever trusted." His voice sounded shaky to his ears, and he didn't even know if Kate was still listening. She'd been holding him motionlessly for such a long time.

"You don't have to a talk about it, Jason." Her hand moved again, a sweet touch against his hot forehead.

"I know. But I want to." He started to look in her eyes but found he was too ashamed. A man didn't break down, not even a very young man who was only ten and had just lost his parents. He'd learned that lesson early from his aunt and uncle. "Do you mind?" he whispered, afraid she'd give the wrong answer.

"I want to know. But not if it hurts too much." He looked in her eyes then and discovered, not the scorn, the contempt, he'd expected. Instead, they were shining with tears of compassion.

Hesitantly he began moving back to the moment when his life had been shattered, pouring it all out on Kate with an inward prayer that she would understand....

HE'D BEEN WAITING for this moment since Friday noon, dreading it, but wanting it nevertheless. Now it was Sunday night. He had so many questions and didn't know if he could handle the answers.

Why had Beth been kissing another man in Central Park?

There was only one possible answer, and his stomach churned as he thought of it. He felt trapped, with nowhere to turn, just as he had felt when he saw them.

It was a rare day when he had a break in his schedule, but that had been such a day, and he'd taken a walk through the park to clear his mind of the never-ending details of his job. He had just purchased a hot dog from a street vendor and was preparing to take a healthy bite when he saw them.

At first they caught his attention because the woman resembled Beth so much. But he knew it wasn't her, not his Beth, walking arm in arm with another man. Curious, he turned to get a better look. Suddenly the day turned black.

The couple had stopped and the man turned the woman toward Jason before blocking her face with a deep, long kiss.

The jolt felt like a comet striking him, a powerful thudding force, burning and blinding. Primitive, alien emotions coursed through him. He wanted to run over to them, bash the man into smithereens and drag Beth away by her hair.

He always worked hard not to feel, not to reveal emotion, not any at all, and his love for Beth and Stacey was the only feeling he allowed in his life. Now he realized it was his Achilles' heel, because new, unfamiliar feelings overwhelmed him.

Rage, murderous rage, consumed him along with unbearable pain at her betrayal. Oh, the betrayal. It cut through him like hard steel, and he wanted to sink to his knees, roar out his agony and demand retribution.

But he didn't. Instead, he dropped his hot dog and ran back to his office, unable to accept what he'd seen with his own eyes.

He sat behind closed doors in his plush corner office for a long, long time, doing nothing until Les Epstein, his boss, rapped on his door, reminding him they would be working all weekend.

Summoning tremendous control, he had called Beth and told her he wouldn't see her until Epstein's command performance lawn party on Sunday afternoon. She hadn't shown any of her usual disappointment. She had simply accepted his news cheerfully and told him she'd see him then. But before she'd hung up she'd said, "We have a lot to talk about."

Talk. Yes. They had to talk.

Now the moment was here. As Jason carried their daughter to the car, all that was left of his raging jealousy was a churning knot in his stomach that he had tried all day to relieve with Scotch. But it hadn't gone away.

"I'll drive." Jason started to take the keys from Beth's hand, but she resisted his insistent tug.

"Let me. You've had too much to drink."

Not nearly enough, thought Jason, but mindful of the sleeping Stacey cuddled against his shoulder, he released his grasp on the keys.

"Whatever you say." He could hear the weariness in his voice. "Would you mind unlocking the back door so I can lay Stacey down. Poor baby, she's tuckered out."

"She's not the only one," Beth muttered harshly as she inserted the key in the lock.

Jason chose to ignore the words. He placed Stacey gently on the bench seat. She looked so sweet and beautiful as she stirred in her sleep, and it occurred to Jason that his lovely four-year-old daughter was nearly a stranger to him. What did she think about in that little head of hers? Did she wonder what Daddy did all day? Why he was away from home so often?

He thought about making her sit up so that he could put on her seat belt, but it was just a short drive home and she slept so peacefully that he didn't want to disturb her. Removing his jacket, he arranged it around her sprawling body, then placed a gentle kiss on her cheek. Her eyes fluttered and she sighed softly, then tucked her hands under her head, falling immediately back into a deep slumber.

Strange, how little he saw of her, even though they lived in the same house. The prospect of seeing even less of her put a lump in his throat.

He shut her door and locked it, knowing he couldn't delay the confrontation anymore. The memory of what he had seen in the park erased his tender feelings. He opened the front passenger door, which he noticed Beth had so graciously unlocked for him.

Slipping into the seat, he laid his head against the headrest and sighed, forgoing the confines of a seat belt. His body ached with fatigue and the night wasn't over. Yet.

He waited until Beth fastened her seat belt and pulled the station wagon out of the driveway before bringing up the subject that had been burning his soul.

"Tell me about him." Although he spoke softly to avoid disturbing Stacey, even he could hear the menace in those words. Several emotions flickered across Beth's face—fear, guilt and, finally, relief.

"So you know." She kept her eyes on the road as she drove onto the highway, and Jason thought she was waiting for him to comment. But then she spoke again. "I want a divorce, Jason."

Divorce! The deceptive calmness of her voice belied the devastation of her meaning. Jason felt as if a steel fist had punched his stomach.

"You've slept with him, haven't you?" Suddenly he forgot about Stacey, about civility, about everything but her betrayal. His voice rose as he asked the question. Beth glanced toward the back seat, reminding him of their daughter's presence and angering him further. "Answer me, damn you."

"It's not important, Jason. Our relationship or, to be precise, our lack of a relationship is what's important. I've found someone who wants the same things I do, someone who believes in building a home, spending time with his family. I want that. For myself and for Stacey."

"Are you sleeping with him?" Jason shouted, a small part of him incredulous that he was fixating on this single aspect of the problem when his whole life was falling apart.

Beth expelled a long breath of air. "Yes. I have. Just once. And I felt terrible about it. But then David said he wanted me to leave you and marry him. He's offering me a better life, Jason, and that's what I want."

David. So that was the name of this man he wanted to kill. Jason buried his hands in his face, unable to revive the rage he'd felt when he first saw them together. Nothing remained but gaping emptiness.

What had gone wrong? He worked night and day providing for them. They were the reason for his existence. Didn't Beth know he loved them both?

And what should he do now? Give her the divorce or try to rebuild their relationship? Forgive and forget?

He didn't know if he had it in him.

"You feel terrible?" He spit out an ugly laugh. "How do you think I feel? Why, Beth?"

"When was the last time you reached for me at night, Jase? I can't remember. You come in so late and you're too tired. Your work is everything, and when I try to talk to you about it, you brush me off." She smiled wryly. "How can I compete against that kind of mistress? I want to be the center of a man's life." She thumped her fist lightly against her breasts. "Me. Not a career. Just me. Is that too much to ask?" She stared at him solemnly, waiting for his reply.

"I trusted you," Jason screamed. His fury returned, and he clenched his fists to keep from wrapping his fingers around Beth's delicate neck. "I trusted you!" he roared again, then let out a string of curses.

Beth still stared at him, now with outright terror on her pale face. He never behaved this way, and he knew his unexpected outburst frightened her. As his anger spewed forth, he found a part of him enjoying her reaction, and he began another series of epithets. Then a flash of brilliant light assaulted his eyes. He blinked, momentarily blinded, before he saw the car veering back and forth across the center line.

"Beth!" he shouted, his rage replaced by horror. "Watch out!"

Her head whipped forward instantly, her foot hit the brakes and she swerved the car to avoid the collision. But the other driver swerved also, flooding their car with light, bearing down on them.

Tires screeched, glass shattered, steel crumpled, all with sickening clamor. Jason's shoulder slammed first into the dashboard, then the door. He saw the hood crumple, accordion-fashion, and his door popped open, throwing him into the street. An excruciating pain tore at his arm as he rolled onto the pavement, then echoed when his forehead struck the gritty tar. Jagged lines ran across his eyes, blurring his vision as he watched the station wagon roll. Once. Twice. A third time. Beth! Stacey!

Did he cry the words aloud, or were they just in his head?

He tried propping himself up with his hands, but his arm dissolved into pain and sweat beaded on his forehead. The cacophony of more squealing breaks brought intense light and another flash of jagged lines.

Ignoring his throbbing arm, he scrabbled to his feet. Where were Beth and Stacey? As he ran to the car, he saw a small, twisted form lying near the rear wheel, which still spun as though the car was trying to go somewhere upside down. The back door gaped open.

"Stacey. Oh, dear God, not Stacey, please!" He was unaware he'd spoken the words aloud as he knelt beside the small body, his own pain completely forgotten.

Stacey whimpered. "Daddy. Oh, Daddy, it hurts." Blood trickled from her tiny nose and from the corner of her rosebud mouth, and Jason gathered her in his arms.

"Daddy's here, honey. It will be all right." She looked so pale, nearly blue, and by the twisted angle of her leg, he could tell it was broken. Something wet ran over his eyebrows, obscuring his sight. Vaguely he realized it was his own blood. A siren wailed in the distance.

He had never been a religious man, but he prayed fervently as he held his daughter in his arms. The injured limb pounded mercilessly, but he didn't care. If he held tight, real tight, he could keep her here, safe. Suddenly Stacey shuddered violently, as though freezing cold, and he brought her closer, willing the heat of his body to keep her warm. "Hang on, Stacey. Hang on," he repeated again and again until a hand tapped his shoulder and he looked up to see a paramedic.

"Thank God you're here. Do something, please." He stood up and moved away to give the man access. "She's all right, isn't she? Tell me she's all right."

The man knelt and placed his fingers under the curve of Stacey's jaw, then quickly bent over, cleared her throat with experienced fingers and began breathing into her mouth. Jason stared helplessly. Between breaths the man bellowed, "Oxygen. Quick."

Without hesitation Jason bolted to the ambulance door. "My daughter. Oxygen. Hurry." He babbled repetitive directions, afraid he wouldn't be understood. But the driver instantly grabbed a tank, hopped from the van and ran toward the paramedic and Stacey. Jason stumbled after them.

When he caught up with the driver, both men stood above Stacey, staring down. The paramedic crossed himself.

"Why aren't you doing something? Why—" Jason demanded.

The driver stepped forward and touched him. "I'm sorry, sir. It's too late. She's gone."

Beth stood beside him now, clothes torn and face scratched, but apparently otherwise unharmed. She clutched his arm, sobbing convulsively, but Jason wasn't moved to comfort her.

"No! She can't be dead!" He rushed forward and picked up his daughter's body, shrugging away the shrieking protest from his injured arm. Why hadn't he told her he loved her more often? Why hadn't he spent more time with her? "Someone can help. She isn't dead. She's only a baby."

He wanted to run with her, take her some place safe, but his body was incredibly weak. And then Beth was pulling Stacey from his arms, crying and shrieking almost unintelligibly, but through his pain Jason heard her words, and they hit him with the force of a physical blow.

"You coldhearted bastard," she screamed. "You've killed her...."

"SHE BLAMED ME," Jason said, thinking his words sounded like a death knell in the otherwise silent hotel room. Then he stopped talking. He didn't repeat Beth's hideous accusation to Kate; he could hardly bear to think about those words, much less speak them.

He heard Kate's irregular sniffles, distantly aware that she'd been crying. He still clung to her, and she stroked his hair as she had throughout his oppressive story. She hadn't spoken the entire time.

"The other driver was drunk, wasn't he?" she asked, her voice sounding thick.

"Yes."

"It wasn't your fault, Jason. There's nothing you could have done. Nothing anyone could have done."

"You know what bothers me most?" He continued talking without looking at her. Now that he'd begun, it was hard to stop. "I forgot to tell her I loved her that day."

Kate turned suddenly, pulling her shoulder from beneath his head, and lay on her side, pressed flat against him, arms pulling him close. "Listen, Jason. Before Lee died...before he left for that last flight...we had a violent argument. He flew that plane still angry at me, and we never made up."

Kate's voice choked and she stopped for a moment. "The next time I saw him he was lying in a casket. I can't take back the words I said. I know losing a husband isn't the same as losing a child, but the point is, Jason, it wasn't my words that killed him. And the words you said, or didn't say, didn't kill Stacey, either. A drunk driver did."

"I know you're right...." Jason's voice trailed off. Kate had assumed he felt guilty, but that wasn't what he felt. No, he felt cheated. Beth had lied, betrayed and blamed him, then snatched his daughter from him before he'd even been able to say goodbye. But he didn't tell Kate that. Instead, he rolled away and stared upward. "I can't even remember her birthday," he said to the ceiling. "It was sometime in March, but Beth always reminded me of the day. I was just too damn busy."

Kate felt her heart breaking, as it had during his entire revelation. The horror she experienced at the idea of losing a child was almost overwhelming. She understood his regret at the things left unsaid, undone. Especially for a man like Jason—a man so consumed by his career that he let everyday things slip by him.

"Don't talk about it anymore," she said, reaching over and pulling him against her.

"Yes," he said, burying his mouth in the curve of Kate's shoulder. He didn't want to talk. He suddenly felt unburdened, released by the rush of his words, and he wanted to hold on to that feeling. Finally relaxed, he felt himself drifting away, lost in Kate's hair, comforted in her arms.

HE DIDN'T KNOW how long he'd slept, but when he awoke, Kate was resting against his shoulder. He could hear the sweet, even sounds of her breathing and, assuming she was sleeping, he carefully shifted his position.

"Hi," she said with a breathy whisper.

Jason smiled, overwhelmingly glad she was awake. He needed her to be with him tonight. He needed to talk. He needed ... Suddenly, with an urgent ache, he understood what he really needed. Shifting, he placed a hand under Kate's chin and lowered his head to kiss her. Her eyelids fluttered closed, and just before he closed his own, he saw her lips part invitingly. He moaned as his mouth touched hers.

She shuddered sweetly and arched her body against his. Placing a hand on his hips, she brought the length of him fully against her, insinuating her soft curves against every inch of him. Hungrily he ran a searching hand across the bare expanse of flesh above her scanty briefs. Her skin felt velvety smooth beneath his fingertips. He shuddered also.

Desire had never felt like this before, a languid, smoky heat inching its way through his body, making him feel as if he were floating. It wasn't an urgent heat, more like charcoal, igniting lazily and gradually burning hotter. Kate moved her hand down the length of his body, her feathery touch creating tiny sparks in his every nerve. Her fingers moved to his taut, sensitive abdomen, starting to go lower, and he groaned with deep pleasure, then grasped her hand gently.

"Not yet," he murmured. "Let's make this last." With another moan he enclosed the back of her head with his large hand and pulled her mouth to his again, whispering, "Forever."

His lips were hot and moist. Kate opened her mouth hungrily to accept his seeking tongue. She wanted to taste him fully and ran her own tongue across the incredibly smooth underside of his lower lip and the lightly serrated edge of his teeth.

She curved eagerly against him, wanting to feel the hardness of his muscles cutting into the soft, aching fullness of her breasts and belly. She whimpered weakly as he forced his hand between their bodies and tugged insistently on the edge of her briefs, pulling them over her hips. Kicking them off frantically, she ground her hips against his. Longing had become insistent need, a need so demanding that she could deny it no longer.

"Now," she whispered hoarsely. "Please now."

He stopped for a minute and raised himself above her with both arms, gazing down on her face. A violent shock passed between them. Kate cried out from its sweet aggression, pulling his hips on top of hers with a demanding grasp that both thrilled and shocked her.

He entered her then, sliding smoothly inside without assistance, and she felt an exquisite heat growing at the center of their joining. She cried out again and wrapped her arms and legs around him, trying to pull him closer and closer. Suddenly her consciousness receded. She was no longer someone's widow, someone's mother or someone's daughter. She was only Jason's woman, and she thrust her hips savagely beneath him, needing to show him she never wanted to be anything else.

Jason felt her explode under him. He'd been holding himself back, wanting nothing more than to see her pleasure. A low groan rose from his gut as he watched her face contort from the force of her climax. The coals inside him burst into flames, and he no longer resisted their heat. His cry followed Kate's, and as he erupted inside her, he felt his grief and anger dissolve in the steamy warmth of their lovemaking.

He knew, then, that this night had changed him forever. His life had begun anew.

IT WAS AWFUL DARK up here, not even a sliver of moon to see by. The drifter aimed the flashlight his "employer" had given him onto the rocky ground in front of him, wishing the beam were wider. Could there be rattlesnakes ahead? A gila monster? Or even a timber wolf? Arizona was supposed to have some dangerous animals.

Hell, how was he to know? When he came to this state, he'd expected sand dunes and an occasional oasis. Instead he found rocky dirt and scruffy trees, then, as he headed north, pines and wild grass. What kind of desert was this? And what was he doing climbing a mountain in the middle of the night?

Sure, the pay was good. Two hundred dollars could probably get him to Amarillo. The offer had sounded mighty tempting while sitting on a bar stool in that roadside tavern outside Lakeview, nursing the one beer he could afford. But that was before he'd been dropped off at the side of this mountain road.

The transformer lay ahead, its support beams sprinkled with red lights. He searched his fuzzy brain for the directions he'd been given, hefting an ax and hacksaw in his free hand. He'd been instructed to sever the beam and cut the guy wires. He mouthed the numbers as he counted. Six, just like his employer had said.

Finding a rock, he propped up the flashlight. The tunnel of light streamed skyward and didn't really help much. But, although he'd been told to turn it off when he got here, he was damned if he'd do this job in the dark. Putting down the ax, he grasped the hacksaw in both callused hands and began to cut. The first grating noise made him jerk nervously. God, he was jumpy. He'd give anything to be back in that tavern with another beer.

He took a deep breath and started sawing again. Trickles of sweat began running down his face. The steel was strong, the going slow. He needed to dig in at least a quarter inch and weaken the beam enough to use the ax.

Was something rustling behind him? The saw made so much noise that he couldn't tell. He stopped his labor for a moment. Nothing. His imagination was beginning to get

the best of him. What did he expect up here, anyway?
Killer tomatoes?

Returning to work, he was pleased to see that he was
making a dent in the metal. Just a little more, then use the
ax and on to the next beam. Ah, there it was. He put down
the saw and picked up the ax.

Just as he raised the ax, readying himself to heave the
final, destructive blows, the brush behind him rattled.
Once, twice, the sounds came from everywhere. And followed by more. He froze in midswing, his heartbeat suddenly erratic.

What was out there? There had to be hundreds of them
to make such a commotion.

He swung around and broadened his stance, preparing
to fight. Easing over, he leaned and picked up the flashlight, swinging the beam over the top of the growth. The
rattle became louder and closer.

What the hell was it?

Then his attacker emerged. The most god-awful ugly
rabbit he'd ever seen, its ears nearly as high as its body was
long. A jackrabbit. He let out a long sigh of relief as the
jackrabbit stopped inside the beam of his light, lurched to
the left, then leapfrogged out of sight. A small dog immediately popped from the undergrowth and, without
pausing, veered left, obviously intent on catching the
rabbit.

The drifter dropped his ax. Enough was enough. The
money was already in his pocket. Leaving his tools behind, he started for the road. With any luck he could hitch
a ride and be at the New Mexico border by morning.

CHAPTER NINE

THE RINGING WAS INSISTENT, annoying. Kate buried her head under her pillow, unwilling to leave the sweet, floating peace of her slumber. But the ringing didn't stop, so she finally rolled over to reach for the phone.

As she grasped the receiver, Jason's hand covered hers, reminding Kate where she was.

"'Lo," he said sleepily into the phone, his body arched over Kate's. He smiled down at her, and she felt a warm sense of belonging. The room was dark, and the sliver between the drapes was just as dark. Too early for the wake-up call. She looked at the clock. Its red digits said it was only five-thirty. Who could be calling at this hour?

"Just barely, Woody," Jason said, obviously responding to a question about his sleepy tone. He nestled lazily back into his pillow, then, abruptly, shot upright, feet on the floor, his formerly relaxed body now visibly tense.

"What?"

At his reaction Kate sat up, too, staring at Jason's rigid back. Something was wrong. Very wrong. She listened intently as Jason went through a series of who, when, where and why questions.

"What is it?" she whispered. But he simply raised a finger, asking her to wait.

Kate slid out of bed, walked to Jason's side and sat next to him. The night silence hung around them like a smothering cloak, interrupted only by Jason's infrequent terse questions and the unintelligible hum of Woody's voice on the other end.

The air conditioner kicked on, the noise making Kate jump. Jason placed a comforting hand on her thigh. The small gesture eased her edginess.

"I'll tell Kate and then catch the next flight back." With those words Jason leaned over the bed and hung up the phone.

"Chuck E. Squirrel?" Kate asked.

Jason nodded, then pulled Kate against his bare chest. His skin, warm against her chilled, naked body, was firm and smooth, and the contact sent a surge of desire through her. He stroked her hair. "He popped up again last night. Even worse, someone attempted to cut down the transformer. Fortunately, for some reason, the vandal just stopped in the middle. But this isn't a prank anymore."

"We could have been off the air for days, Jason. Why would anyone do this?"

"That's what we need to find out." He tightened his hold around her. "But right now what I regret most is that I'm going to have to cut my trip short."

She had known that the moment she realized the caller was Woody, but the open regret in Jason's voice pleased her. And it echoed her own. "Rats!"

"Yeah, rats." He placed a kiss on the tip of her nose. "I was looking forward to playing hooky and staying in bed all day. I had planned all sorts of wanton, lascivious acts."

"Do they involve anyone I know?" This playful side of Jason delighted Kate. He kept it well hidden during business hours, but, seeing how Jason often was with Tommy, Kate had suspected that it lurked beneath the surface.

"A certain freckle-faced redhead. Do you think she's interested?" His lips moved to her neck, leaving nuzzling, nipping kisses in their wake.

"Yes, oh, yes. I think she is." Kate said with only partially mock breathlessness.

Jason lifted his head. "Unfortunately my first order of the day is to change my plane reservations. Woody wants you to stay long enough to have dinner with Erika, then fly back tomorrow."

"Oh, Jason! I don't want to go back. I want to stay here forever!" Kate flopped back onto the bed, torn between desire and duty. "Oh, well, I guess there will be plenty of time for wanton acts in Lakeview."

"Let's not kid ourselves, Kate." His playfulness was gone, and Kate felt a twinge of regret. "Once we get home we've got a big set of problems."

She sighed. He was right, of course.

"Tommy, for one," he continued. "Then there's the gossip. If we're seen together, the whole town will be buzzing. I'm not exactly a favorite with some of your friends."

So he knew. His calm acceptance of the fact amazed her. She would have been devastated by such knowledge.

"We'll find a way." She sat back up, not quite believing her own words. And Jason's skeptical expression told her he didn't believe them, either. They both knew how important it was to her to be liked. "Make the phone call to the airline, Jason. We might as well get started."

But somehow Kate didn't feel this was a start. It felt more like the end.

WHEN SHE GOT BACK to Lakeview the following afternoon, things had already settled down. But, as with the previous three incidents, no one could figure out how Chuck E. Squirrel had gotten into the broadcast.

Per instructions, all the tapes in the jukebox had been previewed before and after the incident. None contained the offending outtakes. Nor had the master control unit contained any switching commands for remote broadcast.

The incidents reminded Kate of that old television series *Outer Limits*. The outtakes seemed to come from some force totally outside the planet.

The day she'd returned, Jason had taken her up the mountain to the transformer. The damage was minor and could be repaired without affecting broadcasting, but the incident had moved this problem into a whole new realm. This was more than someone expressing a sick sense of humor. Obviously the intent was to damage the station, critically, and the Lakeview police couldn't find any clues as to who the perpetrator might be.

"The person doing this is very clever. Will a security system control it?" Kate asked Jason as they stood in the lobby by the coffee maker. It was the day following her return, and the sabotage was still heavy on everyone's mind.

"I have doubts," Jason replied. He lifted his hand to touch Kate's shoulder but dropped it before he made contact, gazing past her to Rhonda Weatherby.

Kate ached to feel his hand against her skin, but she, too, had noticed the disapproving scowl cross Rhonda's face as she looked up from her desk. Rhonda's animosity puzzled Kate while it clearly told her that an open relationship with Jason would irreparably harm their friendship.

"Still, a security system is the best deterrent I can come up with," Jason continued, as though he hadn't noticed

Rhonda's reaction. "But I'm afraid we have a clever hacker here, and a security system probably won't stop him."

"Or her," Kate responded, immediately horrified at what she'd said. Rhonda's head shot upward as Kate realized she'd unintentionally sounded as if her friend might be a suspect. Rhonda stared at her pointedly. Kate smiled and shook her head slightly.

Jason saw the interchange and took Kate's arm, steering her into his office and shutting the door. "It would be better if we didn't discuss these things in front of the other employees anymore. We were both remiss."

Oh, Lord, Kate thought. Secrets. There had never been secrets at the station before, not until Jason's arrival. Again she felt that tug between her old loyalties and this new attraction. Where was the middle road? The one she always took?

But she knew Jason was right. To talk about this openly was inviting speculation about the guilty party. Although they had tentatively narrowed the list to the six people known to be familiar with the computerized animator, any computer expert could be guilty. And since lots of people played with computers at home, the lack of formal credentials didn't necessarily absolve anyone.

"You're right," she conceded, but she felt that familiar churning in her stomach and wished she had an antacid handy. "It's going to be hard to change my ways, though. We've never conducted business behind closed doors before." There was accusation in her voice, and the hardening of Jason's eyes told her he recognized it.

"Uh-huh," he mumbled. Then, with transparently studied casualness, he walked to his chair, sat, picked up a folder from his desk and began leafing through it. "It's going to be a full day. We both better get back to work."

She hesitated, feeling contrite. She hadn't meant to hurt him. She moved to his side and placed a hand on his hair. He looked up, golden eyes softening, and took her hand. Turning it palm up, he place a kiss in the center. A shiver ran from Kate's toes, ending with a jolt in her solar plexus.

"I'll see you later." His voice was a promising purr.

Kate nodded and reluctantly pulled her hand from his.

Later, she thought as she walked to her office. Oh, Lord, she hoped so. Her body tingled with need. But the obstacles Jason had brought up in Seattle were here. Large and looming. They seemed to preclude any "later." Not unless she made a choice.

Her stomach twisted and she quickened her pace. The antacid tablets were in her office.

KATE HAD SHUT his door when she left, and Jason stared at it, his mind whirring, and thought about the comment she had made a few weeks earlier about the sabotage having begun within days of his arrival. Everyone had dismissed it at the time, but Jason now thought Kate might have made a valid point. There seemed to be no purpose or pattern behind these incident. Still, he couldn't ignore the nagging thought that his arrival at the station was the impetus.

But why?

He slumped over his desk, twirling his pencil in one hand. It was becoming a struggle, presenting this calm exterior. What if he failed to bring this station around? The fear ate into his confidence, making him feel mangled inside, raw and bleeding. But he couldn't let it show. His enemies—whoever they were—would look for weakness, exploit it and destroy him.

Whoever they were? He almost had to laugh. It wasn't his enemies he needed to count. It was his friends. And he could run through them by counting his ears and nose. Kate, Woody and Harry. Everyone else fell into the other camp. And he wasn't totally sure about the two men.

Only Kate stood by his side. But could he count on her forever? He didn't think so. The strain she was under because of his unpopularity would eventually cause a crack that could easily widen into a chasm. He knew how much she valued relationships. She was very well liked at the station but, with the exception of Harry Bingham, her co-workers disliked Jason to an even greater degree than they liked Kate.

He examined the situation with harsh realism. No one had ever sacrificed their own needs for him before. Should he expect any more of Kate?

A picture of her damp, hungry body pressing against him leapt into his mind. She was so giving, so tender, and her compassion when he poured out his grief had bound him to her in a way he had never thought possible. Just telling her about Stacey's death had lifted an enormous burden from him. Because of that, he'd felt light and carefree, when he first returned to Lakeview. But the pressure from Mayor Creighton had revived his old, heavy feeling, and he'd anxiously waited for Kate's return, knowing he needed her.

Was he falling in love?

He laughed softly, filling up with happiness. Of course he was, and it really wasn't so frightening. Then the laughter faded, and once again he saw the all-too-real obstacles in their way. If he wanted Kate Gregory, he didn't dare falter along the path.

"HERE IT IS, Jason!" Tommy triumphantly pulled out the fishing pole and held it above his head. "It was my Dad's. Kinda neat, isn't it?"

"Sure is!" Jason felt a warm glow at Tommy's transparent pleasure in being able to do something for him. They had been rummaging in Kate's storage room for over fifteen minutes, ever since Tommy had invited him to go fishing and he'd replied that he didn't have a pole. Now that Tommy had found the pole, Jason had to confess. "But I've got to admit I don't know how to use it. I've never been fishing."

"Never been fishing?" Tommy's gray-green eyes widened in astonishment. Then he looked down and began flicking dust and cobwebs from the pole, examining it intently. "Well, no problem. I'll teach you. Grandpa and Uncle Cory taught me everything they know, so now I know a lot."

"Even how to fix this string?" Jason hooked his index finger around a tangled wad near the tip of the pole.

"Line," Tommy corrected. "It's called a line."

"Oh, yeah. A line." Jason suppressed a smile. "Well, can you fix it?"

Tommy rubbed his fingers against his shirt and looked up with a smug grin. "Sure. There's a fishing knife in the tackle box."

The box, along with Tommy's pole, had been left on the back deck. Tommy headed toward the storage room door, with Jason following. The sunlight and clean air were a shock after spending time in the dusty storage room, but a pleasant shock, and Jason breathed deeply.

"Find it?" Kate asked, while she briskly swept leaves from the deck. She wore cutoff jeans and an oversize tank top. Jason thought she looked beautiful. He and Tommy climbed the stairs, and Kate spied the pole in Tommy's hand. "I guess you did. What kind of shape is it in?"

"The line's tangled." Tommy answered. "But otherwise it looks good." He opened the tackle box, took a fishing knife and cut the line.

"Be careful with that knife, Tommy," Kate warned, a nervous expression on her face.

"Ah, Mom! I'm not a baby. Uncle Cory let me do this all the time."

"Yeah. Well, your uncle isn't a mother. Moms worry."

"I know," Tommy said in a give-me-strength tone, rolling his eyes toward the heavens.

Jason smiled at that. So did Kate. A smear of dirt covered Tommy's nose, and she stepped forward, wiped it off, then took the knife from Tommy's hand. "You finished?"

Tommy nodded with a wry grin as Kate put the knife back into the tackle box. Kate's protectiveness amused Jason. Still, if Tommy were his boy, he was sure he'd feel the same. The thought brought back memories of little Stacey. How was it that he'd lived with her more than four years, yet in a few weeks he already felt he knew this boy better than his own daughter?

For a moment it seemed as if the sun had vanished. The day became dank, overcast, and he felt the same oppressive pain that he'd lived with before he'd bared his soul to Kate. He shook off the feeling, and the sun returned.

Tommy deftly rethreaded the fishing line, then rummaged through the tackle box and attached a weight and hook. A look of satisfaction crossed his face. "Good as new," he proclaimed.

"I wouldn't know. You think I'll catch any fish with it?" Jason asked.

"Depends." Tommy made a mock cast over the rail of the deck.

"On what?"

"On whether you follow my instructions." The devil glinted in Tommy's eyes as he spoke, and Jason recognized the words he so often used when coaching the boys in baseball.

"Okay, wise guy. I'll show you what following instructions is all about." Jason bent over and picked up the tackle box. "Bring those poles, and let's get this show on the road."

"Would you like to stay for dinner when you guys return?" Kate asked with a wistful expression that puzzled Jason.

But she had said the magic words, the words he'd prayed to hear. Since their return from Seattle, she had somehow avoided any personal contact with him. It had been nearly a week and a half, and except for work and Tommy's ball games they hadn't seen each other. He wouldn't even have seen her on this Sunday afternoon if he hadn't offered to bring Tommy home from ball practice.

He had wondered if she were deliberately avoiding him, and her invitation meant more to him than he was willing to admit. "Depends," he answered, mimicking Tommy's tone.

"On what?" she responded in an imitation of a deep, masculine voice.

"On what you're serving." Jason laughed, and Kate took a playful sweep at him with the broom.

"Fish!" she said haughtily. "That is, if you catch any."

"Oh, we'll catch 'em all right," Tommy interrupted as he tugged on Jason's hand. "Let's hurry before they stop biting."

"Impatience, the curse of youth." Jason followed Tommy to the deck stairs, looking back. "Set the table for three. I shall return, with or without fish."

"I'll plan an alternative just in case," Kate called after them as she leaned over the railing and watched Jason and Tommy head for the car.

Jason continued looking back. The late-morning sun glinted in pink-gold prisms off Kate's untamed curls, the clear sky seemed to reflect in her blue eyes and a creamy expanse of bare legs peeked through the slats of the rail. He felt a sudden surge of desire. God, he missed her—and they hadn't really even been apart.

Kate watched them drive away. Her son and her man.

Her man?

Surely that archaic term hadn't waltzed through her head? She wanted to deny it. He wasn't her man. One night of passion didn't constitute a relationship and, of course, that was what the term implied.

She wasn't ready for this. Not ready at all. Too much was happening too soon: the sabotage at the station, Tommy's reading problems, Jason and his lonely, tragic past.

So many problems and so few solutions. Uneasily she realized that soon she would be forced to decide between Tommy's welfare and her father's approval, between the acceptance of her co-workers and the company of Jason Brock. A bone being pulled between two dogs couldn't feel as uncomfortable as she did.

Somewhere deep inside, in a hidden place she wanted to avoid, Kate knew where her choices would lead. But, on a conscious level, she only knew the decisions would have to be made soon.

For the next several hours Kate puttered around the house, restless, slightly bored, but unwilling to do anything to relieve that boredom. She made macaroni and cheese and thawed out some hamburgers in case the boys didn't bring back any fish. Finally, when she heard Jason's car pull up out front, her heart leaped in anticipation.

Silly, she told herself. Plain silly. But she couldn't wipe the stupid smile from her face as she stood at the open door, waving.

"So you caught some."

"Five, Mom! Count 'em. Five!" Tommy held a string of fish in front of him like a warrior's prize as he trotted in front of Jason up the walk.

"My hero!" Kate cheered. "You put dinner on the table, after all."

"I didn't catch them all. Jason caught two. He learns real fast." They reached the door, and Tommy thrust the dripping string into Kate's hand. She grimaced and held her bundle away from her, making sure it didn't dribble onto her feet.

"Ah, shucks," Jason said in mock modesty. "Tweren't nothing. I just followed instructions."

Actually, Kate thought, he looked pretty proud of himself, and she couldn't help noticing the affectionate bond developing between him and Tommy. It occurred to her that if she chose not to keep Jason in her life, Tommy would be bereft. He'd already lost Cory; losing Jason would really hurt. Quickly she buried the thought, reminding herself to tackle one thing at a time.

"Followed instructions," Kate repeated. "That's good, because I'm issuing new ones. Take these babies out back. I don't want them dripping on the rug." She smiled teasingly, anticipating his reaction to her next question. "Do you think you can clean them?"

Jason's horrified expression caused her to laugh. "Clean them? Are you out of your ever-loving mind, woman? Isn't it enough that I caught them?"

Still laughing, Kate handed the drippy mess back to Jason and dolefully intoned, "A man works from sun to sun. A—"

"Woman's work is never done," Jason finished, his throaty laugh echoing Kate's.

Tommy started laughing, too. "Poor Mom," he said, wrapping one arm around her waist and the other around Jason's. "My two favorite people."

The gesture brought them all very close, Kate's head near Jason's, with Tommy's between them. Jason looked down at Tommy's upturned face, and Kate thought his eyes shimmered a little too brightly, his smile looked a shade too vulnerable. She suspected that her own feelings were just as close to the surface, and she blinked rapidly, glad that Jason was looking at Tommy and not at her.

But Tommy noticed. "Hey, I didn't mean to get you guys all mushy." He released his hug and ran toward the back of the house. "Let's clean fish."

"Yeah," Jason said. "Let's clean fish."

He took Kate's hand in his, and they strolled to the deck.

"THAT WAS GREAT." Jason leaned back in his chair, looking for all the world like a big satisfied cat.

It had taken over an hour to clean, bread and fry the fish. Tommy had assisted with the cleaning, and Jason had helped. Some of the filets had been ragged, but once they were cooked nobody noticed. Now Jason rose and stretched, and Kate expected him to lick his chops at any moment. Instead, he reached down and picked up his plate. "Let me help you clean up this mess."

"You promised to play Mario Brothers with me, Jason." Tommy seemed to be trying to control the whine in his voice, but it broke through, anyway.

"Tell you what. Why don't we both help your mom? When we're done, I'll play you a couple of games. It's not fair that she did all the cooking and has to clean up, too." Jason stacked another plate on top of his own. "I'll wash and you dry."

"We don't do that stuff. We have a dishwasher."

"Then I'll rinse, you load. How's that?"

"What's Mom gonna do?"

Kate watched the interchange with amusement. Jason didn't really try, but he seemed to have a knack with kids and disciplined without effort or conflict.

"Kick back and watch the tube. Don't you think she deserves a rest after slaving over a hot stove?"

"Yeah," Tommy muttered, not too graciously. "But it was a barbecue grill, not a stove."

"Same, same. Let's get hopping. The sooner we're done, the sooner we can play Mario."

"Sounds great to me," Kate interjected lazily. And, to her amazement, the logic seemed to appeal to Tommy. He jumped up and carried a serving dish to the sink, then returned for another one.

"You're a real wizard," Kate commented as she stood. "I'm going to take you guys up on your offer before you change your mind." She glanced at her watch. "I'm dying to watch *Murder She Wrote*."

She walked into the living room and settled comfortably in front of the television set. Sounds of Tommy and Jason's laughter drifted into the room and brought a smile to her lips. But under the circumstances, was it wise to let Tommy get so close to Jason?

They were so different, she and Jason. Night and day. Dog and cat. She strove for a balanced life, friends, family, work. Jason's entire life seemed to revolve around the station, and he was so driven.

At least that was how he seemed. But was it true? His affection for Tommy was obvious, and in Seattle he had seemed more disturbed about their interrupted week than about the sabotage taking place in Lakeview. Maybe that devotion to duty was simply a shield, a way to keep people from hurting him.

She recalled his tortured confession that night they'd made love. He'd been scarred deeply by his wife's infidelity and his daughter's death, and the infrequent comments he'd made about his childhood—his parent's early death, his aunt's indifference—told her that he'd never known love and support. She wanted to give him those things but was afraid of what it might cost her.

She heard the guys coming out of the kitchen and looked away from the program she wasn't really watching. Tommy was carrying a bowl of popcorn, and Jason followed with a tray of soft drinks.

"We decided to forget Nintendo tonight, Mom." Tommy grinned ear to ear, apparently pleased at taking care of her for a change. "Thought you'd like us to hang around."

"Thanks, guys. I always hate being a Nintendo widow." Kate smiled in return. This was family life, the way she'd always envisioned it. She sat up and patted the spot beside her.

"So sit, you two."

They joined her on the couch, munching popcorn and guzzling soda until the show was over.

"Bedtime, Tommy."

With his usual groans of protest Tommy reluctantly trudged to the hall. Kate followed, not wanting him to dawdle tonight. After ushering Tommy through face washing, teeth brushing and pajama getting-into, she tucked him under his blankets.

"Those were some dandy fish," she said, planting a kiss on his forehead.

"Yeah." Tommy's eyelids drooped; he was obviously already sleepy. "But two of 'em were Jason's. He's real cool."

"He sure is, kiddo." Kate rearranged the covers around his sleepy face. He was always so endearing when he was like this—tired, forgetting his "little man" ways. She kissed him again, then stood, ready to leave the room.

"Are you gonna marry him, Mom?"

Already at the door, Kate turned, shocked by Tommy's question. "What?"

"Are you gonna marry him?" His eyes were wide open now, studying her carefully, looking for a reaction.

"It's not likely, Tommy. Why?" Kate tried to keep her tone cool, even. Tommy had just voiced a question she had been avoiding.

"I just think he'd make a rad dad."

"Well, he makes a rad friend, too. Doesn't he?"

"Uh-huh." Tommy closed his eyes again and wriggled deeper into his covers. "But dad would be better. Night, Mom."

"Good night, Tommy." Kate shut off the light and closed Tommy's door behind her.

Rad dad. The rhyming words rang in her head as she walked back to the living room. Rad husband didn't have quite the same flair but, still, it did have a certain charm of its own.

"UM, TASTY," Jason said, playfully nipping Kate's earlobe and sending delightful shivers down her spine.

She felt alive, electric. The cotton fabric of the couch seemed like silk, the low hum of voices coming from the television like a seductive siren's song. Kate lifted her shoulder and arched against his arms.

The pressure of his firm, contoured muscles soothed that aching need inside her, simmering for days—a need begun in Seattle and not fulfilled since. Suddenly she wanted to be crushed against him. She twisted and touched her lips to his.

"This will taste better," she murmured against his mouth. His lips softened at her touch, mouth widening, and he took her lower lip between his, released it, ran his tongue over the sensitized surface, then roughly devoured her.

Now her entire body pulsated, culminating in a throb deep in her center. She wanted him close. On top of her, inside her. She pulled her mouth away and ran little, nibbling kisses down his neck, across the hollow of his throat. She pulled the knit fabric of his shirt aside and rained those kisses over the smooth, rolling muscles of his upper chest. The smell of him—spice and musk—filled her with joy. Jason moaned. He buried his hands in her hair and pressed her tightly to his chest. The hardened buds of her breasts flattened, causing exquisite sensations to consume her body.

She was losing control, her senses had dimmed, and nothing seemed to matter except Jason. Her consciousness faded except for one tiny flicker in the corner of her mind: Tommy.

"Oh, stop, Jason, please. I can't stand this."

He pulled away with obvious reluctance, his golden eyes dazed. His uneven breathing reminded Kate that his arousal was as great as hers.

"Tommy might wake up," she offered lamely.

He nodded and rubbed his forehead. "Get a sitter tomorrow night, Kate. Let's go to my place."

Kate's eyes widened. His place? To risk being seen going to his apartment? After that, how could she publicly deny the relationship between them, pretend that his friendship with Tommy was the only thing keeping them together? She searched her mind for words to tell this to Jason without hurting him. "I'm not ready for that yet," she finally offered.

Slowly the cold shutters closed over his eyes. "Can't let people know you're bedding down with the hatchet man, can you?" Bitterness laced his tone.

She picked up his hand and studied the palm. He had a long lifeline, or at least she thought it was a lifeline. "Let's not fight, Jason. It's just too soon, that's all."

He nodded. "But we can't go on like this. I'm not a monk. And after last week I know you aren't a nun."

She giggled weakly, slightly embarrassed, but the appreciation in his voice also pleased her. She wanted to make him happy. It was just that—

"There's got to be a way." Apparently no longer annoyed, he enclosed her in his arms. "I'm going mad trying to keep my hands off you." He kissed the tip of her nose, then stood. "On that note I'll be leaving. If I stick around, things are sure to get out of hand."

Kate smiled regretfully and got up also. They walked to the front door in silence, and after Jason opened it, he pulled her against him, enveloping her in a big bear hug.

"Keep the faith, baby," he said. "I'll think of something."

CHAPTER TEN

JASON TURNED DOWN the threadbare bedspread. The pattern, which must have once been vivid orange and green, was faded into a dingy brown mass. But then the whole room was brown and dingy. The town of Globe wasn't known for its plush hotels.

At least it was clean, he thought as he sat on the bed and removed his shoes, wondering if this was such a hot idea. He could hear water running in the bathroom where Kate was washing up.

What were they doing here? This wasn't what he wanted. Clandestine, stolen moments. It wasn't what she wanted, either, he was sure. But it was her insistence on discretion that had brought them here in the first place, to a town over fifty miles from Lakeview, a town where nobody went, a town where they wouldn't be seen.

What did he want? What did *they* want?

The bathroom door opened with a protesting squeak. Jason resisted an impulse to jump up and oil it as Kate stepped out wearing a silk teddy. The muted mint-green shade enhanced her fair coloring, and desire replaced his former urge.

"You look like wedding candy. Good enough to eat."

A smile crossed her face, followed by a flush. Her eyes looked like robin's eggs and contained a shy invitation.

He got up and padded in stockinged feet to where she stood. A strange feeling overcame him, a kind of reverence. For a moment he was almost afraid to touch her. As if sensing his apprehension, she lifted her arms and wrapped them around his neck, drawing his head down to her waiting mouth.

He couldn't taste enough of her. Her breath held a hint of peppermint toothpaste, and her hair smelled like wildflowers. She opened her mouth to accept his eager tongue, whirling her own frantically around his. He moaned and pulled her roughly against his body, suddenly annoyed that he hadn't removed his clothes.

But she took care of that. Her hands slid to his sides and tugged his sweater upward in quick, jerky motions. With an impatient gasp she pulled away just long enough to allow him to bring it over his head.

Then she reached for his waistband, but he grabbed her hands and swept her into his arms. Tracing a line with his tongue along the curve of her throat, he carried her to the bed where he placed her in the center.

"No," she moaned when he failed to follow her. Jason thought he would explode from the naked need in her voice. He nearly ripped off his pants, then lowered himself beside her, his desire almost uncontrollable.

Only an act of will kept him from taking her right then. She deserved more than a rapid coupling. She deserved hours of stroking. She deserved tenderness and time. He took handfuls of her tousled hair and pulled her mouth to his, trying to devour her and trying not to.

But she reached down and unfastened her teddy. "Now, Jason. Please." Her voice was harsh and hungry. "Please."

Jason's control vanished.

He started to bring her under him, but before he could she rolled on top of him and took him inside her in one quick movement. His responding moan filled the room and mingled with hers.

Suddenly the room was no longer shabby. Beauty surrounded them as they completed their act of love with slow, deliberate strokes, their hands actively exploring each other's bodies. And as Jason soared to his shattering climax, he thought that with Kate he would live in beauty forever. "I love you," he whispered just before he cried out.

Her scream followed his. Then she collapsed against him, her chest heaving, sobbing for breath.

He held her close like that, on top of him, her head resting against his shoulder, overwhelmed with how precious she was. She hugged him tightly but was very still. A drop of moisture struck his chest.

"Are you crying?" He released his hold and lifted her head. A tear ran from the corner of one eye. He wiped it away. "Why?"

"It...it was so...spiritual," she finally said, another tear welling up in her eyes.

"Spiritual?" He smiled. Somehow he had never thought of sex as spiritual. "Seemed pretty carnal to me. Wonderfully so." He placed a kiss on the track of her tears.

"I knew you'd think it was silly." She smiled back, apparently not offended, her tearfulness vanishing. "Not to speak badly of all things carnal, but it was as though, for a moment, we went somewhere else. Like we were one person, not two."

He held her face between his hands, becoming lost in those clear blue eyes. He couldn't have found the words himself. He no longer felt amused. "Yes." His voice was almost inaudible. "That's how I felt, too."

And then he remembered his words. *"I love you."* He had only said that to one other woman—Beth, his ex-wife. Now those former feelings he'd once called love seemed incredibly shallow compared to what he felt for this woman lying on top of him. He shivered beneath her, suddenly afraid of hurting her.

Hurting her? It had been Beth who'd hurt him, Beth who'd betrayed him, Beth who'd caused the accident that had killed Stacey, not the other way around. Why should he fear hurting anyone?

But the thought destroyed his mood. The tenderness, the closeness, seemed cloying now, suffocating. He shifted his weight and placed a quick kiss on Kate's nose, then rolled her off him.

She sighed in protest, bringing back memories of all the women who had protested his actions throughout his life. Getting close meant obligation, divided priorities, recriminations.

"It's late. Time we were getting back." He sat up and reached for his pants.

"Already?" Kate glanced at her watch, avoiding looking at Jason. She sensed the change in his mood, unable to understand what brought it on. Was it something she'd said? Did? Had he been shocked by her aggressive lovemaking? Or was it the reference to its spirituality? No. He had said he felt the same.

She wanted to ask him what was wrong. But fear stopped her. It had been a wonderful, awkward, passionate, sad and silly evening. She didn't want to destroy it with unpleasant truths. She turned her head to look at him. He was briskly getting into his clothes, apparently anxious to leave. She looked down again at the watch on her wrist.

"Goodness. Is it really almost ten?" She forced cheer-fulness into her voice, suddenly feeling sordid. The room looked shabbier than ever and smelled of stale cigarette smoke and sex. "You're right. It's time to get back. Mom and Dad still have fits when I stay out past midnight." Her following laugh sounded hollow to her ears, but Jason smiled as though he didn't notice.

I've hurt her already, he thought, instantly consumed by a need to rush to her side and comfort her. She was sitting up now, a fake smile pasted on her face. He walked over, lifted her to her feet and enclosed her in his arms, inhaling the fragrance of her hair. "I wish we could stay the night. Like Seattle."

He felt the tension leave her body as a part of him marveled at the truth in the words he'd only spoken for comfort. He did want to sleep beside her, to awaken to the sight of her face.

"Me, too." She felt slim, almost weightless in his arms. A perfect fit, in more ways than the physical. She had an ability to speak his thoughts before he even thought them, as though she could read his mind. His love for her resur-faced, and this time he didn't fight it.

"We'll go away for the weekend sometime. Maybe take Tommy."

She pulled away and looked at him, shocked. "We can't do that, Jason. Tommy wouldn't understand."

What was it with them? One minute they were like puzzle pieces, fitting perfectly, joining flawlessly. Then, the next moment, things changed and they were two wrong pieces trying to force themselves together.

"I wasn't suggesting we share our room with him, Kate. Tommy's old enough for an adjoining room of his own."

His tone annoyed her. He could tell by the sudden stiffness of her back. "Don't be sarcastic, Jason. It's just that—"

"News of our relationship will get around? Isn't that what you're trying to say?"

"It's not that. But we don't know where we're going and . . . I'm just not ready."

"Where *are* we going, Kate? When will you be ready?" He stepped back from her, trying to get some perspective. To see himself the way she did. To see her the way she was, not the way he hoped she would be. But it didn't work. His question hung in the air, unanswered. "I'm not the kind of guy who enjoys back-alley trysts in cheap motels."

"That's my line," Kate snapped. Then she laughed. A mild laugh to be sure, but a laugh nonetheless. "Let's give it some time, okay?" She reached out a conciliatory hand and touched his shoulder.

And Jason remembered why he loved her. She saw the humor in life. She didn't nurse grudges—defend her *rightness*. This was a special woman, and he'd be a fool to let her go. He should ask her to marry him right now. Let the opinions of her friends be damned. Do away with all this hiding. Nothing was stopping him.

Except himself. And Kate. He didn't recall that she had said she loved him, too.

KATE YAWNED. Late hours didn't sit well with her, and it had been well past midnight when she finally fell asleep. Tommy, unusually cheerful about his fate, had spent the night with her parents and had waved her and Jason off with a hearty goodbye. When she called this morning to see how he had fared, he enthusiastically asked her how the evening had gone. Not in those words, of course, but his intent had been obvious. Her devious son was into a little matchmaking. So were her mom and dad. If her mother had uttered "Don't worry" one more time, Kate thought she would have screamed.

Still, she couldn't help smiling. The loving afterglow of Jason's touch still lingered on her skin. Despite all their problems and her undeniable fatigue she was deliciously happy this morning. But she couldn't sit here all day daydreaming like a lovesick teenager.

She got up from her desk and entered the lobby where carpenters were noisily installing doors to the entrances of both the operations and production wings.

"Good morning, Rhonda," she called over the din. Rhonda stood at the office supply cabinet, counting. Must be time for monthly inventory, Kate thought. Rhonda was a stickler for keeping track of things—even pencils and paper clips.

"My, you're cheerful this morning." Rhonda turned and gave Kate a steady look. She didn't smile, and Kate felt that sinking feeling once again. She and Rhonda had been so close. Now they were nearly strangers. This couldn't go on.

"Rhonda," she said, her heart thumping a little at the thought of a confrontation. "Could we go to lunch? Talk?"

Her friend's expression softened a bit, but she paused before answering. "Yes. Talk would be good." One of the carpenters started an electric saw, and Kate barely caught Rhonda's words, but heard enough.

"I have to review *Small-Town Women* for the last time, then I have a quick staff meeting. We could go after that," she shouted over the buzz of the saw.

"Okay!" Rhonda shouted back, then turned around and began counting again.

The clerk was busily logging in new tapes as Kate entered the tape library. The girl looked up and smiled, her dark bob reflecting in the fluorescent lights overhead. Her name was Lisa. She was young, fresh out of college, and Kate recognized the hero worship in that smile. She'd often told Kate that she admired her and hoped she could achieve as much in her life.

"Here for your cassette?" Lisa asked.

"Yes. For the last time, I hope."

"Oh, it's going to be a hit, I'm sure. You're so talented, Kate." Then a frown crossed her unlined face. "But I hope Jason doesn't squash it. This cost-cutting stuff could go too far."

"Squash it?" Kate laughed. "That's ridiculous! We're way too far down the line for that."

"I suppose." Lisa's face brightened a little. "Besides, you really know how to handle that guy. I don't know how you do it. Nobody else can stand him."

"That's not true," Kate said quickly. "Harry thinks a lot of him. Says he's a terrific boss. And Carlton likes—" She stopped, realizing that Carlton's endorsement wasn't exactly high praise. "Besides, Woody thinks he's doing a great job."

"Maybe. But, in my mind, anyone who nearly fires Steve Karako isn't doing a great job." Lisa got up and headed for the tape library, saying, "Let me get you that tape," and leaving Kate with the distinct impression that she'd just lowered her image in the girl's eyes.

A few hours later Kate slipped her cassette back into its case. Maybe she wasn't being objective, but she thought the project was dynamite. Some minor editing and it would be perfect.

Her triumph was a little marred, however, by the recollection of her encounter with Lisa. How many other employees would lower their opinion of her a notch if her relationship with Jason became public? There was something else that bothered her about that conversation, but she couldn't quite put her finger on it. Something Lisa had said. She felt that familiar rebellion in her stomach. She'd consumed more antacids since Jason's arrival than ever before in her life. When was it going to end?

When you take a stand! The answer popped out like the proverbial groundhog on Groundhog Day. She wanted to shove it back into its hole but couldn't. Indecision was tearing her apart. Not Jason. Not the conflict. Just her own indecision.

But, Lord, which decision was the right one?

She wrapped her notes around the cassette, left the previewing booth and placed the cassette in the rack Harry reserved for tapes needing his attention. It felt good to do that, knowing that Harry would take care of it when he started his shift and do everything superbly. At least Harry didn't share everyone's view of Jason, and if others disapproved...well, that didn't bother him. He just followed his heart.

Followed his heart. Yes, that was what Harry did, and others be damned. Maybe she should do likewise. Unlike her mind, her heart knew exactly where it wanted to go.

Glancing at her watch, Kate realized it was time for the staff meeting. Walking around the workmen's tangled cords, she made her way to the lobby where she saw Carlton and Jason filing into Woody's office.

"Close the door, will you, Kate?" Woody asked over the noise as she trailed in behind the two men.

"Thank God this will soon be finished and we'll be rid of that blessed racket." Woody waited while they all took a seat before he continued. He got right to the point. "The security company's representative says everything will be in place by midday tomorrow. We're putting coded locks on the doors to the operations and production wings, the master control room and the editing booth. The only way to enter will be by using a card. A password system is being programmed into the master control unit, the animator and all the editing equipment. No one will have access to anything without identifying him or herself first.''

''Seems like overkill, Woody.'' Carlton clasped his hands almost primly across his knees. ''Do we really need a system this elaborate?''

''Yes, we do.'' Woody looked grave. ''The mayor called a few days ago. Seems he was contacted by Bruce Connolly's lawyer.''

''Chuck E. Squirrel's creator?'' Carlton's usually haughty expression was now replaced by a look of surprised concern.

''Why?'' Kate asked at the same time.

''Connolly's claiming copyright infringement. His lawyer wanted to know what we're doing to stop these episodes. They want assurances and they want them quick. That, coupled with the media's speculation that we're doing this purposely as a publicity stunt, is turning this sick joke into a piece of serious business.''

''Hence a security system that would make a nuclear armory proud.'' Jason's comment made it clear that he'd known about the copyright problem for a while. Carlton glanced at him sharply. Was that resentment on his face? Kate wondered. The man was losing his edge. Usually he allowed no stray emotion to mar that supercilious mask.

''Did you put this system together?'' Composed again, Carlton turned toward Jason, who nodded. ''Nice work.'' The compliment was brief, direct and seemed sincere. ''I told Mayor Creighton it was a good move hiring you.''

"Thank you, Carlton." Jason smiled in appreciation. "But we all do good work around here."

Kate suppressed a snort. Carlton was always quick to express his admiration for Jason. He almost seemed to worship Jason, as demonstrated by his attempts to dress and act just like him. She wondered if Carlton had noticed how Jason had changed since his arrival. It was almost as if he had drained the essence from the old Jason, leaving a kinder, more relaxed, man behind. If that were the case, Kate should thank Carlton. She liked the new Jason better.

"Glad to see you folks getting along." Woody said. "But that's not why we're here. Each time someone enters one of the wings or accesses the computerized equipment, they'll identify themselves. The passwords will be on a master list. Only two of us will have access to that list. By studying entry and exit patterns, we may discover the responsible party."

"I guess you and I have our work cut out for us, Woody." Carlton leaned forward, obviously assuming that he would be one of the privileged two. "Reviewing that list will eat up a lot of time."

"Lucky you," Woody answered. "You're going to get out of this one. I've assigned that responsibility to Kate."

"Kate! But she's in programming!" Carlton was definitely losing it, Kate concluded. Not even attempting to control his look of open shock, he stared at Kate accusingly, as though she had deliberately outmaneuvered him. "This falls within my duties."

Woody put out a hand as though trying to stave off Carlton's outburst. "I realize that, Carlton. But this is touchy. For the sake of...well...appearances...this list can't be accessible to anyone who has the ability to produce those cartoon outtakes. Since both you and Jason are trained on the animator, neither of you should know what the passwords are.''

"Are you saying we're suspects?" Carlton asked huffily.

"It's for your own protection."

"Well, if that's the case, you can have my resignation right now." Ignoring Woody's last comment, Carlton stood, made a great show of adjusting the fall of his jacket, then reached for the doorknob. Woody remained silent.

"For heaven's sake, Carlton." Kate stood also as Carlton started to turn the knob. She'd never seen him so emotional. While a part of her wanted to let him march out that door and out of the daily life of KZET, another part couldn't let that happen. Not over something like this. "Woody isn't accusing you. He's just stating the obvious. Jason's excluded, too, but he isn't causing a fuss."

The flicker of animosity in Carlton's eyes, so strong that she resisted an urge to flinch, startled Kate. Then it vanished. He smiled ingratiatingly. As he did so, Kate wondered at Woody's reticence. Why hadn't her boss said something when Carlton started for the door? He still didn't say anything, and Carlton shifted uncomfortably, then returned to his chair.

"Guess I am overreacting." Carlton sat back down and crossed his legs.

"It's a tense situation," Jason commented. "But these new security measures might just stop the sabotage altogether."

The other three looked at him, and Kate wondered what they were thinking. He was right, of course. With equipment access tightly controlled the saboteur might decide the risks were too great. But then they would never know who it was. That was an unsettling thought.

Woody broke the silence. "I hope so," he said. But his voice contained little conviction.

JASON TAPPED his pencil against his temple as though trying to dislodge a stubborn thought. He didn't know which problem to tackle first: the station's sorry financial state, the vandalism problem or the state of the union between Kate and him. The state of the union. That was a laugh. There wasn't any union.

At least in anything but the physical sense. But he had to admit that despite all these weighty matters he felt good, energized—no matter that he had only had five hours' sleep. And he felt content. Just like a fat, old cow, he thought. Even all these negative thoughts about his future with Kate couldn't pull him down. And that was unusual. If Jason did anything, he planned for the future, tried to mold it to his liking and became very disturbed when he didn't like what he saw. Still, if his future held nothing but secret meetings in sleazy motels, it was better than nothing. Besides, the motel wasn't really sleazy. In fact, it had a nice pool, and Jason looked forward to sharing midnight swims with Kate as an interlude between more interesting activities.

He might as well dismiss this particular quandary about his future with Kate. Nothing could be done about it, anyway. He'd have to accept things on Kate's terms—at least for now.

The first worry dismissed, Jason directed his attention to the second: the mysterious appearances of Chuck E. Squirrel and the recent attack on the television transmission tower. Someone obviously meant business here. But what was this someone trying to prove?

They weren't any closer to discovering the brains behind all the destructive activity, and he wasn't sure they ever would. All he knew was that these preventive measures were costing the station a whale of a lot of money. Money it didn't have.

He reviewed the March financial reports and winced. Ninety-seven thousand dollars in the red, year-to-date. Add eighteen thousand for the security system, forty-two for salary and benefits for the twenty-four-hour guards, another thousand for carpentry and other miscellaneous work, and it all made Chuck E. Squirrel one expensive intruder!

It now took three people to man each shift—one to preview the tapes just before airtime, another to check the switching commands continually and a third to carry out routine duties. Of course, it wasn't as if they didn't have the manpower. Prior to automation, a three-man shift had been standard. But these people wouldn't be needed now if it weren't for Chuck E. Squirrel.

At least half of these salaries could have been cut from the payroll. But not anymore. Under the circumstances, layoffs were now out of the question, at least until they were certain the security system would work adequately. And Jason didn't know how they could ever be sure.

Still...he tapped his temple with his pencil once again. Perhaps there was a way. He began making notations along the margins of the financial report. Was it possible? Could he turn around the station's precarious position without laying off a single person?

Several major businesses in the area used television advertising and had to go to Phoenix to get their ads produced. What if they did the production here?

On a yellow ruled pad he scribbled projections of possible revenue and expenses. A few minutes later he looked up at his blank, ugly wall and smiled.

Wouldn't it be nice, he thought, if he could trade his hatchet man label for another?

Magician. That had a nice ring to it.

IT WAS A TRENDY, tourist-trap restaurant, just now opening for the season. The plant-filled dining room, furnished with antiques, was nearly empty.

"For two?" the hostess perkily asked Kate and Rhonda. At their mutual nods she led them to a window table.

They were immediately seated and, after ordering coffee, stared at each other over their enormous, padded menus like two distant relatives thrown together at a family gathering.

"How's *Small-Town Women* coming along?" Rhonda asked.

Her tone carried a stiffness that set Kate on edge, but the topic of the question made her heart lift just a little. If they could talk about old familiar things, then maybe they could close this distance between them.

"It's almost ready to go to the mayor's office for approval, isn't it?" Rhonda added.

"Yes. It goes tomorrow." Almost forgetting that she and Rhonda were no longer on good terms, Kate began her habitual confessing of all her thoughts and actions. "I'm as nervous as a cat. I think it's really good, but I'm not sure the city council will think so, too."

"They will. You did it, so it's got to be good."

The confidence that Rhonda always expressed in her abilities was one of the things that made Kate value her friendship. This latest statement made her realize how sorely she missed it. "Thanks," she said with real feeling. "Cross your fingers for me."

"It'll take more than crossed fingers."

Before Kate could ask what that meant the waitress interrupted their conversation. Kate ordered poached salmon, while Rhonda chose a Mexican-style luncheon special. As soon as the waitress left, Kate eyed Rhonda directly.

"Why do I get the feeling that your comment had nothing to do with *Small-Town Women?*"

"You always were astute." Rhonda smiled, and there was no malice in that smile, just a touch of sadness. "You know, we should have talked sooner. I don't usually let things go on this long." There was a slight emphasis on the "I," as though Rhonda was saying that Kate usually did.

And Kate knew it was true but refused to accept the subtle admonishment. There wasn't anything wrong with trying to preserve harmony.

"So what's your point?"

"Jason almost fired Steve Karako." The horrified expression on Rhonda's face clearly expressed how deeply she felt about this. "And for something that wasn't even his fault. For God's sake, Kate, why are you friends with that man?"

"He's just doing his job." This was a question she didn't quite know how to answer. But she was coming to understand Jason. He looked at the broad picture. Not always the best approach but at least his intentions were good. "He does it the only way he knows."

A salad plate suddenly appeared in front of Kate, and she paused in her defense. She wasn't doing a very good job of it, anyway. As she waited for Rhonda to be served, she stared at the chintz pattern on the tablecloth, a nebulous thought stirring in the back of her mind. When the waitress left, the thought took form.

"Rhonda, how did you know about Steve? That meeting was confidential." Besides herself, only Jason, Woody and Carlton had attended the meeting.

Rhonda stirred uncomfortably, then forced a smile. "I have my ways."

"I hope you haven't taken up eavesdropping."

"Eavesdropping! Me?" Rhonda's denial was so exaggerated that it was obvious she wanted Kate to disbelieve her. Kate decided not to press the question. Rhonda wasn't above spreading a little gossip, but Kate knew she guarded a confidence as though it were her firstborn and wouldn't say how she'd really found out about Steve, no matter how hard Kate pressed.

But an uncomfortable thought entered her mind, and she realized why her earlier conversation with Lisa had disturbed her. Lisa had also commented on Steve's near-firing.

"Who else knows about this?"

"It's all over the station."

Kate groaned, and suddenly her salmon became very unappetizing.

"What's wrong, Kate?" Rhonda reached over the table and touched Kate's hand. Kate blinked rapidly. The familiar gesture made her realize again how much she had missed Rhonda's friendship.

"They'll think I'm the one who told you."

"Who?"

"Jason, Woody, Carlton. Neither Woody nor Jason would have told you." She laughed sarcastically. "And could anyone even imagine Carlton rushing to *you* with gossip? The way you two hate each other?"

"I hadn't thought about that." A frown creased Rhonda's pancaked complexion, then vanished. "If it comes to that, I'll just tell Woody I listened at the door."

"Is that what happened?"

"Ask me no questions, I'll tell you no lies." Rhonda shook her head. "The news didn't start with me, Kate. But that's all you get."

The main course arrived, and for a few moments she and Rhonda ate in silence. Then Rhonda looked up from her meal. "Now back to Jason."

"I really don't want to talk about him, Rhonda. This is obviously a sore spot between us, and I don't know what talking about it will accomplish."

"It's for you own good, Kate. You're ruining your friendships with your open support of that man. You talk about him all the time. Like he's some kind of god."

"I do not!"

"Yes, you do. It's 'Jason said this.' " Rhonda bobbed her head from side to side in imitation, an expression of contempt on her face. " 'Jason did that.' All day long it's Jason, Jason. If you aren't hanging around the coffeepot with him, you're in his office. Or he's in yours. And do you know what really bugs me? Harry defends you guys. He thinks the world of Jason."

A hot flush crept up Kate's neck and flooded her face. My God, Rhonda was right. She had thought she was being so discreet. Instead, she was as transparent as cellophane. "I can't help it, Rhonda. Jason isn't as bad as people think. He's been good to me. Good to Tommy. What am I supposed to do? Tommy adores him."

"Tommy adores him," Rhonda repeated, her contemptuous expression vanishing. "Harry adores him. You adore him." She stopped for a moment and sipped some coffee. Kate was grateful for the momentary silence to allow the embarrassed heat to leave her face.

Rhonda put down her coffee cup. "Maybe if the three people I like the best in the whole world like this guy, I'm missing something." She stared out the window momentarily, as though her thoughts were drifting far away. Then she came back. "But tell me something, would you, Kate?"

"What?"

"Are you in love with this guy?"

CHAPTER ELEVEN

"IT MIGHT WORK." Woody lifted his shaggy head from the papers he'd been studying. Jason had hurriedly put together a proposal, then buzzed Woody to set up a brief meeting. Now they reviewed the proposal together.

"That's what I thought." Jason smiled broadly. "This could take a while to set in motion, but if we rent out studio time and can book even, say, forty hours a month, that will bring in several hundred grand a year. We keep two more technicians on the payroll and let attrition take care of the others. I know for a fact that Mark Bishop wants to move down to Phoenix. He's bright. It shouldn't take long. Also, we could ask for voluntary layoff."

"Let's put out some feelers for clients." Woody leaned back and clasped his hands behind his head. Like Jason's chair, his squawked loudly, but Woody didn't seem to notice. "How much time did you put into this proposal?"

Jason grinned. "Oh, about an hour." He knew the thing was pretty sloppy, but he had wanted Woody's input right away. A quick and dirty job was better than no job at all. Or jobs, in this case. That was what he was trying to do—save jobs.

"You're kidding!" Woody whistled, sounding impressed. "I thought you'd put in a couple of days. Mayor Creighton said you were good. I should've believed him."

"Thanks," Jason murmured. He shifted on his hard chair, embarrassed.

"But this isn't your usual method of cutting costs, is it? Why this sudden shift in direction?" There was no animosity in Woody's voice, merely sincere interest.

"KZET isn't like the other stations I've been to. The employees here are dedicated and loyal. In bigger cities television people play musical chairs with the stations in the area, so it's no great shock to them when they lose a job. It happens all the time." Jason shifted in his uncomfortable chair and rubbed his scar. It ached today, probably the result of too little sleep. It wasn't the only reason he was uncomfortable, though. The motives he was giving Woody were shallow, only skimming the surface of the truth. "It's different in Lakeview. Like you said a while back, laying someone off is almost like running them out of town on a rail. Where else can they go?"

Woody listened closely, tilting his head to one side as Jason talked, regarding him carefully with those observant hazel eyes. Jason had the sinking feeling the man knew he wasn't telling all.

But what could he say? That a blue-eyed, strawberry blonde and her green-eyed son were causing him to examine his attitudes? That a part of himself would die if he had to lay off Kate? He truly wished his reasons were grander in scope, more altruistic. But the bottom line was that Kate's welfare was his primary concern here.

And that internal admission bothered him. He had always operated on the premise that personal concerns shouldn't affect business decisions, and this change of heart made him feel as if he was betraying himself.

"I'm glad to see this shift in your thinking, Jason," Woody finally said. He leaned forward, swept some papers out of the way and propped his elbows on the desk.

Resting his head on clasped hands, he continued. "We can present your program to the city council at our monthly meeting next week. I have to tell you, though, I don't think they'll be very receptive while this squirrel thing is hanging over our heads."

That had also occurred to Jason, and he nodded at Woody's words. "I've run through this again and again, Woody. As yet I haven't a clue as to who could be doing it. Or even why. Do you have some ideas?"

Woody shook his head, but slowly, as though holding something back.

"You sure?"

A long pause. Woody eyed him critically, as though assessing him. "I have one idea. We know that only Harry, Carlton, Rhonda and you know how to operate the animator. That kind of narrows the field."

"Don't forget Amy Herrera and Steve Karako."

"I didn't forget. It's just they're almost always chained to the master control unit. When would they have time to produce the clips?"

"You have a prime suspect, don't you?" Another pause. Woody wasn't giving this up easily. Jason couldn't blame him for his lack of trust. Suspicions could easily grow into accusations, accusations into charges. "This is just between you and me, Woody. You have my word."

"I hate to think it." Woody ruffled his graying hair. The mild gesture seemed, to Jason, to reveal his agitation. "I've worked with Harry for nearly ten years now. The man's good. Damned good. He should have gone places."

"He should have had my job, you mean." Jason felt his defenses rise but, at Woody's questioning glance, he brought them under control. His boss was opening up, and he didn't want to do anything to close him back down again.

"Harry said he didn't care about the promotion," Woody continued. "And I believed him. He loves tinkering with all that equipment back there. Being a desk jockey isn't really his style. But his talent is what causes me to suspect him. Who but Harry could come up with this screwball method of sabotage? Those wacky quips the squirrel spouts have Harry written all over them." Woody flopped against the back of his chair, placed his feet on his desk and stared at the ceiling. "Don't tell me you hadn't thought of that."

"Yes, it occurred to me."

"And it will occur to Mayor Creighton or some member of the city council, too. Harry's crazy ways are what cost him this promotion. Revenge is a powerful motive."

"Do you really think he did it?"

"Harry loves this station," Woody hedged. "I can't believe he'd do anything to hurt it." He swung forward and planted his feet on the ground. "Who do you think is responsible, Jason?"

"I don't know. Rhonda has opportunity. So does Carlton."

"Rhonda isn't skilled enough. Besides, what reason would she have?"

"I can't believe you asked that," Jason shot back with a laugh. "The woman hates my guts."

"There's still the ability thing. These latest attempts are so skillfully done that we don't even know where they're coming from."

Jason couldn't argue Woody's point, but he also thought it possible that Rhonda could be self-taught. She was always nosing around the station and seemed to have an aptitude with computer equipment. Then, dismissing that idea as farfetched, he brought up another possibility. "How about Carlton?" As soon as the question was out, Jason shook his head. "No, absolutely no motive. His job's as secure as Harry's."

But Woody's forehead had puckered as Jason spoke, and Jason wondered why.

"Between you and me, Jason?" Woody paused until Jason nodded, then went on. "I've been a little uncomfortable about Carlton lately. True, he's a top-flight fundraiser, but he's a little careless with his other duties. We've had a couple of talks about that."

"I see," Jason replied. "Did you say anything that implied his job might be at risk?"

"No way. Carlton brings in so much money that I could never let him go. No, we just talked about transferring some duties, maybe to Kate." Woody shook his head ruefully. "No matter which way I take this speculation, it always leads back to Harry. I can't even stand to think about it anymore."

"I understand," Jason said, but he really didn't. How could a manager refuse to face a problem and still think he was doing his job? Not that Jason thought Harry was responsible. Such malice seemed too out of character for his laid-back assistant manager. "You know, Woody, it really wouldn't take a lot of skill to pull outtakes of *Candy Cane Lane*. Just because the quips are zany doesn't mean Harry dreamed them up. They could be stock lines from the show. When's the last time you watched it?"

"Never." Woody smiled regretfully. "We don't have any kids."

"I've never watched it, either. Maybe we should do that. It could answer our primary question."

"Which is what? Who's the guilty party?"

"No." Jason suddenly realized why all this speculation was getting them nowhere. "The primary question is what is the motive."

ARE YOU IN LOVE with this guy? The words replayed in Kate's mind like a broken record, gaining a kind of rhythm as they repeated again and again. Of course, Kate had denied any such thing, but Rhonda had looked at her skeptically and, although she hadn't said so, Kate knew Rhonda didn't believe her.

Now Kate was safely back at work, safe in her cramped office where Rhonda couldn't ask any more probing questions.

At least she hadn't asked if Kate was sleeping with this guy, sparing her the necessity of lying. Sex and love. Did they necessarily go together? Kate had always thought so. So why was the idea of loving Jason Brock so frightening?

She shuddered then. Pictures of Jason's golden eyes—open, vulnerable, glazed with passion—filled her vision. She could feel him. Feel his legs, lightly covered with hair, their texture coarse against her own legs as she wrapped them around him. A deep yearning stirred within her.

In Seattle he'd lain beside her, weeping like a child, exposing the raw pain he felt inside. Her yearning had dissolved into an ache of sympathy. How had he survived such a background without being terribly damaged?

Perhaps he hadn't. The picture vanished, replaced by another. This time Jason's eyes were cold, a hard, flat surface that nothing could penetrate. He talked of profits, futures and bottom lines, while his eyes shut out any contact with his soul.

Is that what frightened her? Was Jason capable of sustained intimacy? Would he allow her to get close, only to pull away and shut her out?

She picked up the programming schedule, determined to get back to work. This line of thought was getting her absolutely nowhere, and she needed to finalize the next quarter's schedule.

She almost crushed the papers in her hand as a realization hit her. Jason wasn't shutting her out. No, he was pursuing her openly. He'd even said he loved her.

She was the one doing the shutting out. And for what reason?

Fear of censure. That was the only honest answer. She had wanted, at almost any cost, to avoid the disapproving expression she'd seen on Rhonda's face, on Lisa's and on the faces of many of the other staff members.

Fear was ruling her life. Like some inner tyrant, it sat on an ugly throne demanding that she conform, be liked, win approval. A sudden anger erupted inside Kate's chest. Damn! It was as if her dad walked beside her every day reminding her to watch her step! Or was it her mother? Her dad seemed to do pretty much as he pleased, but Rita constantly fussed and fretted over the opinions of others. She clenched her fists, stunned by her rage. In a flash of insight she realized it was directed at herself. It was she who was reacting like an obedient child instead of the adult she was, an adult capable of directing her own life. She. Not her dad. Not her mom.

No matter, she decided with firm conviction. Today was the day Kate Gregory was going to take charge. At that she began lightly fingering the neckline of her dress, then yanked her hand away. That habit belonged to the old Kate.

She roughly pushed her chair back from her desk, stood and walked to her open doorway. The lobby was empty, and Kate started to head for the operations wing when Rhonda appeared in Woody's door. Partially hidden by the doorframe, Rhonda seemed to cringe for a moment, a tense expression on her face. Something black jutted from her hand, and she turned quickly before Kate could see what it was. When she came back out of Woody's office, her hands were empty.

"Just tidying the boss's office a little," Rhonda said cheerily as she returned to her desk. "I don't get this opportunity often."

She seemed a bit high-strung, but Rhonda had been acting that way a lot since Jason had been hired, and Kate dismissed it as a result of their luncheon talk. Although it had seemed to ease some of the strain between them, Kate knew that everything wasn't settled. Not yet. Even at the risk of opening that rift again, some things had to be said.

She smiled at Rhonda's comment, then walked over and stood in front of her desk. Rhonda looked up.

"To answer your question," Kate said without hedging, "yes, I'm in love with him."

Something flickered across Rhonda's face. Disappointment? Pain? Or even envy? "You're sure?" she asked.

"I'm sure," Kate answered. And joy followed that answer. Joy and a supreme sense of freedom. Now she wanted to tell Jason, let him know she wasn't a coward anymore.

"I guess we know where you stand then."

Kate had expected anger, an argument, anything but this quiet acceptance.

"I hope we're still friends, Rhonda." Was there also something else in Rhonda's eyes—something that bordered on admiration. "I value your friendship very much, but I have to live my own life."

A faint smile crossed Rhonda's face. "It's hell when you hear your own words come back to haunt you."

"What?"

"That's what I told you the day you met with Tommy's school."

"So it is." Now it was Kate's turn to smile. "I hope you meant it."

"I did." Rhonda inclined her head back over her work, her usual signal that she was done conversing. But then she looked up again. "Just protect yourself in the clinches, honey. I don't want to see you get hurt."

"I'll be fine. You'll see," Kate replied softly. She felt a subtle shift and knew that something was now eternally altered in her relationship with Rhonda. She hoped they would rebuild on more solid ground. "Is Jason in his office?"

"No, he and Woody are in the operations wing." Rhonda frowned in confusion. "Said something about watching cartoons. Can you imagine? Fine way to waste an afternoon."

Now she sounded like the old Rhonda, and Kate grinned affectionately. She really did love this old bat. "I'll find them."

As Kate walked down the hallway to the studio her heels clicked on the linoleum floor. The sound seemed brisk, purposeful. Cheerful. Just like Kate felt inside. A burden had taken wing, releasing her, allowing her to fill with the happiness that had been waiting for her all along.

She saw Jason and Woody in the previewing booth. Its soundproof walls prevented any noise from escaping, but she could see they were laughing riotously. She knocked on the door, and when it opened, she saw Chuck E. Squirrel rollicking on the monitor.

"What are you doing?" she asked. Jason and Woody sat there with tears of mirth running down their faces. Chuck E. had just walloped his arch enemy Sneaky Pete, and Pete was slinking off, a sizzling stick of unexploded dynamite in his hand. When the dynamite exploded, the men roared again.

"Sneaky keeps trying—" Jason tried to talk between spurts of laughter "—to do Chuck in." More laughter. "But the guy's so stupid he's killing himself...instead." Jason slapped his leg and Woody punched him.

"Think we...could keep the...the employees in line this way?" Woody asked between his own gasps of laughter.

"It's a...a thought," Jason stuttered between giggles. Kate had never seen him like this before. He was laughing just like Tommy did when he watched this stupid show. Although she'd never thought it was quite so stupid until the squirrel had begun his impromptu commentary during Channel Seven's nighttime programming.

"Two grown men! You should be ashamed." But Kate began laughing, too, from the sheer infectiousness of their amusement.

"It kind of loses something out of context." Jason's laughter subsided some. "But you should have been here, Kate. You'd have loved it. Don't know why I've never watched cartoons before."

Because you've never been a child. An overwhelming love filled her as she watched Jason's adolescent amusement with the slapstick antics on *Candy Cane Road*. He had never been young, the way a child should be. Loved. Protected. Entertained. She wanted to fill that void in his life, not as a mother, but as a friend, lover, companion.

Her smile, so broad that it ached, consumed her face. Jason turned his gaze on her and his laughter faded completely. Their eyes locked.

Woody must have noticed the change of mood, because his laughter subsided also. "That's enough for today, don't you think?" He turned off the monitor, and for a moment silence filled the small booth.

"What?" Jason asked. "Oh, yes, I suppose it is."

"What were you guys doing, anyway?" Kate asked, painfully brought back to the matters at hand.

"Gathering evidence," Woody answered.

"Were you going to make Chuck confess? Get him to tell you how he did it?" These two goofballs amazed her. Taking an hour off and trying to pass it off as work.

"More like why." Jason spoke this time. "We thought we might get a clue if we knew a little more about the show. Neither Woody nor I have ever seen it."

"That's a shame." Kate suppressed a urge to stroke the strong angle of Jason's jaw. "Now you have."

"Yep," Woody said. He stepped into the open doorway of the booth. "Who were you looking for, Kate, me or Jason?"

"Jason."

Oh, was she ever looking for Jason!

"Then I'll leave you guys to discuss your business." He walked away starting to laugh again, and the sound echoed off the prefab walls, growing fainter and fainter until it disappeared.

"Well?" Jason looked at her expectantly, his expression clear and open. He looked young, carefree. "What is this important business?"

"Do I have to have a reason to see you?" Kate looked at him with mock flirtation though lowered eyelashes.

"No. Not unless it's to invite me for another glorious night at one of the city of Globe's finest resorts." There was still a hint of laughter in his rich voice.

"I have a better idea." Kate shut the door of the pre-viewing booth, then closed the few inches between Jason and her and wrapped her arms around his neck.

He kissed her nose. "And what's that?"

"How about Friday night you cook dinner for me?"

"What?" The laughter bubbling beneath the surface emerged again. "For you and Tommy. At your house?"

"No." Kate nibbled at his lower lip. She couldn't believe she was doing this, kissing her lover—yes, her lover—in a minuscule booth during working hours. But she couldn't resist. "At your house. Alone. Just you and me."

Jason should have smiled. Instead he looked at her seriously, obviously realizing the importance of her invitation. "This is what you want to do? No doubts?"

"No doubts." Her heart soared as she realized it was true. "I love you, Jason."

"I love you, too." He brought her tightly against his chest, and Kate could feel, more than hear, the sigh of relief escaping his throat. Releasing her, he smiled into her eyes. "But I have to warn you." He wore a loving grin filled with expectation.

"About what?" A sudden tightness gripped Kate's chest.

"I'm a terrible cook."

"Who plans to eat?" With a delighted laugh she sank into his arms.

Jason kissed her then. Right there, while on the payroll, he kissed her deeply, passionately, completely.

JASON SHIFTED restlessly and wished he could open the window of his stuffy little office. The month of May was nearing and the weather was warming up. Too cool for the air conditioner, too warm without it. Although he'd abandoned his business suit over a month ago, even his chambray shirt and cord jeans seemed too much. He wondered now how he'd ever stood all those years in that three-piece suit of armor.

But the weather wasn't causing his restlessness. And he didn't know exactly what was. His life was purring, running so smoothly that he wanted to give thanks every morning. Since that first sultry invitation in the previewing booth, Kate had visited his apartment often. He smiled as he thought of the silky feel of her skin against his, of that tangled mass of curls wound around his fingers. Yes, he was a sexually satisfied male.

But besides a wonderful bed partner, he had a true friend. He could talk with Kate about anything, something he'd never been able to do before with anyone.

And work was going well. He had investigated his plan for renting studio time and had already lined up several prospective clients. If Kate's series was successful, the combined revenues of those two efforts would bring Channel Seven back into the black. Even without Kate's series, the studio rental alone would keep them on an even keel.

Sure, many of the employees still treated him as if he were Stalin reincarnated. But time would take care of that. And, although they still hadn't discovered who had introduced Chuck E. Squirrel into the station's programming, there hadn't been any more incidents since the security system had been installed. Maybe they'd never discover who did it but, if it stopped, it really didn't matter.

So why this sense of impending doom? This feeling that he should prepare himself for the worst?

His telephone buzzed, and Rhonda coldly informed him that the manager of a large equipment dealership was on the line. His heaviness immediately forgotten, Jason pressed the flashing button and presented his studio rental proposal to the calling businessman. The man was quite interested, and after Jason showed him how it could save him several thousand dollars a year, he told Jason to "count him in." Pleased with himself, Jason hung up. But the pleasure was short-lived. His heaviness descended again.

He got up to the inevitable wail of his aging chair and opened his door. The door to the lobby was open also, and maybe some fresh air would chase away this gloom.

He stared out the lobby doorway at the landscape beyond. The deciduous trees were sprouting new growth—shiny, soft green as only emerging leaves could be. It reminded him that life was springing anew for him, giving him a chance at rebirth. He'd be a fool to let it get away.

An absolute fool, he realized, knowing then what had been bothering him. Every transcendent moment in his life had been followed by disaster.

He thought of the day he'd been drafted into the baseball minor leagues. His parents had gone sailing that day while he'd stayed home for the tryouts. After his acceptance, he'd waited eagerly at his friend Sammy's house for his mother and father to come home, anticipating the "pizza celebration" that would follow his announcement. Daylight had faded to dusk, dusk to total darkness, and Jason had noticed the uneasy expressions that Sammy's parents had worn as they had all continually glanced at the door.

When the knock finally came, Jason had run to answer it, expecting to see his parents sunburned, apologetic and ready to dispense their generous ration of well-deserved praise. Instead, a uniformed, grim-faced officer had greeted him. Sammy's mother had tried to draw him aside, to shield him from the words.

"Freak storm. Capsized." His parents were gone. Gone.

He hadn't believed it. Not then.

The next time he'd seen them they were in twin caskets. Only then had he begun to accept the truth, his fate. Not until he'd been dispatched to the hatchet-faced Aunt Phyllis, who had often acted as if she'd wished he'd drowned with his parents, had it truly sunk in.

Throughout his life it seemed that disaster followed triumph. Even Beth's betrayal and Stacey's death had come after he was riding high on a new promotion.

Now, as he relived his earlier pain, he realized the time to lay those ghosts to rest had come. Kate was here now, willing, he was sure, to start a life with him.

What was he waiting for?

He would buzz her on the intercom right now and plan a dinner at a fancy restaurant for Saturday night. What kind of ring would she like? Should they pick it out together or should he surprise her? Would she want a large wedding or would a small, informal ceremony suit her better?

He reached for the telephone, but it buzzed before he lifted the receiver. Rhonda told him the mayor was on the line.

He picked up the phone. "Jason speak—"

"I want to see you in my office right away, Brock," the voice bellowed. "Just what the hell is going on?"

MAYOR GEORGE CREIGHTON'S scowling face, as he shouted at Jason and Woody, belied his good-ol'-boy appearance. His office, Jason noted peevishly, was lusher than the vinyl cubes that Channel Seven's staff occupied. Although it didn't match the luxury of Jason's former penthouse suites, it did have thick carpeting, decent drapes and furniture with varnish intact.

God, his hands were shaking. Why? He'd had worse dressing-downs in his lifetime. His hand went instinctively to his scar, which was throbbing unmercifully.

"Shake your bootie, babe?" Creighton roared. The man's chest was larger than a rain barrel, providing ample room to develop a roar, and he slammed his fist on his desk as if the power of his voice wasn't enough. "You have got to find out who's doing this! This has got to end!"

Jason's mind swirled as he tried to figure out what had happened. "George—"

"Don't George me, Brock. We're paying you big bucks to keep that station's operations running smoothly. Now earn them!"

"This isn't getting us anywhere," Woody interjected in a quiet, placating tone. "Settle down, George. We don't even know what you're talking about."

Jason shot Woody a look of gratitude for smoothly diverting George's attention. He felt himself shrinking inside, cringing from George's verbal assaults as though they were physical blows. From what he could gather, Chuck E. Squirrel had appeared again, right in the middle of Kate's production.

The mayor took a deep, long-suffering breath. "The council and I were reviewing *Small-Town Women*. When that guest, Erika something—"

"McCardy," Woody provided.

"Whatever." George waved impatiently. "Anyway, she came onto the set. Then, boom, that freaking squirrel appeared, saying, 'Shake that bootie, baby.' We kept watching, of course. A few minutes later he showed up again. This time . . . Lord, it's ridiculous. Erika was leaning into the camera, and that creature screeched, 'Show us some cleavage, doll!' My God, a pornographic cartoon character." George then launched into a string of obscenities that aptly described what he thought of the entire situation.

"Thousand of dollars, which, I might add, we can sorely afford, went into a security system that isn't doing a damn bit of good! This has gone way beyond a practical joke. As if being hounded about copyright infringement isn't bad enough, the network has told us that our license is in jeopardy. The FCC is breathing down my neck, and you guys still don't have a clue who's doing this!"

A clock ticked solemnly on the mayor's desk. A wooden circle on a bronze base, it appeared to be antique and bore a plaque of appreciation dedicated to George. Jason fixated on it, trying to use his old trick of focusing on the exterior to bring his shaky emotions under control. It wasn't working. He knew he should say something. He just didn't know what. The ramifications of this incident were overwhelming him. This project—Kate's baby—had been compromised. She hadn't heard yet, but he knew she'd be devastated.

"We don't even know why they're doing it," Jason finally commented. "I can't deny it, George. This whole thing has me at a loss."

George straightened in his chair at Jason's words. There was a long silence. The ticking clock suddenly sounded like a time bomb, and Jason had a creepy intuition, a chilling feeling that he wasn't going to like what the mayor was about to say.

"Yeah." George broke the silence. "The council and I talked that over, Jason. We, uh, er, think this has... something to do with you." The final statement was rushed, as though George was afraid he'd never get it out.

"Me?" Incredulous, Jason shot back in his chair as though he'd been slapped. From the corner of his eye he could see Woody looking at him in shock. "The council thinks I've been doing this sabotage?"

George shook his head. "We think you're the target. Someone wants to be rid of you. Bad."

Just as Kate had suggested, Jason thought, remembering his own speculation along those lines. Now the idea had occurred to the others. He had the sinking feeling he was being set up, not only by the saboteur, but by the mayor.

"Now, George, there's no way of knowing that," Woody said, rushing to Jason's defense.

"Powers of deduction, Woody." George tapped his temple. "Powers of deduction. This didn't start until Jason arrived. We've been hearing rumblings about employee discontent, and the whole town knows Jason isn't very well liked at Channel Seven."

"Given his reputation, that's pretty easy to understand, isn't it?" Woody eyed the mayor with the hardest stare Jason had ever seen on the man's face. The silent message was unmistakable: *You hired him, George. You knew what he was, and that's why you hired him.*

"Uh, well, yes." George looked down and fiddled for a moment with a document lying on his otherwise clear desk. "We had to have someone who could bring these runaway costs under control. But employee satisfaction is important to the council. And to me. This is a small town. We can't have these—"

Voters dissatisfied. Jason mentally filled in George's unspoken words. The mayor's message was becoming increasingly clear.

"We didn't realize he would cause this big a ruckus," George finished. "The crux of the matter is that you guys have to find out who's doing this. And soon. How about that Bingham guy? Wasn't he the last one who handled the tape? He's an oddball if I ever saw one."

Jason almost laughed at that. How could a mayor who presided over town activities wearing paint-stained overalls and a workman's hat call Harry an oddball?

"Harry's our most competent worker, George," Woody responded quickly.

And one of the few friendly faces I meet all day, Jason thought.

"If Jason's the target, we should look for people who dislike him." Then, echoing Jason's former thought, Woody added, "Harry supports Jason."

"Yeah, well, there's something screwy about that guy. Who else you got on that suspect list?"

"We've been over this before, George." Woody's usually relaxed posture stiffened. He leaned forward almost challengingly and, with amazement, Jason realized he was angry. He hadn't thought Woody ever possessed an angry thought. "What good will it do rehashing old stuff?"

"It's like this. Either you and Brock fix this quick or the council has decided that we'll find a team who can." The mayor pointed an accusing finger at Jason. "And you," he said evenly, "mend your fences with the staff. Make 'em like you."

How the hell was he supposed to do that? He looked at Woody, hoping for support, and saw there was none. His boss's anger had vanished. He looked close to shock, opening his mouth as if to speak, then closing it again.

When he finally did speak, his voice was hushed, as though his throat had closed firmly over his vocal cords. "I can't believe what I'm hearing. George, you and I have been friends for years." A white ridge appeared around Woody's mouth. Jason recognized that sign of fear. How often had he seen that same reaction when he spoke similar words in his years as the network's cleanup man, their hatchet man? Too many times. How strange to be on the other side of the table. How strange to see someone he considered an ally demonstrating that back-to-the-wall behavior.

He didn't feel anything himself except numb—as though a barrier had arisen, shutting off his anxiety. But he had seen this coming earlier in this conversation. Obviously Woody hadn't.

"You're saying you'd fire us?" Woody's voice was a mere whisper.

The mayor looked away, but Jason saw the raw pain in the beefy man's eyes. Why? Jason had never found this kind of encounter painful.

You and I have been friends for years. Woody's words resurfaced, containing the answer to his question. In all his time in network management he had carefully avoided friendship, thinking he didn't have time. He now realized he'd been protecting himself from the agony George was clearly feeling. His relationship with Kate, along with his sense of comradeship with Woody and Harry, was now making that difficult. When had he lost his objectivity?

George looked up. "I've been protecting you from the council for months, Woody." A bright sheen reflected from George's eyes, but his expression was stern, uncompromising. "No more. The bottom line is that you two have to fix this problem. Or else!"

CHAPTER TWELVE

IT WASN'T POSSIBLE. Just wasn't. Kate sat crammed into the previewing booth with Woody and Jason, watching the butchered version of *Small-Town Women*.

"Hot stuff!!" Chuck E. Squirrel crooned as Erika crossed her shapely legs. The fuzzy creature disappeared from the screen, and the camera zoomed in on the curve of Erika's calf. This had definitely not been in the original version!

"Enough. Enough." Kate waved her hands in frustration and, in response, Jason leaned over and shut off the monitor.

"A work of art, isn't it?" A wry, unhappy grin crossed Jason's face.

"Whoever's doing this is very skilled."

"Who could it be besides Harry?" Woody looked unhappy at his own question. Deep lines etched his forehead, and he seemed terribly tired. "This contains voiceovers, splicing, high-tech stuff. I've been away from the production end so long I'm not even sure how it was done."

"It's not hard on the new animator, Woody. Anyone could figure it out after a basic introduction." Jason massaged his scar as he spoke, and Kate could tell it was bothering him. She wished she could ease his anxiety. He and Woody were both unusually subdued since returning from their meeting with Mayor Creighton. Neither had said what had happened, but Kate knew it wasn't good.

"Then it could be anyone." Kate leaned back against the booth's wall and lifted her cotton knit sweater away from her skin. She felt sticky and uncomfortable. The tiny cubicle was stuffy, and if their topic hadn't been too sensitive to risk the chance of someone overhearing, she would have opened the door. "Rhonda, Harry, Amy or Steve?" She repeated the litany of names they'd gone over so often.

"Don't forget Carlton. Or even me." Jason's bitter laugh sounded warning bells in Kate's head. "Or so I've been accused."

The sharp glance that Woody shot Jason confirmed Kate's suspicion. Whatever had gone on when they visited the mayor had disturbed Jason deeply. She had a feeling he wasn't going to tell her. When she asked him about it, he'd simply muttered, "Nothing more than I expected," then had changed the subject. Woody wasn't unaffected, either, judging by his uncharacteristic tenseness.

"According to George," Woody said, "the motive is probably to get rid of Jason and possibly stop the layoffs in the bargain. Harry's job is secure, so why would he want to do this? The only things implicating him are the squirrel's off-the-wall comments and his losing the promotion because of Jason."

"Could someone be trying to set Harry up?" Kate asked. "Everyone knows about his weird sense of humor. It's not as if no one else ever thinks things like that. They just don't usually say them."

"We're going in circles." Jason stood, his head nearly touching the ceiling of the cramped booth. Kate looked up at him, wishing they were someplace else. Someplace where she could touch him, hold him, help erase the tightness around his eyes. Anyplace but this tiny, distress-filled room. "And it isn't getting us anywhere. The only way to stop this is to catch the person in the act."

"Why don't we put a security guard on nights?" At her suggestion Woody and Jason both paused, as if considering it. "Maybe someone undercover."

"It's a possibility." Woody scratched his chin. "What do you think, Jason?"

"We're making the assumption that this is happening at night. How do we know that? That animator is a slick piece of equipment. By using the in-line monitor, this stuff can be produced anytime, even during working hours, without anyone ever seeing."

Woody shook his head. "That means it would take a full-time crew to keep an eye out. Almost one person for every employee who has the skill. George would explode if we even suggested it."

"But these incidents are getting more and more sophisticated, Woody," Kate said. "This guy's got to slip up sooner or later. The security measures are making it harder, too."

"We'll put the idea on the back burner," Woody said, obviously closing the subject. He stood up beside Jason, making Kate feel suddenly small. "The security is just getting operational. If you and I review the password entries every day, Kate, we might spot unusual activity." Woody opened the door to the booth and took a deep breath. Apparently the stuffy room had bothered him also. "In the meantime, can you stay late tonight? Work with Harry to put your pilot tape back into shape? George said he wants to see it again tomorrow."

"Did they like it?" A frisson of dread shot down Kate's spine. The city council hadn't been especially enthusiastic about her project at the outset. Would this destroy her chances?

"I don't know. Chuck E.'s commentaries didn't exactly present it in the best light. But they're willing to give it another shot."

"I'll stay and help, Kate." Jason's sympathetic expression told Kate that he recognized her apprehension.

"Thanks, Jason." His offer eased her worry, but she needed him elsewhere. "Could you pick up Tommy instead? Mom has bingo tonight, and I don't want to ask her to give that up."

"Sure. We can throw a few balls." But Kate noted an underlying sadness in Jason's eyes as he agreed. Whatever could be bothering him? Surely he'd had his hind end chewed before and by bigger bullies than George Creighton.

Jason's cheerlessness notwithstanding, Kate felt more secure as the three of them filed out of the booth, but when they reached the door to the lobby, her sense of well-being faltered. At least a half-dozen employees huddled around Rhonda's desk, listening to Amy Herrera with great interest.

"About to be fired. My sister knows the mayor's secretary. She called me right away. Soon as she heard."

Kate saw someone tap Amy on the shoulder, and the woman turned, her face becoming blood-red. Turning again, she bolted for the entrance to the operations wing. Following Amy's lead, the group immediately dissolved.

Woody and Jason were a few steps ahead of Kate, and she had seen them exchange startled looks on hearing what Amy had said.

She followed Jason into his office before she said anything. "Who's going to be fired?"

"I don't know, Kate." Ignoring convention, Jason sat, trying to find the words to cover up what they had just heard. Damn small towns. Nothing was ever a secret. He didn't want to share this with Kate. Not yet. He hadn't failed so far. He still had this job. Still had a chance to straighten out this slapdash station. "Rumors get started. If you want to know, why don't you ask Amy?"

Had it just been a few hours ago that he'd been thinking of what kind of engagement ring Kate might like? As he sat there, feeling as if he were once again beneath his aunt's oppressive shadow, it seemed like days, years even.

Well, he could forget about that until he got this mess straightened out. Kate didn't need a failure as a husband. Tommy needed a better father image than that. Besides, if he lost this job, where would they live? Would Kate follow him? Uproot Tommy? He didn't want the answers. He might not like them.

Kate wondered why Jason was being so short with her. He had a lot on his mind, to be sure, but didn't he know she was on his side?

"Jason, please." Kate swung her arms in frustration. "You don't need to go through this alone. Tell me what's wrong."

"We both have heavy schedules today, Kate. Can't we talk about this later?"

Knowing she'd lost this one, Kate nodded, but before leaving Jason's office she looked back. "We *will* talk later. Trust me on this one."

Jason watched Kate's retreating figure. Where had this sudden feistiness come from? She seemed to have gathered an inner strength lately, was more direct, outspoken. And he rather liked it. He'd never been fond of the way she allowed people to walk all over her. But why now, of all times? Right now he needed her to be docile, accepting, and leave him alone to work out his odious predicament.

If he could. The possibility of failing was something he didn't want to think about.

KATE MADE one final note on her comment sheet, then turned off the monitor. She stretched long and hard, her muscles stiff from both fatigue and outrage. Someone had butchered her production! Not only were the outtakes dubbed in, but certain scenes had been enlarged so that the camera seemed to be constantly zooming in on Erika's breasts and legs. A program designed to show women succeeding in the business world had been turned into a parody. No wonder the mayor and city council members had been inflamed. They had no way of knowing those shots weren't in the original tape.

Scrunching her shoulders, Kate stood and checked the time. It was after six, and she knew Harry should be in by now. They still had a lot of work ahead of them if this was to be finished by morning.

She stepped into the production studio, but Harry was nowhere to be seen. The studio was silent save for the omnipresent hum from the equipment. Maybe Harry had gone to the bathroom. Kate sat down, flexing her legs. Lord, she was tired. It was a pervasive ache spreading throughout her body. Relieved at getting a moment's respite, she leaned back in the chair and waited.

Ten minutes passed. No Harry. This respite could be turning into an all-night affair, and she wanted to get finished and go home. She got up and walked to the production room door, grateful she didn't have to pull out her card to get out of this room. It was bad enough using it to get in.

"Harry," she called. The hallway was silent, and Kate was wondering if she shouldn't head for the men's room and rap on the door. Maybe Harry was sick.

Having decided that was exactly what she should do, she started down the hall in the opposite direction from the main lobby. The sound of the lobby door opening stopped her. She turned to see Harry lumbering toward her. He looked surprised to see her.

"Didn't Woody tell you I'd be working with you tonight?" Kate asked.

Harry grinned. "Yeah, he told me. But you were so quiet in your little cube that I guess I forgot you were here." He had a cassette in his hand, and he slowly lowered it, moving it slightly behind his body.

"What's that?" His action had drawn Kate's attention to the cassette, but her question was only idle curiosity. Most likely he'd been in the control room and was bringing back an already aired tape.

"Nothing." Harry lifted the tape back up, and Kate noticed it wasn't labeled. "Woody was looking at this tape today. I guess he forgot to return it. I've been hunting all over for it."

"So that explains your absence." Kate smiled. "I thought you were sick, and I was about to invade the men's room to hunt for you."

"Well, don't pay any ransom—I escaped."

Harry returned her smile, but Kate noticed it didn't quite make it to his eyes. He looked sad tonight, somewhat harried, and his usually unruly hair was more unkempt than usual. "Are you okay?" she asked.

"I'm fine, babe. Just a little tired tonight." He took her elbow and guided her to the studio door, then patted his pockets with his free hand. "Where's that damn card? God, I hate these things."

"Never fear. It's in here somewhere." Kate rummaged through her bag, finally unearthing her own card. "Think I'll have to put this on a string and wear it around my neck."

"Yeah, me, too. Just like dog tags." Usually Harry made comments like that lightly, but tonight Kate thought he sounded cynical. "Nothing like being a suspect in the great cartoon caper."

So that was it. Carlton wasn't the only one who was taking all this security stuff personally.

"No one thinks you did it, Harry." She touched his arm consolingly. "We all have to use these things." She placed her card in the slot, then opened the door, stepping through and allowing Harry to follow.

"Tsk-tsk, Kate, you're violating security. I'm supposed to use my own card, you know." He made a big show of gazing around the studio for his missing card. "There it is."

As he passed the videotape storage rack, he deftly slid the tape in his hand into a vacant slot, then bowed dramatically in front of the console. Picking up his access card, he waved it. "Should I leave and reenter, madam?"

Kate didn't think she had it in her to calm down one more set of prickly feelings, but she tried, anyway. "Stop it, Harry. I told you before that no one thinks you're the culprit."

"Would you tell me if they did?" He looked at her levelly, no longer clowning. "Would you, Kate?"

The question threw her off balance. There had never been a reason for this line of thought before. "Jason doesn't think you did it, either, Harry." Sidestepping the issue was probably the best way to handle things.

"But somebody else does. Right?"

Were they all feeling this way? she wondered, thinking of Carlton's show of defensiveness and Rhonda's testiness. Could this also be what was bothering Jason? What kind of speculation was going on behind closed doors?

"I don't know, Harry." She was too tired now to search for the right words to salve hurt feelings, so she simply lied. "I honestly don't know."

"WHEW! I'm glad that's over." Tommy lifted his head from the book he'd been reading and looked over at Jason. They sat at the kitchen table where the light was good but, good lighting or not, Tommy's eyes were red. They hadn't been like that at the beginning of the session.

"Is it that bad?" Jason knew it had been. The way Tommy struggled over every word had tugged at his heartstrings. "Aren't your new classes helping?"

"It's a little easier. At least the teacher doesn't tap her foot when I'm slow," Tommy answered. The night air was pleasantly warm, and a breeze entered the open window, lightly sifting through the pages of Tommy's book. He closed it with an air of finality. "She gives me this stuff to help. Like little signs showing me which way the *e* is supposed to go. But it doesn't help much."

"What do you see when you look at words, Tommy?" He'd promised Kate he would stay out of this, but he just couldn't overcome his impulse to offer the help Tommy so desperately needed. Why couldn't Kate see that? "Do they turn backward, or do they kind of move around?"

"Move around?" A funny, embarrassed smile crossed Tommy's face. "Nah, that's dumb. Words don't move around. Everyone knows that."

But his face flushed a little, and Jason knew he'd hit a nerve. He'd just driven a small wedge into a massive logjam. Well, he wouldn't press any more tonight. Give the boy a break. But he decided to broach the subject with Kate again even at the risk of an argument. Besides, maybe she was ready to confront her father about getting Tommy evaluated. She certainly had developed some new assertiveness, and he smiled in spite of his heavy worries, thinking about her insistence that they would talk.

"What are you smiling about? Was it what I said?"

Tommy's mouth was set in a hard, proud line, and Jason regretted his lapse. "No, no. I was thinking about something else for a minute." Jason looked at the kitchen clock. It was after eight, nearly Tommy's bedtime, and Kate was a stickler about bedtime. But looking at Tommy's hurt face, Jason wanted to make things better. "Want to play some video games?"

"Yeah!" Tommy jumped up. "How about that new boxing one. I bet I can beat you."

"I bet you can." Jason got up and followed Tommy into his bedroom. Tommy was way ahead and already had the unit turned on when Jason entered the room. The room looked typically boy. Toys littered the floor, and Tommy had obviously made his bed himself, probably at Kate's insistence. Jason sat beside the boy on the rumpled spread and took his control unit. This kid was going to wallop his pants off.

A few hours later Jason heard footsteps in the hall. He glanced at his watch. Lord, it was nearly ten o'clock.

"Yikes, Mom!" Tommy punched the off button on the Nintendo, then shut off the television. "Hurry. If I'm under the covers, she'll think you just came in to check on me."

"Are we in trouble?" Jason laughed. He couldn't believe a nine-year-old was dragging him into cahoots against his mother.

"Big time!" He started tugging at the spread, but Jason sat where he was, creating an insurmountable obstacle. "Hurry, Jason," Tommy urged before turning to look at the door. "Oops, too late. Hi, Mom."

"Hi." Kate stood at the door, a half smile on her face. Jason thought she looked very tired. "I guess I don't have to ask what you're still doing up." She didn't seem to have the energy to look stern. Shadows darkened the little hollows beneath her eyes.

"Did you finish?" Jason asked.

"Yes." Weariness pervaded her tone. "Get into your pajamas, Tommy. You have enough trouble in school already without adding sleepiness to your problems."

Why did she have to remind Tommy like that? At this moment she sounded like Jason's aunt. Then Jason felt a tug of remorse. Kate was obviously exhausted. Being a mother took tremendous patience. He couldn't expect her never to falter.

"I guess I'm not a very reliable baby-sitter," he said.

"Yes, you are," Tommy piped in. Already caught, he obviously wasn't too worried about being punished. "I can beat you at everything."

"I'm not sure that's a criterion." Kate opened the closet door and pulled a pair of pajamas from a hook. "Pajamas," she said firmly. "Teeth brushed. Lights out."

"Okay, okay." Tommy took the bundle from his mother's arms and bolted for the bathroom, leaving Kate and Jason alone.

"I'm sorry," Jason said. "I shouldn't have let him stay up so late. It's just . . . well, we were having a good time."

"One night won't kill him." She began picking up toys from the floor.

"Leave it be, Kate. Tommy can do this tomorrow. Go fix yourself a drink. I'll put him to bed."

An expression of extreme gratitude filled her eyes, and it made Jason happy to do this small thing for her. Somewhere, deep in his mind, it occurred to him that this tiny gesture was something he'd never done for Beth. But then Beth had never worked as hard as Kate, either.

"Thanks." She left the room, and Jason started picking up the toys himself, throwing them into Tommy's already crammed toy box. How could one kid have so much stuff?

A few minutes later he had Tommy settled for the night and headed for the living room where Kate sat on the chintz sofa, feet curled beneath her. "Was it that bad?"

Kate's woeful expression answered his question wordlessly.

"Didn't you have a backup tape?"

"Not an up-to-date one. Harry did the final editing just last night. The council wanted to review it first thing this morning." For a moment Jason thought Kate was going to cry. She blinked rapidly, then continued. "The tape was just going down the street for one day. Who would think anything could happen to it?"

Jason sank into the cushion beside Kate and encircled his arms around her. She sighed and rested her head against his chest. He loved the way she felt in his arms. Even after slaving all day she still smelled sweet and fresh. Her curly hair lightly tickled his nose, and he brushed it back from her face. Suddenly a thought occurred to him. "You must be right, Kate."

She lifted her head and flashed a weak half smile. "About what?"

"The sabotage has to be happening at night while we're off the air. This had to have been done between sign-off and sign-on."

"Yes! That's it!" Kate shot straight up, silhouetted by the lamp behind her. A soft halo of light framed her pink-gold hair, and Jason thought she had never looked more beautiful. "Harry would have put the cassette in the storage rack when he was finished working, so the changes had to be made after he left and before the sign-on shift arrived. Oh, Jason!" She gestured widely with her arms, then wrapped them around Jason's neck, raining happy kisses all over his face.

Wonderful. It felt totally wonderful. He wanted to do this for a lifetime. Hold her like this, soothe her when she was tired, feel her lips against his skin like this. Forever.

He let out a small, desperate sigh. It wasn't possible. At least not yet. Not until his job was secure again.

"Are you ever going to tell me what's wrong?" Kate pulled back and looked at him, concern filling her big blue eyes. He loved those eyes. They reminded him of antique stained glass, all the possible shades of blue reflecting in them. He hated seeing worry dim their luster and wanted to placate her with reassuring words, but he couldn't. Nor could he tell her the truth. This was his problem and he'd solve it alone.

"It's something I can't talk about just yet." Lord, how he wanted to. But how could he tell her he was failing...again?

"Is it something to do with your meeting with George?"

He pulled her back against him. "Yes. And I'll tell you about it as soon as I can." He had a little more hope now. At least they had determined when these incidents were occurring. "Soon, I promise you." He kissed her pert little nose.

"All right. I won't push." She snuggled back into his arms, and it seemed to Jason as if she had always belonged there. "Jason?" She arched her neck and looked into his eyes. "I just want you to know, whatever it is, I support you. You can count on that."

Yes, he knew he could, and it filled him with a glorious power, a certainty that he would overcome this obstacle, succeed and ask Kate to be his wife.

She deserved all the good things in life, and he was going to give them to her. It just had to be.

CHAPTER THIRTEEN

"WHERE'S RHONDA?" Kate asked.

Lisa, the girl from the tape library, sat at Rhonda's desk, answering phones. She looked subdued, perhaps a little sad, and Kate wondered if she'd had a fight with her boyfriend the night before.

"In Woody's office," the girl answered quietly. "They want you to join them."

Kate cringed. What a way to start her day! Exhausted from the previous night, she'd overslept, forcing her to rush Tommy through their morning routine and causing her to be uncustomarily late for work. With little enthusiasm she headed for Woody's closed office.

As the door opened, she was confronted by Rhonda's red-eyed face. Tears had caused little rivulets in her makeup, and smudges of mascara pooled around her eyes. Harry, looking as grim as death, Carlton, looking typically smug, and Jason and Woody all stared also. A somber silence filled the room. A sudden tremor of fear raced through her body. What on earth—?

"Sit down, Kate," Woody directed. Kate picked up a wooden chair to bring it closer to the desk, and one of the crosspieces fell off, clattering to the floor and breaking the ominous hush.

"Damn," Kate whispered under her breath.

Jason scrambled to his feet, picked up the errant board and helped Kate reassemble the chair. That done, Kate sat and glanced around.

"Would someone tell me what's going on?"

Woody cleared his throat. "Carlton, would you fill Kate in?"

"This morning I got here early, probably about seven. I'd just pulled into the parking lot—"

"Could we speed this up a little, Carlton?" Kate snapped, her skin crawling with apprehension. Tears had welled again in Rhonda's eyes, and Harry gazed intently at his hands.

"I saw Harry walk out the side door of the production wing. It made me wonder. What was he doing here so early?" Carlton was clearly enjoying this. He sat ramrod straight in his chair and, in Kate's opinion, was practically preening, appearing determined to drag this out as long as he could. Kate gave him a sharp glance, and he sped up his narrative. "Anyway, I walked over and saw him throw something into the garbage bin." He gestured to a broken cassette on Woody's desk. "That."

Kate leaned over and picked up the cassette, which seemed to have been crushed by a giant hand. Jagged edges of plastic jutted from one end. It looked like the same cassette she'd seen in Harry's hands the night before but, unmarked, all cassettes looked alike.

"So I asked him—" Carlton paused and directed a hard stare at Harry, who continued to examine his hands "—what he was doing. He said the tape was broken and he was throwing it away. When I asked why he was here..." Carlton looked at Kate. "It wasn't his shift, you know." Kate nodded. This was the first thing from Carlton's mouth that made sense. "Well, I didn't like his answers, so I asked him to come inside. We went into the studio, and I looked at some of the frames." A satisfied smile crossed Carlton's face. "Guess what I found?"

Kate didn't have to guess, but Carlton provided the answer, anyway. "Chuck E. Squirrel!" he proclaimed dramatically. "Harry's our culprit."

"Harry was...just...protecting me." Rhonda's soft voice drew attention away from Carlton. The pathetic hitch between her words caused a stab of pain in Kate's chest.

"Don't cover up for him, Rhonda," Carlton said sharply. "It will go bad for you if you do."

"I'm not," Rhonda wailed. A single tear flooded over her lower lid and ran down her already streaked face. "It's the truth!"

"Let Kate hear the other side of this story." Woody raised a hand to stop the bickering and directed his attention to Kate. "I'm sure you have questions."

Shock and disbelief jumbled Kate's mind. Questions? She had dozens. Had Harry really done this? Or Rhonda? No, it wasn't possible. They were her friends. She knew them as well as herself, or thought she did. There had to be an explanation.

"Why was Harry protecting you, Rhonda?" Kate struggled to keep her voice gentle and not let any of the hysteria she was feeling bleed through.

Rhonda was obviously about to weep again. Struggling to compose herself, she took several sharp intakes of breath before speaking. "I found that tape in my desk about two weeks ago while the security locks were being put in."

She stopped for another deep breath, then continued. "It was in my bottom drawer, the one where I keep all the forms, way in the back. I was cleaning it out—" she stopped and a weak smile appeared "—and there it was.

Woody was out and I was curious, so I went into his office and played it on his monitor. It wasn't broken, then,'' she added, looking over at the cracked cassette. ''Harry must have done that to make it look as if there was a reason to throw it away.

''Anyway, when I realized what it was, I took it out of the player and shoved it back into my drawer.'' The long-suppressed tears burst through and became tiny sobs. Kate took Rhonda's hand in hers and didn't say anything, remembering the afternoon when she'd seen Rhonda leaving Woody's office, now knowing the real reason for her friend's tense behavior.

''Oh, God, I was so scared. Everyone knows I hate...I don't like Jason. I knew I'd be blamed.'' Rhonda stared at Kate imploringly as she spoke. ''I don't even know how to do something like that. I just use the animator to make little cartoons for the patrons' newsletters.'' The sobs started once more but subsided quickly.

''Harry must have found the tape and thought I did do it, because the next thing I know, Carlton's marching in here saying he found the perpetrator.''

Rhonda had said the word disdainfully, an exact imitation of Carlton's prissy voice, and Kate saw Carlton stiffen. She felt no sympathy for him. His ego was larger than Arizona. He could withstand a little mocking.

Kate looked over at Harry, who'd abandoned the inspection of his fingernails while Rhonda talked. ''What do you have to say about all this?''

''I found the tape. It was broken. I threw it away.'' Stubbornness had settled over Harry's features, and Kate was certain she wasn't going to get much from him. ''What's wrong with that?''

''Harry, stop it,'' Rhonda cried. ''I won't let you take the blame for this.''

"What were you doing here at seven in the morning, Harry?" As far as Kate was concerned, his presence during his normal sleeping hours was the most damaging piece of evidence.

Harry fidgeted and began examining his fingernails again. Kate was about to repeat her question when he said, "I forgot something."

"What was so important that you gave up sleep to get it back?"

Harry was lying. But why? Rhonda said he was trying to protect her, but now Kate wasn't sure.

"Probably he wanted to talk to me." Rhonda's tears had vanished, and a protective expression rested on her face. "He knows I always come in early."

Kate nodded. Yes, that would explain it. But it was so complicated. How were they going to handle this?

"You've got the picture, Kate?" Woody had been silent during the whole interrogation, and his voice brought all eyes to him.

"I think so."

"Good. We've heard enough for now. Harry, Rhonda, you both go home now." Woody ran weary fingers through his hair. "You're both suspended pending further investigation. The rest of you," he said with a wide sweeping gesture, "stay put. We need to hash this out."

Rhonda wiped her face with both hands and stood. With poignant dignity she straightened her shoulders before turning to leave the room, with Harry right behind her. Before closing the door behind him. Harry glanced back at Woody. "I didn't do this. I swear."

Woody nodded, and they all remained silent until the door clicked closed.

"Oh, God, Harry." Rhonda's voice filtered into the silence. "What are we going to do? I love my job. What will I do without it?"

A lump formed in Kate's throat as she wondered the same, and when Woody spoke, Kate noted he was unusually hoarse. "Two weeks suspension without pay. Isn't that what your new policy says, Kate?"

The words sounded almost accusing, and Kate looked at him in astonishment. But before she could ponder that injustice, Jason's voice interrupted.

"Termination."

"What?" Kate's head snapped in Jason's direction.

"The policy states that termination occurs when deliberate misconduct is involved."

Frigid words, spoken smoothly, unemotionally, destroying people's lives. Kate thought Jason had changed since he had first arrived. She also thought she knew her friends. Now she didn't know what she thought. "Are you suggesting we fire them?" she asked.

"We've found our guilty parties," Jason replied. "I think they did it together."

Kate stared at Jason's eyes as he spoke. Yes. Those shutters were back. Hard. Impenetrable.

"Let's just get this behind us and return to business as usual," he added.

"Amen," Carlton said.

It didn't surprise Kate that he agreed. After all, this little "collar" was Carlton's coup. "But we don't know for certain that they did it," she said. "Both say they didn't. We're talking about their lives. We can't just *terminate* them." Kate hated the word. It sounded too much like an execution.

"You both have points," Woody said. "But I prefer to take the conservative approach here. Kate's right. There is reasonable doubt. We'll suspend them until we can determine what really happened.''

"Doubt? Carlton caught the man with the tape in his hand," Jason responded firmly.

Woody's raised hand was just as firm. "Suspension, Jason. There's no hurry here."

But the dismayed look on Jason's face made Kate wonder if he did have something to hurry about. He seemed so anxious to get this behind them. Why? Did it have something to do with yesterday's meeting with the mayor?

When the group adjourned, Kate followed Jason into his office. He didn't look particularly happy to see her there, but he gestured toward a chair, listlessly inviting her to sit.

"Okay, Kate. You might as well get it out." From the set expression on her face he could tell she didn't see his point of view.

"Why are you so quick to take extreme action, Jason? Rhonda and Harry need their jobs," she said sharply.

Jason rose, walking to the door to close it. He remained standing, drawing on his early business training. The standing opponent always had the advantage.

Lord, why was he suddenly seeing Kate as an opponent? He didn't want this. He wanted her on his side. But that, he knew, was too much to ask. These were long-term friends whose lives were being affected. Her loyalties would naturally be torn.

"This little caper, Kate, has cost Channel Seven thousands of dollars, approaching six figures. It's not a practical joke. The station's funding is stretched to the limit and other people's jobs are at stake. Innocent people, I might add."

"And you think by firing Rhonda and Harry it will end? You heard them. They both said they didn't do it."

"Well, I don't believe them. But I'm sure you do." He knew his tone had been condescending, and the quick flash in Kate's eyes told him she recognized it.

"Don't talk down to me, Jason Brock. I've known these people for years."

The implication was that he hadn't. The reminder annoyed Jason. "So does that make them innocent? I'm sure there were people who knew the Boston Strangler, too."

Kate blew out a frustrated breath, then said in a calm, tightly controlled tone, "No, it doesn't make them innocent, but it does give me some perspective to judge their characters. I know neither would do anything like this."

Jason sat then. "Look, Kate, I don't want to believe this, either. While Rhonda hasn't exactly been a favorite of mine, I like Harry a lot. But I can't let that cloud my judgment. This station is a business, and I can't let a bleeding heart dictate my actions."

"And I do. Is that what you're saying?" His patronizing attitude struck an ugly chord and reminded Kate of her father's offhand way of treating her opinions.

"No. No." He slumped forward, resting his head. God, he just wanted this behind him. Discovering who was responsible for the sabotage would do a lot to secure his job. Then he and Kate could get back on track.

"Yes, that's what you're saying. But if I have to be a coldhearted bastard like you to be a success in business, I'd rather be a failure."

Her remark jabbed at Jason like a rusty knife, pulling, tearing, bringing with it images of Stacey's lifeless body and Beth's twisted, angry face. He lunged upright, enraged and hurt.

"I'm trying to save your neck, you stupid goose. Don't you realize that if your series isn't successful, you won't have a job anymore?" Was his voice rising? He struggled to contain its volume as he saw, without satisfaction, the bewildered, stunned reaction on Kate's face. "You let everyone else run your life. Rhonda. Harry. Your parents. You won't even let Tommy get the testing he needs because you're afraid your father won't like it. The kid's dying in school, and you refuse to see it. If that's the way to run a life, no thank you." His fist pounded the desk and he stared at it in dismay. He was losing control. This had to end. He lifted his hand.

"Kate—"

"You leave Tommy out of this. How can a man who can't even remember his daughter's birthday tell me how to raise my son?"

Turning on her heels, she stormed out, slamming the door behind her. Jason stared at the dirty wooden surface, then sank slowly back into his chair, the sting of Kate's words still burning. He'd been a fool to confide in her, to confide in anyone, and the way she'd used his own confession against him made him recognize that his hope for a future with her was futile.

But he also knew she was right. He hadn't been able to understand his own child, and now it was too late. What made him think he understood Tommy?

Lisa gaped at Kate, openmouthed, as the slamming door heralded her exit from Jason's office.

"Kate?" she asked weakly, as if afraid she'd be the next target.

Taking a calming breath, Kate headed for her own office, ignoring the girl. "Kate," Lisa said again.

"What?" Had she snapped? Her heart was still pounding in outrage. How had Jason dared...*dared* to suggest that she wasn't raising Tommy properly? And what was that comment about her job? After what they had felt for each other, how could he have kept that from her?

She *had* snapped. The look on Lisa's face told her that. "What?" she repeated, more gently this time.

"There's a telephone call for you. Tommy's school."

Tommy's school? Telling Lisa she'd take the call in her office, she walked in, sat down and picked up the phone.

The caller identified herself as the school secretary and quickly told Kate that Tommy hadn't returned from recess.

"I'm sure nothing has happened to him. We searched the grounds, all the bathrooms. He isn't here." The woman spoke rapidly, as if afraid Kate would interrupt her. "Holly said one of his classmates was making fun of him at recess for being in remedial class. He probably just has a case of hurt feelings and ran away."

Kate wanted to screech at the woman, ask her why they didn't keep a closer eye on the children. But she forced herself to say a calm thank-you, then hung up.

Where could he have gone? Home? To her parents' house? No, he wouldn't go there. He would have to explain why he wasn't in school. Quickly she dialed her home, tapping her foot as the phone rang and rang. Even though the logical part of her brain realized that if Tommy were home he probably wouldn't answer, another part pictured him floating facedown in one of the many ponds surrounding Lakeview, while yet another horrified part visualized a sobbing, shrinking Tommy trapped in the car of a threatening stranger.

The phone continued ringing. Finally, the frightening images still hovering before her, she hung up and called her father.

"Dad, Tommy's run away from school," she blurted after the interminable wait while her father's clerk located him.

"Run away?" Sam paused a moment after asking the question, as if thinking. Then he chuckled. "The kid's played hooky, Kate. I bet you'll find him at the Circle K playing those video games of his."

"The convenience market? Why didn't I think of that?" While she might not like it, it was still true that boys sometimes played hooky.

But she couldn't lay the fears completely to rest. "Would you come get me, Dad? Help me look for him?"

"Sure, hon, if it will make you feel better. Give me ten minutes."

He hung up, and Kate leaned back, no longer quite so frantic. She needed her father's calm steadiness to lean on. She didn't have anyone else. With a shock Kate realized that until a few moments ago she would have instinctively turned to Jason. A nearly overwhelming pain followed, slicing through her fear for Tommy. How was she going to survive without him? For, in the hidden corners of her mind, lay certain knowledge that today's confrontation signaled the end of something precious. Fighting a rush of tears, she stood. She needed to tell Woody what was going on. She walked into the lobby and saw that she wouldn't have to hunt for her boss.

He leaned against Jason's doorjamb. "I've asked a technician to repair the tape so we can view the whole thing. The few frames that Carlton saw aren't enough to convince me," Woody was saying through the open doorway.

Kate approached and touched Woody's elbow. He turned, and his sudden change in expression informed Kate he knew something was wrong. Before he could ask, Kate told him. As she spoke, she heard Jason rise and walk toward them.

Why didn't he just stay put? This was none of his business. But he didn't, and soon he stood by Woody's shoulder, paying close attention to her story while she studiously ignored him.

"I'll hunt, too," he said when Kate was finished speaking.

Kate started to blurt out a definite no when she noted the concern filling his eyes. He sincerely cared for Tommy. That she knew. And she wanted his help, his support. She'd come to rely on him so much during these past two months. "It's not necessary," she finally said, carefully keeping her voice soft.

"Don't be silly. I'll take my car. You take yours, and your father can take his. With three of us hunting we'll find Tommy in no time."

"Yes." Woody said. "Both of you go look for the boy. You've got to be worried sick, Kate."

"I am." Kate knew she couldn't continue to refuse Jason's generous offer, not with Woody and Lisa staring at her. And she didn't want to, anyway. She needed him.

She nodded. "Thank you."

The lobby door opened and her father entered. He greeted Jason's suggestion heartily. Within a few moments they had developed a search plan and began heading to their respective cars. As Kate slipped into her driver's seat, Jason said, "Don't worry. We'll find him."

Simple words. Meaningless words. But for some reason Kate felt better as she drove to her first destination.

TOMMY WASN'T at the Circle K. The proprietor hadn't seen him for several days. Kate tried her next spot—their house. Tommy might simply have not answered the phone, knowing Kate was looking for him. But she didn't quite believe that.

She pulled into the driveway. Her street was empty and eerily quiet. A few birds chirped happily in the overhead pines, and the crunch of her feet on the fallen cones seemed as loud as gunshot blasts.

Keys still in hand, she unlocked the door. "Tommy," she called as she stepped inside. "Tommy!" she cried again, this time more loudly.

No answer. She listened intently, hoping to hear video music coming from Tommy's room, but the empty living room remained silent. Late-afternoon sun filtered from the loft, casting shadows from the windowpanes, and the room seemed, then, like a prison cell. Vacant, lonely, un-friendly.

"Tommy, are you here?"

She thought of milk cartons plastered with pictures of lost children. She thought of bogs and marshes and the many ways a small boy could be hurt. Hurrying now, she scrambled up the loft stairs.

No Tommy.

She skittered down, rushing toward the bedrooms, slamming each door as she moved quickly through the hall.

No Tommy.

Back in the living room she searched her mind, seeking one small clue as to where Tommy might have gone. The search seemed fruitless, and she drifted toward the kitchen. Of course, it, too, was empty.

Jason and her father were checking the other places. The creek where Tommy liked to throw rocks. The pond where he often fished. The horse stables where he sometimes helped out. Kate's search was done, and she had nothing left to do but wait. Waiting was worst of all. Despair began seeping into the yawning chasm left by her worry.

Listlessly she opened the door to the back deck and walked outside, her footsteps echoing on the wooden planks. She looked around, scanning the neighborhood for some sign of Tommy. Then she noticed the open door. It was ajar only a few inches, but someone had obviously been in the storage room. Her heart jumped in hope, and she quickly covered the distance to the door, jerking it fully open.

The tackle box was gone. So was Tommy's fishing pole. A folding stool, usually resting just inside the door, was also gone.

Kate smiled.

CHAPTER FOURTEEN

JASON FOUND him sitting on a canvas stool, line in the water, waiting for the big one. Never, Jason thought, in his entire life had he seen such a welcome sight.

"Anything biting?" He kept his tone deliberately casual.

Tommy jumped, nearly falling off his stool, then struggled to regain his dignity as he turned to look at Jason.

"Nah." He gave his attention back to the water.

Jason walked over and hunched down beside the boy. "Too bad I didn't bring a pole. Maybe I could help you out."

"You don't fish too good, anyway." The reply, short, crisp and a little rude, alerted Jason to how badly Tommy was hurting.

"Your mom is real worried."

"She is?" Tommy glanced over at this. Obviously it hadn't been his intent to scare his mother.

"You didn't think she would be?"

"Guess not." Tommy's lower lip protruded a bit, sullenness replacing his studied indifference. "Didn't think about it at all."

"Do you want to talk about it?"

"No." The child fiddled with his reel, making a big production of adjusting the line. After moving it a few inches, he looked down, and Jason noticed he was biting his lip. "He called me a retard!"

So that was it, Jason thought, cringing just a little at Tommy's admission, so reminiscent of his own childhood. "Who?"

"Jimmy Schmidt. He's a retard himself. Big, dumb old stupid dweeb!" The tears came then, streaming out of Tommy's eyes, and he rubbed them furiously as if attempting to push them back. "I'm not going to cry. I'm not," he wailed between sobs.

"Of course not." Jason wanted to pull him into his arms, comfort him, then go wallop the tar out of Jimmy Schmidt and make sure the boy never hurt Tommy again. Since the day the kids had encircled him on the playground, Jason had faced his own share of Jimmy Schmidts. But no one had offered to fight for him, so he'd become quite handy with his fists.

Well, Tommy had someone who would fight. Jason gave in to his urge, lifting Tommy off his wobbly stool and encasing him in a protective embrace.

The boy sobbed piteously against his shoulder, no longer even pretending he wasn't crying. The sound mingled with the slap of water on the pond's bank and the chirrups of crickets. Jason thought he'd never heard such a mournful melody. "You're not a retard, Tommy. You're not," he intoned fiercely over and over, his own eyes misting as he spoke.

Finally Tommy's heaving chest grew still, but he remained huddled against Jason's chest. "What's wrong with me, Jason? Why can't I read? Micky Laughton's little sister is only in second grade and she reads better than me."

Jason lifted Tommy's chin and tried to wipe the tear from his face. He was certain he could help if only the boy would answer his questions honestly. "If I ask you something, Tommy, will you tell me the truth?"

The bravado was gone, and Tommy shuddered in his arms. "I'll try."

"First, there's something you probably don't know about me. When I read, I wear a patch over one eye."

"A patch?" Tommy brightened a little bit. "Is it black? Like a pirate?"

"Yes. But I don't wear it to look like a pirate. I wear it so that letters don't move all over the page."

A tiny flash in Tommy's eyes told Jason that he was getting the point. "So what did you want to ask me, Jason?" The tone, though slightly wary, was promising.

"Do letters move around when you read?" No sense in delaying this any longer, Jason thought. Tommy was bright. He already knew where this was leading. "They move for me."

Tommy felt a weight lifting from his shoulders. So this happened to someone else. Not just anyone. To Jason. And Jason was cool, almost as cool as Uncle Cory. If this could happen to a guy like that, well . . . maybe he wasn't stupid, after all.

But Jason could read. When they worked together, Tommy could tell he could read. "You never wear that patch when you help with my homework."

"I had lots of therapy. Now I only need the patch when I read for a long time." Tommy knew he'd practically accused Jason of lying, but Jason didn't seem to notice. If Tommy had ever said something like that to his grandpa, he would have gotten real mad.

"So will you answer my question?" Jason asked. "Do the letters move for you?"

Tommy nodded, looking down, afraid Jason would laugh just like the kids did that day on the playground.

But he didn't, and Tommy felt suddenly relieved. He didn't have to keep this a secret anymore. Maybe he could even tell his mom. Or his teacher. "They crawl around like ants."

Jason did laugh then, a hearty, booming laugh that Tommy could feel bouncing against his shoulder. He shrank away, sorry he'd confessed until Jason said, "That's exactly what I said when I was a kid."

Tommy hugged Jason real hard, happy at finding someone he could talk to. Then he pulled away, embarrassed. But Jason hugged him back tightly. It felt safe and warm in that hug, and Tommy hoped Jason would stay around forever.

"Let's go talk to your mom." Jason released him and stood up, pulling Tommy to his feet along with him. "You need to see a psychologist."

"No!" Tommy cringed at the word. "Grandpa'll have fits. And Mom won't like it, either. Besides, I don't need anyone to shrink my head. You can help me. I can wear a patch."

Jason cursed himself for his impulsiveness. The boy wasn't ready for this. Sam Springer's outspoken disapproval when Tommy's uncle had sought counseling had conditioned Tommy against the mental health profession. But maybe Cory was the answer. "Your Uncle Cory has seen a shrink, Tommy. Do you think anything is wrong with him?"

"Well, no-o-o...." The answer was thoughtful, considering.

"I think you have something called dyslexia, Tommy. You need to have some tests to make sure. Not have your head shrunk." Jason almost smiled then, not believing he was using these words. But he needed to talk to Tommy on his level, and that was what the boy had been hearing most of his life. "Will you think about it?"

"Dyslexia?" Tommy repeated, stumbling a little over the word.

Jason nodded and Tommy stared at him. The sun was beginning to set, a glorious pink-and-lavender skyscape, and it highlighted the smooth contours of the boy's face. "Will you agree to have the testing, Tommy?"

"We better get home so Mom won't worry anymore." Tommy turned to pick up his fishing equipment. He handed the tackle box to Jason, tucked the pole under one arm, then picked up the stool with the same hand.

Tommy slipped his other hand into Jason's. As he tightened his own fingers around the little hand, Jason felt the warm, slightly scratchy, callused texture of it.

"Okay, I'll think about it," Tommy said as, together, they walked to Jason's car.

Tommy didn't talk on the drive home, just sat and stared out the window. Jason didn't push him. He'd given the boy a lot to think about.

Hell, he had a lot to think about. Tommy shouldn't have to carry this burden. This wasn't the nineteenth century, for God's sake. Didn't Kate realize how Tommy's study problems could ruin his life? The kid shouldn't have to grapple with questions about whether to see a psychologist. He was only nine years old! That decision should have been made for him without hesitation.

His anger at Kate erupted again, and he felt the muscles of his jaw tighten. He'd done his best not to interfere, to stay out of Kate's way where Tommy was concerned. But this was a special boy. Too special to allow his life to go to waste like this.

A car honked. He ignored it. But the noise continued and, annoyed, he looked around. Kate was following him, waving out her window and leaning on her horn. Sam Springer sat in the passenger seat, also waving.

She was worried—he knew that—but he wanted to whisk Tommy away and get him the help he needed instead of returning him to his mother's arms. Suddenly he understood why ex-spouses kidnapped their children. With a pang he wondered why he'd never felt this fierce possessiveness for his own daughter until the night she'd died in his arms. A nearly unbearable stab of pain provided the answer.

It hurt too much.

When he pulled over, he was still prepared to do battle. Then he looked at Tommy solemnly watching his mother drive in behind them and realized that after what he'd gone through today, Tommy didn't need to witness a scene. Jason would talk to Kate later, after Tommy was in bed, when they could speak privately.

Kate leapt from her car and ran toward them. Sam followed behind at a more sedate pace.

"Tommy!" Jason could see tears streaming down her face as she yanked open the car door and pulled Tommy into her arms. "Oh, my God, I've been so scared. Oh, Tommy, Tommy, are you all right?"

She ran her hands over his hair, his face and his square little shoulders, checking every inch of him. Her father stood behind her and winked at Jason as if to say, "See how these women are." The act annoyed Jason, and he didn't wink back. Of course Kate was frantic. What mother who loved her child wouldn't be? His own mother had been nearly hysterical that time he'd wandered off at the state fair. A faint twinge of wistful envy pricked him as he realized how early that had ended.

Now satisfied that Tommy was unharmed, Kate grasped his arms and moved him away from her. "Don't you ever do that again. Do you hear me, Tommy? Do you?'' Hysteria edged her voice, and she frowned at Tommy in anger, but it mingled with relief, and she didn't seem able to maintain it. She jerked him back into her arms. ''Oh, thank God you're not hurt.''

''I'm sorry, Mom.'' The words were muffled against Kate's shoulder, and Tommy's arms wound around her neck. ''I'm really, really, really sorry.''

''He didn't mean to scare you, Kate.'' Jason, having gotten out of the car to join Sam at the roadside, could see fresh tears filling Tommy's eyes. The urge to protect him arose anew.

Kate released Tommy and turned to look at him, heart full of gratitude. ''Thank you, Jason, for finding Tommy.'' She looked back at her son. ''Where were you, kiddo?'' But she could no longer force any sternness into her voice.

A ghost of a grin crossed Tommy's face. ''Fishing.''

''I knew that.'' Kate's hands kept shooting out, lightly touching Tommy, trying to reassure herself that he was truly there. ''I knew that,'' she repeated. ''You should have closed the storage room door. It was a dead giveaway.''

''Let's get this truant boy home, Kate,'' Sam interrupted.

Kate stood up, taking Tommy's hand in hers. ''Okay, Dad.'' She noticed that her father's eyes seemed a little too shiny. Maybe he'd been more worried than he let on.

Jason was still waiting, wearing a polite, shielded expression, shutting her out again. But even as the knowledge stung her, gratitude flooded back. The last tinges of the sunset stained the sky. Soon it would be dark. If Jason hadn't been here to help, Lord only knows how long Tommy would have stayed at the pond.

"I can't tell you how grateful I am, Jason. Words just—"

He raised his hand. "I was happy to do it, Kate. Tommy's a great kid." The tension was there, hanging in the air, palpable, and Kate wished she could take back her ugly words, return to a time when he would have been encircling them both in his arms, taking them home himself in place of her father.

"Good night, then." Not knowing what else to say, she turned to follow her father back to the car, holding Tommy by the hand.

Usually she buckled Tommy into the back seat. This time she pulled him into her lap after asking her father to drive. Tommy didn't voice the complaint she expected; he just settled against her docilely, clearly glad to be home. Then he stiffened. "My fishing stuff! It's still in Jason's car."

Jason was already driving away, his car now several hundred feet down the road. "We'll get it tomorrow," Kate said. His fishing stuff could wait. He and she had plenty to talk about when they got home.

The answer apparently satisfied Tommy. He leaned back, and she held him loosely as Sam steered the car off the shoulder.

"Do you know how to deal with this, Kate?" Her father glanced at her from the corner of his eye as he carefully aimed the car forward. He was a strong believer in never taking his attention from the road. "Maybe this needs a man's touch."

Something tightened inside Kate. Her mother always thought she could do anything. Her father, obviously, thought the complete opposite. "I can handle this, Dad," she responded evenly. His attitude shouldn't even bother her anymore. She should be used to it. But she wasn't.

"Just thought I'd offer."

"Thanks. But we'll be okay." She patted his arm. He meant well and tried very hard. She was just edgy. This had, after all, been one of the worst days of her life.

Sam didn't say anything and just continued driving. Kate drifted off into a peaceful netherworld, wanting, for a few moments, to forget the day. Tommy was also quiet. Kate imagined he was afraid to say much, knowing he was in serious trouble.

Her daydream had something to do with Jason helping her tuck Tommy in, barbecuing on the deck and kissing her with wild abandon. Then Tommy's voice interrupted.

"What?" Kate wasn't sure she'd heard correctly.

"Jason says I might have dyslexia."

Kate saw her father's head snap in their direction, his expression pure astonishment. She caught his eyes, and suddenly she was very, very angry. Jason had once again barged right in and imposed on her life.

JASON TIGHTENED his arm over the camp stool and walked to Kate's door. The stool shifted uncomfortably against his armpit and threatened to tumble from his grip at any minute. The trek up the gravel path reminded him of another night—the first time he'd dined at Kate's, when he carried a box of chocolates and a bottle of wine instead of a stool, tackle box and fishing pole.

He had realized that Tommy had forgotten his gear even before getting back into his car. But it presented the perfect excuse to talk to Kate without Tommy around, so he hadn't attempted to return it.

Undoubtedly Kate had put Tommy to bed by now. He was probably sad again after Kate's inevitable grilling about why he'd run away.

Or maybe not. Her joy at seeing him unharmed may have overridden her anger at his truancy. But Jason doubted it. Sometimes she was just too hard on that boy.

He set down the fishing equipment and rapped on the door. He hoped to catch her off guard so that she wouldn't coolly dismiss his advice. Lord, her thank-you had been so formal, so polite, as if he was some distant acquaintance.

What had he expected? A grateful embrace? A...a what? He didn't know what he'd expected. The door opened.

"Jason."

For a moment an awkward silence hung between them. She had on baggy prison-gray sweats, and her hair was tousled. What little makeup she wore had long vanished under the strain of the day. She looked wonderful! He wanted to wrap his arms around her fleece-covered body and just drink her in.

"I brought Tommy's fishing gear. He left it in my car."

"So he told me." Her voice carried extreme reserve.

Another pause, long, heavy. Jason shifted his weight, looking down for a moment, waiting for her to ask him inside.

She didn't.

"May I come in, or am I persona non grata?"

"Yes. That might be best." Her enigmatic reply took Jason off guard. What did she mean by that? But he didn't ask; he simply bent to pick up Tommy's gear. She bent also, reaching for the stool, and their hands met. She pulled back as if shot, taking the canvas stool with her and brushing Jason's hand aside.

What had happened? She hadn't been like this when he returned Tommy. Hesitant, yes, even distant, but this chilly reception went way beyond hesitation or distance.

"You can leave the stuff there. I'll put it away later."
Kate gestured to a spot beside the coat closet. Normally
Jason would have argued, insisted on placing the things
in the storage room. But this time he was too taken aback
by Kate's behavior to argue with her about something so
small.

"Sit down, Jason. We need to talk." It was more like
an order, and it made him tense up, but he complied, reminding himself he was here for Tommy's good. Getting
Kate mad would achieve nothing.

"Yes, we do," he agreed, sitting obediently where Kate
had indicated, although his rebellious streak bridled.
"Tommy and I had a long talk today."

"I know."

"You do? Good. Then we can get right to the point."
He had expected to ease into the subject. This made things
easier.

"Please, I've asked you to stay out of this problem
Tommy's having." She spoke softly, too softly, as if she
was making an effort to stay calm, and she pulled away
from his touch. "I'd like to remind you that he isn't your
child."

Her words stung, but he couldn't argue with them, although they didn't make his opinion any less valid. "Kate,
I'm not trying to undermine your position here, but you
can't keep ig—" He changed his approach. This wasn't
going to work. "Have you any idea what happens to kids
who fail in school?"

"You act as if I'm totally blind here, Jason, and I don't
appreciate it. Tommy and I also had a long talk. He told
me what you said about dyslexia and the psychologist."

"You have to get him tested, Kate." Jason could see her
stubbornness rising. The velvet glove wasn't going to

work. "You have no personal experience with this and you refuse to listen to someone who does."

"Tommy's life isn't a replay of yours. He has a mother and grandparents who love him, support him. We won't let this ruin his life." Her words came out rapidly, laced with anger.

"You will if you don't drop that archaic attitude. Psychologists aren't monsters who play with people's heads." Jason felt his control slipping. His voice rose, and although he wanted to subdue it, another part didn't mind if the world heard him roar. "If you cared about Tommy at all, you'd see that. You wouldn't neglect this the way you do."

Kate's hand flew to her face. "If I *cared?* What the hell do you mean by that, Jason Brock? Night after night I've worked with him. Neglect?" She stood abruptly. "Get out of here, Jason." She marched to the door and opened it, speaking in a menacing hiss. "Tommy isn't some alter ego that you can fix up so that he doesn't make the same mistakes you did, and he isn't a replacement for your daughter. He's my son, Jason, and don't you forget it. We don't need you in our lives. Tommy and I were doing just fine before you came along."

He jumped from the couch. "Just fine? You have a kid who can't read, a job that's about to end and a father who dictates your every move. That doesn't sound peachy-dandy to me."

His temples throbbed, his scar ached, and this impossible woman was throwing him out, refusing to listen to something very important to her. And to Tommy.

"You need me, Kate Gregory. You need me bad." He stood beside her now, looking down, and he grasped her chin. Barefoot the way she was, she suddenly seemed very tiny. How could this small creature unsettle him like this? "So does Tommy."

"Out!" She jerked her chin from his hand and spoke through clenched teeth. Then, catching him unprepared, she shoved him so hard that he stumbled through the door. It slammed lustily behind him.

For a long while Jason just stood here, staring at the closed door. Clenching and unclenching his fists, he squelched his urge to pound on that slab of wood until Kate let him back in.

After a while, he realized his breath was coming in painful heaves, his anger monumental, way beyond reason. He hadn't felt this kind of rage since—

Since he'd seen Beth kissing another man in Central Park. Since he'd confronted her about it and distracted her so that she didn't see the weaving car in time.

Lord, the causes weren't even of the same magnitude. His shoulders slumped as shame flooded through him. Why had he bulldozed Kate that way? He'd completely ignored her feelings as he'd blurted out his viewpoint. As he walked to his car, a niggling thought occurred. Wasn't this his usual mode of operation—bulldozing people?

Sliding behind the wheel of his car, he dismissed the idea. The object was to solve Tommy's problem. Jason knew, without doubt, that if there was anything he did well, it was solving problems. His mind flew to possible alternatives. Maybe he could talk to Tommy's teacher. He dropped that idea. The school probably wouldn't take kindly to interference from an outsider.

Perhaps Woody might talk some sense into Kate. No, Woody made it a tight policy to keep out of people's personal lives.

Then the solution hit him. Sam Springer. Jason was certain Kate would have already had Tommy tested if not for her father. All he had to do was persuade Sam to see things differently. The rest would take care of itself.

Jason started the car. He looked at Kate's front door. Had the curtain on the living room window moved? He was sure it had, and he smiled. Yes, Kate Gregory did need him. Very much. And he was going to prove that to her.

The brief drive was quick, and as Jason pulled up in front of the Springers' house, he hesitated for a minute. Was he about to go too far? After all, as Kate had so often reminded him, Tommy wasn't his son. Also, considering the way he had lost his temper with Kate, there was the possibility that he would do the same with Sam. Perhaps he should save this for another time.

No. Something needed to be done. Soon. And Jason wasn't going to let this just drift along, ignored. He got out of the car and walked to the door.

Sam opened it, greeting him with a surprised smile. "Wasn't expecting *you*," he boomed. "But it's a pleasant surprise. Come in, come in," Sam swung the door wide. "Have you heard the one about the guy who applied for a job as a bellringer?" Sam asked as Jason moved inside. Jason hadn't, but to avoid getting into a string of jokes, he said he had.

"Well, how about a beer then? I got some strong German brew in the fridge."

Jason accepted, and Sam led him into the kitchen, moving energetically, then making a big production out of opening the bottles. He seemed on edge, Jason thought, almost as if he'd anticipated this visit.

He handed Jason the bottle, not offering a glass, and led him to the table. As Jason sat down, he asked where Rita was.

"Bingo," Sam replied. "That fool woman plays bingo three nights a week. She wins sometimes, though, so I guess it ain't all bad."

"I guess not," Jason replied, then looked around the kitchen for a moment, trying to focus his thoughts. The room was filled with ducks. They hung on the wall, sat on top of the cupboards and marched along a border beneath the ceiling. "She likes ducks," he commented.

"Yeah." Sam took a deep swallow from his bottle. "I'm getting so I never want to see another one. But I love her, anyway."

Jason smiled politely, taking a drink from his own bottle. The sting of the hops was refreshing and had a calming effect on his nerves. He was about to broach the subject of his visit when Sam asked, "You think Kate has the boy in tow by now?"

Jason paused. The opportunity was now. "Actually," he said, "no, I don't think so."

"Yeah?" There was no hostility in Sam's tone, just a hint of mild curiosity and . . . something else. Was it apprehension?

"Sam, this isn't just a friendly visit," Jason began.

"Somehow I didn't think so." A rueful smile crossed Sam's face.

"I'm concerned Tommy has a serious learning disability that's keeping him from reading. Similar to one that I have. Maybe even the same."

"You have a learning disability?" Sam whistled incredulously. "An educated guy like you. Who would've thought it?"

"Yes. It's called dyslexia, and it can ruin a kid's life." Jason almost sighed in relief. Sam appeared receptive, so he launched into a recap of his conversation with Tommy and a brief history of his own experience with dyslexia.

Sam listened without interruption, but Jason noticed that he frowned frequently. On several occasions he appeared about to speak and then stopped. Taking advantage of the man's attention, Jason covered his ground quickly before concluding, "So Kate desperately needs to get Tommy evaluated so that therapy can start right away."

Sam nodded, then took another swallow of beer. He looked tired now and very serious. His shoulders sagged, and he seemed to be supporting himself with the table. Very odd, Jason thought. Something was definitely going on beneath the surface. But what?

Jason waited, hoping for an answer.

Instead, Sam rose. "Thanks, Jason, for letting me know." He tossed his beer bottle into a trash can, then opened the refrigerator and got another. "Think I need this," he mumbled. "You want another?"

"Thanks, no. It's late and I think I'll be going." Jason's nervous energy had dissipated and fatigue was overcoming him. He'd come here for a purpose, and it didn't look as if he'd accomplished it. He needed to press Sam further; he just didn't know what to say.

He was trying to find new words as Sam accompanied him to the door. The man shuffled along, looking tired, old. Jason felt a twinge of sympathy. Jason knew he was asking for a major shift in attitudes developed over a lifetime. Surely that wasn't easy. He thanked Sam for the beer and stepped outside.

"No trouble," Sam responded, and still Jason couldn't find the words. Resigned to failure, he turned. It was no use.

"Jason." There was a raspy quality to Sam's voice, and Jason looked back into an immensely sad face. "I'll talk to the girl."

"Good." Jason smiled broadly, then headed for his car, surprised to notice a sudden spring in his walk. Somehow, though, he didn't think Sam was feeling the same way. Jason's heaviness returned. He had wanted to salvage a life and maybe he'd succeeded, but he had a sinking feeling that in the process he'd wrenched apart someone else's.

CHAPTER FIFTEEN

THE KNOCK INTERRUPTED Kate's brooding. For the past hour she had stared, unseeing, at the television set, replaying the argument with Jason in her head. As she padded to the door, she thought it was probably him, brimming with apologies, wanting to make amends.

Who was she kidding?

Never, since she'd known him, had Jason ever apologized about anything. Why would he start now? Most likely he wanted to shove that damnable testing down her throat again. And he could be right. She couldn't deny he had an insight into this problem that she lacked. Determined to be reasonable, Kate opened the door.

"Daddy!" She was almost shocked out of her sweatpants. Her father never visited this late at night. "What brings you out at this hour?" She forced a smile. Her response hadn't been very polite. "Come in," she said warmly, trying to make up for her lapse. "Would you like a soft drink? Anything? Sorry, I don't have any beer."

Why on earth was she babbling to her own father?

Because she'd been expecting, even hoping, that Jason had returned, that was why. She shook off her pang of loss and stepped back to let her father inside.

"'The way you're acting reminds me," Sam said as he entered the room, "of the one about the guy who went to his friend's house to borrow money. He knocked— Oh, forget it." Sam waved his hand at his self-inflicted interruption, looking suddenly tired. Kate was about to comment on his obvious fatigue, but he spoke first. "I want you to get Tommy tested."

Kate flopped onto the couch, too stunned to respond. Of all the words she'd ever expected to come from her father's mouth, these weren't them.

"Rita and I talked this over." Sam sat down in the overstuffed chair opposite her and leaned forward. "I dragged her out of that cursed bingo game. She thinks I should tell you."

Puzzled, Kate frowned. "Tell me what?"

"There ain't any better way to say it, so I guess I'll just have to say it plain." He was always jovial, her dad. Always. Except when something offended his basic values or threatened his security. From the look of him, perched on the edge of his chair, a crimson blush creeping up his neck, this was one of those times. Kate waited, almost frightened.

"I can't read," Sam blurted out in a rush. "Could be I have dyslexia."

She must be getting numb or perhaps a little spacey from the strain of the day. "Did you say you can't read?" Sam cleared his throat, and as he did, his statement finally sank into Kate's foggy brain. "That's silly," she said nervously. "You ran a successful business. You still do. How could you do that if you can't read?" She laughed as though the thought were ridiculous, her heart still denying what her mind was beginning to accept. "I see you all the time with the newspaper."

"I can read headlines if I try real hard. But it's just for show, hon, just for show. Later I catch the news on TV so I can keep it up."

"You never told me . . . or Cory . . ." It wasn't a question, and she spoke the words in a whisper, almost to herself. How could she have lived with him all these years and not known?

"Cory found out and we fought about it. He wanted me to get tutoring." Sam laughed bitterly. "Can you figure me going back to school at my age?"

"Now you and Cory don't even speak to each other."

"He threatened to tell you. Said if I didn't get help, he wasn't keeping this to himself. I couldn't have that, hon. You always looked up to me, thought I was perfect." There was a hitch in his voice, and Kate thought it sounded almost like a sob.

She felt pity. But she also felt anger, a slow, simmering anger over the way he had duped her. Despite the threat, Cory hadn't told her, for reasons only he could explain. Instead, he had left town in bitter anger, determined to wipe his family out of his life forever—even her and Tommy. And all because of her father's unreasonable pride, his stupid vanity.

"Mom knew?"

"Yeah. She helped me all the way. Long ago we agreed never to tell." He stared at the empty fireplace as if remembering. "Long ago."

"Why are you telling me now, Daddy?" Now she understood the terrified look in her father's eyes when Tommy mentioned dyslexia on the way home. She'd expected his usual tirade, but instead he'd been strangely quiet, dropping them off and leaving quickly without saying a word about it.

"Ever since you told us about Tommy's schooling problems, your mother's been nagging me to tell you. I meant to, but I've been putting it off. Then Jason came to see me tonight," Sam continued, still looking into the fireplace as though unable to meet Kate's eyes. "He told me about his own problem and what Tommy said at the pond today.''

Kate's head moved up and down as her father spoke. She had begun to suspect as much. Her anger increased, now directed at Jason as much as her father. He'd gone over there and started on her father. She could tell by his beaten look that he'd been badgered as only Jason knew how.

Sam's eyes glimmered in the lamplight. Kate recognized her father's anguish and how painful this was for him, but her outrage at Jason became tangled with her sense of betrayal, and her anger started boiling. ''Do you realize what you've done? Knowing that Tommy is having these problems, how could you? Did you know that dyslexia is often inherited?''

Sam nodded. ''I saw it on TV once.''

''If only I'd known. God, I would have had Tommy evaluated the first time the school suggested it. How could you do this, Daddy?'' She pointed an accusing finger and spoke in a rising voice. Sam cringed and shrank back in his chair.

''I was afraid you'd blame me,'' he mumbled.

His reaction punctured Kate's anger. He wasn't supposed to do that. He should have straightened his shoulders, garnered his sternest expression and put her back in her place, the way he had always done. He was Daddy, strong, in command of every situation. Despite his character flaws, which she knew so well—his silly jokes, his stubborn refusal to change with the times—she'd always seen him as invincible.

He'd been right. She had always looked up to him, always asked him to confirm her decisions. This was as much her fault as his. The realization shamed her, and she now accepted the truth of Jason's accusations.

Emotional pain twisted her gut, her heart. Tears, the ones she'd suppressed all day, filled her eyes, burning, ready to burst out.

She couldn't fight them anymore, and a racking sob erupted from her throat. "Oh, Daddy, how awful for you. How awful for all of us."

Quickly Sam slipped out of the chair and into the spot beside Kate, pulling her into his arms. This, Kate knew, was a role he was comfortable with, allowing his broad shoulders to soak up her tears, then kissing them away and telling her everything would be all right. She was comfortable with it, too, but even as she wept she knew this was the last time she would play her part.

Sam murmured all the reassuring little homilies that Kate expected, stroking her hair as if she were still a child and, soon, her sobs subsided.

"Thanks, Daddy," She broke away from his embrace and looked at him. Rivulets ran down both his cheeks. She touched one. "You were crying, too," she said in wonder.

"Don't tell." His attempt to smile failed. "I've been wrong. Real wrong. I tried to do what I thought was best. Guess I don't always know what that is." He brought her against his barrel chest, and Kate cuddled again. "It's not often I say I'm sorry," he continued, "so I'm not too good at it. But please believe me, Kate, I am. And, thank God, it isn't too late to help Tommy."

"No, it isn't," she replied. Tonight was going to change forever the way she saw him. Sam Springer, her father, wasn't infallible. He was just a man with many strengths and many faults, and she loved him, anyway. "So, tell me, Daddy, how did you fool everyone all this time?" Now that her outrage and despair had eased, her earlier curiosity returned.

They talked for several hours as Sam explained how Rita had covered for him in the early years of his business, how he'd learned to get others covertly to read for him, then later hired people to take care of reading related tasks. Some of his stories were very funny, and laughter interspersed their talk. It occurred to Kate that her father had to be extremely intelligent to have successfully run a business, raised a family and covered up this embarrassing disability. Her admiration for him, true admiration based on seeing the real person, increased.

She was also relieved to know that Tommy could be helped and wouldn't be forced to resort to her father's tricks. She thought about Jason, who had benefited from therapy just as Tommy would. Tenderness replaced her earlier anger. Her father wasn't the only one who let pride stand in his way. So did she. She owed Jason an apology—not just to appease, the way she usually did—but a heartfelt one.

"So, Daddy, are you going to get tutoring now that your dark secret is out?" They stood by the door, both having been startled to realize the late hour, and Sam was leaving.

He smiled at her question. "Could be. But you know what they say about old dogs and new tricks."

"You're not old, Daddy. Age is all in the mind."

"Maybe." He reached out and brushed a strand of her hair back in place. "Thanks for the vote of confidence. Tell you what, I will do one thing."

"Which is?"

"Call Cory and mend some fences. First thing in the morning. I've held a grudge against that boy too long."

Kate kissed his cheek. "I think that's a great idea."

After saying good-night, Kate turned off the lights and headed for bed. Her body was heavy from fatigue, but her mind felt very, very light. Tomorrow she would mend some fences of her own.

JASON STARED at himself in the mirror as he shaved and didn't like what he saw. The face staring back looked hard, single-minded and mean. He had gone too far last night. Nothing gave him the right to interfere in Kate's life the way he had. Not even Tommy. She was a good mother. Eventually she would do the correct thing.

But he couldn't let events just run their course. No, he had to try to shove this down Kate's throat, even use her own father against her. A litany of accusations often chanted by Beth paraded through his mind. *Always think you know what's best. Never give anyone else credit for having any sense. Steamrolling things through.* Until now he'd dismissed these complaints as the product of short-sightedness and lack of goals.

What if Beth had been right? He tried to tell himself no, that Tommy's welfare depended on his actions, that he did know what was best and just wanted to get the help Tommy needed.

It wasn't working. Fleeting thoughts of the many decisions he'd made over Beth's protestations intermingled with memories of Stacey's birthday parties and the delight on her face that single time he had attended—late, but there. She'd thrown herself into his arms with a squeal, and he'd been pleased at the time. But now the memory brought a glimmer of guilt, a guilt he tried to shove away. He'd done his best, still did, but he didn't like what he saw when he looked in the mirror any better despite his reassurances.

Disgusted, he gave his face a final swipe, yelping when he nicked his jaw.

A while later, after pulling into his parking place at the station, he peeled the dab of toilet paper from the cut, satisfied it wasn't bleeding anymore. He wondered if the nick showed, then decided he didn't care. He was wearing his pin-striped suit today, something he rarely did anymore, and wondered why he had made that choice. His tie still hung loosely around his neck, but he decided to leave it unknotted. The day was going to be warm, and he would only end up taking it off, anyway. Although he probably looked like some down-and-out gumshoe, he didn't care.

Almost dragging himself from the car, he walked up the steps of the trailer and stepped inside to a flurry of activity. People rushed back and forth between the two wings of the building, and Woody stood at Rhonda's desk frantically punching numbers into the phone. Through Woody's open door Jason could see George Creighton pacing the floor of the small office.

"Damn, Jason, I've been trying to reach you." Woody slammed down the phone. "I've been trying to get Kate, too, and Carlton's not home, either. Where have you been?"

"I stopped for breakfast." He looked around, confused. "What's going on?"

"Our uninvited guest appeared again this morning. At sign-on." Woody ran his hand across his face, then added in a confidential tone, "George is here."

"I saw him," Jason replied, his voice sounding very far away. Something began swirling in his mind, a whirlpool, dragging him down. This couldn't be happening. Harry and Rhonda had been caught. The squirrel episodes should have stopped. "But Harry and Rhonda..." His voice trailed off as the obvious struck him.

"They didn't do it," Woody said flatly, echoing Jason's internal conclusion. "Now George wants to see us."

You were born to fail! His Aunt Phyllis's words screamed in his head, and he felt himself shrinking beneath her dark shadow. Ten years old, scared, alone, lost. He was lost.

"George wants to see us," Woody repeated.

Jason nodded and followed him into the office.

KATE STILL FELT fuzzy from lack of sleep as she drove from Tommy's school to the station. She was over an hour late and had totally forgotten to call to let anyone know. She'd been too intent on seeing to Tommy. First thing that morning she had driven him to school, then gone to the principal's office to request testing as soon as possible. The entire staff had smiled throughout her visit, telling her that Tommy already had an appointment, scheduled by Holly Shortridge, and the psychologist would be there the following day.

Now Kate smiled, too. Today she would set her life back on track. She didn't doubt that Jason would welcome her apology, and she pictured the look on his face when she did so—pleasure mixed with relief. His eyes would soften, and he'd give her that tender look she loved. The vision filled her with intense happiness, making her recall Tommy's question just a few weeks earlier. Yes, she thought, she would marry Jason Brock, even if she had to ask him herself.

As her tires hit the gravel driveway of the parking lot, she promised herself she might do exactly that, and when she opened the door to the station, she was still wearing a smile. The smile vanished in astonishment the minute she stepped inside.

Rhonda sat at the reception desk, busily working.

"Good morning, Kate," she said pleasantly.

"What...? I mean..." Kate stammered.

"You mean, what am I doing here?" Rhonda arched her eyebrow in faint challenge. "You aren't disappointed to see me, are you?"

"No! I'm relieved. It's just...how? What happened?"

"Woody's been trying to reach you. I guess he wasn't successful. Chuck E. Squirrel appeared first thing this morning. Since Harry and I were on suspension, it became obvious we were telling the truth. Harry will be back tonight." Rhonda looked away for a minute, then brought her gaze back to Kate. "It's too bad nobody believed us in the first place."

"I believed you." At Rhonda's skeptical expression Kate added with more emphasis, "I did. Ask anyone."

"Really?" Her defensiveness vanishing, Rhonda looked as though she wanted, more than anything, to believe Kate.

"Really." Kate walked over and hugged her friend. "I'm glad you're back, Rhonda. I knew you didn't do it." Rhonda returned her hug, and after a moment Kate asked, "Is Jason in?"

"Yes. In his office." As Kate turned in that direction, Rhonda called her name.

"Yes?"

"Watch your step. The mayor took a big hunk out of him this morning. Seems the city council wants someone to blame and they want it quick." The hint of smugness on Rhonda's face annoyed Kate. She couldn't deny that her friend had a basis for her antagonism toward Jason, but it was also true that Jason had plenty of reason to believe that Rhonda and Harry had engineered the Chuck E. appearances. Deciding not to pick up that issue, Kate simply thanked Rhonda, then went to Jason's door, rapped lightly and opened it.

"Good morning!" she said cheerfully. She wanted to launch immediately into her apology, but the new information forced her to change her plans.

He stood, back to the door, looking out his dirty window. From behind him Kate could see he was watching a squirrel run up a tree.

"Did you come to gloat?" He didn't turn around, just continued watching.

Kate winced, but she knew she deserved his sarcasm. "No."

"Oh?" He stayed at the window, still virtually ignoring her.

"I came to apologize."

"There isn't any need, Kate." How like her to apologize even though she was the one who was wronged. A small surge of anger caused him to shudder. He didn't want her insincere apologies. "I'm the one who should apologize."

"No, you aren't," she said, walking over and taking his hand.

Her fingers were smooth and warm, and suddenly he realized how cold he was. Deathly cold. He felt warmer from her touch, from the weak sense of joy it created. Then it quickly vanished. In the movies this was the point where the hero and heroine fell tearfully into each other's arms and kissed.

"I know now that you were right," she told him.

"Thank you, Kate," he said weakly. When he saw her puzzled expression, a pinprick of pain stabbed through the fog surrounding his emotions. Clearly this wasn't what she'd expected. She'd expected and wanted that scene from the movies.

He wanted it, too. But a letter awaited his signature, and he needed to get to it.

He untangled his hand from hers and moved away. "I don't mean to rush you, but I have a lot to do today."

Kate's mouth tightened into a grim smile, and he knew she had recognized the brush-off. "I understand," she said. "One gets a lot done staring out a window."

She started for the door, but upon reaching it, she glanced down at the printer on his dented metal credenza. A letter jutted from it, and she read it without attempting to pretend she wasn't. Finished, she looked back at him.

"What's this all about, Jason?" Kate was stunned by the vague, formal resignation letter. Jason wasn't really leaving. She knew he was still angry with her, could tell by the rigid set of his back and the shutters on his eyes, but she'd never thought this was an ending.

"You were right, Kate. I'm the reason for the sabotage." He laughed, but it was an ugly, derisive bark, not the rich thunder Kate had grown to love. "Someone hates me so much that they were willing to destroy the station to get rid of me."

He moved to his chair and sat down, slumping. Kate noticed for the first time that he was wearing his business suit. It was wrinkled, and a stain that looked like coffee marred his white shirt. His tie was loosely knotted somewhere around the third buttonhole. She recognized the signs. He was deeply depressed, and she had a feeling there was more to this than a resignation letter.

"So we'll be hunting for work together," Kate said with a breeziness she didn't feel. She sat down, too, determined to talk this out. "After all, didn't you say I'm a candidate for layoff?"

"Not if your series is successful." His voice sounded leaden, disinterested.

"After yesterday it might be turned down," Kate replied. "The outtakes may have prejudiced the council against it, and with today's commotion I doubt they've even looked at it. Besides, what about the studio rental program you were working on? Without you Channel Seven will go bankrupt."

"Woody will see it through. And once your project goes into syndication the financial problems will get better."

"So you're going to quit without a fight? Just like that?" she asked, not knowing what else to say. Jason seemed so remote and unfeeling. She felt as if she was talking to a stranger. She wanted to shake him, bring him back to the world, but wasn't sure she could reach him.

"Fight for what? Don't you see how destructive I am? You were right last night, you know. You were getting along fine without me. Everyone was." He didn't look at her while he talked; he simply held his hands limply in his lap and stared down at them.

"But I love you, Jason. What about us? Tommy?" How could he leave them? she wanted to ask. And a desire to fall to her knees and beg him to stay almost overwhelmed her, but she fought it back, nearly trembling from the effort.

"I don't deserve you or the happiness you've given me. I love you, too, Kate, but I'm no good for you."

The indifference in his tone nearly undid Kate. Suddenly her frustration transformed to anger. "Why don't you let me be the judge of that?" she snapped, trying to battle her anger.

"I think I'm in a better position to judge than you are." Jason's voice was even, as if was talking about the weather instead of their future.

"Bull!" Kate jumped to her feet, putting her hands on her hips, and leaned over him. "Everyone tells me what's good for me, even you. Well, I'll tell you one thing, Jason Brock. You might not be willing to fight but, by God, I am. This isn't over, and don't for one minute think it is."

With that she spun around and marched out the door, leaving it open behind her, her anger already transforming into hot tears.

Jason got up and shut it behind her. When he came to Channel Seven, offices had always been left open. Nowadays, if he stood in the lobby, he'd see nothing but closed doors.

He had certainly left his mark, barreling in here with his network ways, and he'd caused irreparable damage. But perhaps it wasn't truly irreparable. Not if he left.

"The purpose is to get rid of him"—so said the note the mayor found tacked to his office door, demanding the resignation of Jason Brock. For the past hour Jason had searched his soul and realized that he'd brought the events of the past few days on himself. He was widely disliked, and it was because he put people last. Always had.

It wasn't as if no one had ever told him so. Beth had done so often. His very first argument with Kate had been on that very subject.

He and Woody had agreed on two weeks to allow a replacement search. Two weeks to get his desk in order. Two weeks to allow Jason to find another job someplace else, far away from Kate Gregory.

Lord, that was going to be the hardest part. He didn't think he could bear to see the pain she was trying so hard to cover. Even more, could he bear knowing he would never laugh with her, or hold her in his arms again?

And what about Tommy? The baseball season wasn't over for several weeks. Who would lead his team to a winning season? How would he react to losing yet another man in his life?

This was best, though. After the ugly meeting with Woody, he'd searched hard for the truth about himself, and found it. It was uglier than Woody's request and had almost devastated him.

He had neglected Beth, almost forced her into infidelity. And Stacey, too. He thought of the little things he'd done for and with Kate—helping her filet fish, picking up things in Tommy's room, carrying glasses down from the loft. He'd never done those things for Beth. True, she wasn't the woman Kate was, but she hadn't deserved his indifference, the same indifference he'd lived with for most of his childhood. He knew the pain of that and shouldn't have inflicted it on his wife—or his child.

Where would he go from here? He almost didn't care, and thought it was too bad he couldn't leave himself behind. Because no matter where he landed, his guilt would go with him. It was his forever.

He realized how much he'd hoped for with Kate and Tommy. So much. It was a miracle that Kate loved him. He didn't deserve that love and wasn't going to take the chance of abusing it. What a fool he'd been. As he slumped back onto his chair, he wondered why he'd ever thought that his Aunt Phyllis had been wrong. He was, despite all his efforts to prove otherwise, a failure, after all.

KATE WANTED to go home, throw herself onto her bed, pound on a pillow and let all her grief and rage pour out. Instead, she hurried past Rhonda, entered her office and closed the door. Only then did she let the tears spill over.

Why? Why? The cry echoed in her head. If only she hadn't gotten so angry at him over Rhonda and Harry.

Over Tommy. Or used his tormented confession against him by flinging that ugly accusation about his daughter's birthday. If she'd done things differently—

She ran through their disagreements, looking for some clue, something she might use to turn the situation around. Nothing surfaced except the horrible feeling that this was all because of something she'd done.

Eventually her tears slowed down, her rage and grief ebbed, and she was left with a gaping emptiness. But with the emptiness came reason.

Yes, she'd been wrong. But so had Jason. They had worked out their differences before. She was certain he loved her. Therefore he was leaving in spite of her, not because of her.

His letter had stated that he was leading the station into a direction it didn't want to go and felt KZET would be better off with someone else. Double talk, that was what the letter was. Pure double talk. So what was the real reason? There had to be one. And she had to find out what it was. She got up, marched out of her office and went directly into Woody's.

"Why is Jason leaving?" she demanded.

Woody looked up, obviously shocked by her tone. "Why don't you sit down and stay a while, Kate?" he suggested dryly.

Kate nervously brushed her hair back from her face. "I guess I did come on a little strong."

"Yeah. We're all jumpy these days. But there's no sense keeping you in the dark. It will be out soon enough, anyway. The grapevine around this place is too efficient." He gestured for Kate to sit down. "I take it you've heard that Chuck E. turned up again."

When Kate nodded, Woody went on. "The mayor considered this the last straw. After Rhonda and Harry were caught with the tape, he assured the city council that these episodes were over. When Chuck appeared this morning, it left him with egg all over his face. He stormed in here almost before daybreak, looking for a fall guy."

"Jason?" Kate nearly whispered the name.

"Jason," Woody repeated. "His unpopularity with the staff has earmarked him."

"But Jason didn't do this, Woody. Even if he leaves, it won't stop."

"That's what I told George, and after a bit I calmed him down. He left in a better mood than when he came. I thought we had it handled." Woody toyed with a wooden pencil in his hand, then blew out a breath in obvious frustration. "Not five minutes later George calls me. Seems someone had tacked a note on the city hall door. Fire Jason and this all stops."

"Oh, Lord." Kate's chest constricted. Who could hate Jason that much, enough to jeopardize the jobs of all their co-workers and the very company that paid their salary?

"I had to tell Jason myself. I hated that..." Woody's voice trailed off. "He took it well. Too well. He seems...I don't know, Kate...disassociated or something. He worries me. I think he's about to snap."

"Snap?"

"Yeah." Abruptly Woody bent the pencil. It broke with a pop, and Kate flinched at the sound. "You know, snap." Kate suddenly realized that Woody was deeply angry.

"We can't let it happen." Kate leaned forward, ready to do battle. "We've got to do something. What about the idea of putting an investigator on the payroll?"

"I ran that by the mayor and he vetoed it." Throwing the broken pencil into the trash can, Woody stood. "With

Jason's resignation this thing will stop, Kate. George isn't interested in finding out who did it anymore.''

"I suppose not.'' Kate got up, too. "But, damn it, Woody, it's not fair!''

"No," Woody agreed, "it isn't.''

As Kate left Woody's office, her mind returned to her original thought. Somebody had to do something.

Back at her desk she pulled out the equipment sign-on logs. She and Woody were supposed to review them daily, but it was a monumental task because of the volume of activity. It had been her habit to check for frequency of access only but now she decided to check times, also. If the saboteur was, indeed, accessing the equipment between sign-off and sign-on, it would show up right away.

A few minutes later she sighed in exasperation. Yes, the equipment was being accessed after midnight, but with various codes. She checked the code list and found that Harry, Jason, Steve, Amy and Rhonda had all logged in at one time or the other. In fact, one of the codes was Woody's. Somehow the security of the list had been compromised.

Desolate, she leaned back into her chair, not knowing what to do next. She started reviewing the events since Jason's arrival and instantly got an idea that renewed her energy. She stood up and walked into the lobby, straight to Rhonda's desk.

"Who told you that Jason wanted to fire Steve Karako?'' she demanded.

CHAPTER SIXTEEN

KATE INSERTED her key in the lock. It slipped in noiselessly, and she carefully opened the back door to the production wing. Wearing dark clothes and soundless tennis shoes, she felt like a cat burglar as she stepped inside and hurried to the studio. Her plan was to hide in the previewing booth.

Slipping into the booth and leaving the door slightly cracked, she settled in a spot that give her a clear view of the animator console and waited.

And waited.

Her eyelids grew heavy, and several times she caught herself about to slip off her chair. The nap she'd taken after work simply wasn't enough to let her stay awake all night, especially through such a tedious wait. She blew out a breath of air as she reviewed the facts. The saboteur might never show up. His note had said that once Jason resigned the episodes would stop. Maybe he meant it.

Her mind gnawed at the problem. She suspected there was more to this sabotage than discrediting Jason, although she had no solid reasons for thinking that, at least not until this afternoon. What she'd learned from Rhonda had been very enlightening and had given her an angle she hadn't considered before. The only reason she hadn't made an immediate accusation was because she couldn't find a motive, and premature action might be worse than doing nothing.

Well, if her vigil succeeded and she caught the culprit in the act, she wouldn't need a motive. She stretched, then settled back in her chair, prepared to wait some more.

At four in the morning she gave up. She drove home in the darkness, slipping quietly past the baby-sitter, who was sleeping on the couch. The girl had agreed to stay at the house for the next two weeks and keep an eye on Tommy while Kate worked this problem out. As she climbed into her bed, weary and discouraged, Kate wondered what the baby-sitter had concluded about her nightly excursions and hoped the girl kept her promise to remain silent about them. Kate wasn't certain that this crazy scheme was even going to work, but if her presence at the station became known, her plan would surely fail.

Whoever was behind this was smart, but even the smartest people make mistakes, and this thought comforted Kate as she drifted into a heavy slumber.

A week later, sluggish from lack of sleep, Kate looked over at her son, who huddled against the car seat, arms folded angrily around his body, face twisted into an expression of disgust.

"I'm going to look like a nerd, Mom. Only nerds wear glasses."

Kate wanted to groan. Her nighttime activities were taking their toll, and she was so tired that even this short trip taxed her energy. She struggled to be patient with Tommy. After all, what young boy wanted glasses? "What you wear doesn't make you a nerd, Tommy."

"Yes, it does. You just don't understand."

This was getting her nowhere. As promised, his battery of tests had been administered the day after she'd given permission, and Tommy had been diagnosed as having Scotopic Sensitivity Syndrome—an inability to process light waves adequately. Kate had been relieved to

learn that the disability could be easily corrected with
special glasses, but Tommy hadn't seen it quite that way
and hadn't stopped complaining since.

Now, as they drove to pick up his glasses, his complaints were reaching a crescendo, while Kate's patience
was at an all-time low. She tried again. "You'll only have
to wear them when you read." She suddenly got an inspi-
ration, amazed that her foggy brain could even come up
with a new idea. "They're tinted. They look almost like
sunglasses."

Tommy looked slightly less disgusted and straightened
up a little. "They do?"

"Sure do, kiddo." She reached over to ruffle his hair.

He gave her a warning look. "You can't kid me out of
this, Mom." But now a wry grin toyed about his lips.
"You're telling the whole truth?"

"Promise."

The repugnance disappeared. "That might be cool, ya
know. Wearing sunglasses inside. I could make that cool."

"If anyone could, it's you." They were approaching the
optometrist shop, which was located in a strip center, and
Kate pulled into a parking place, noticing that Tommy still
looked wary.

Without much enthusiasm he followed her inside where
a clerk greeted them. Kate told him why they were there.
The young man went to a cabinet and pulled the glasses
out of a drawer.

As soon as Tommy saw them, his face brightened.
"Wow! Blue glasses. That's rad!" The man behind the
counter smiled.

"Thought you were getting granny glasses, did you?"
He pulled out a soft cloth and polished the lenses as he
spoke. Walking from behind the counter, he directed

Tommy to a chair in front of a small table with a mirror. "Put these on and let's see how they work."

Hesitantly Tommy slipped the glasses on, adjusting the dark aviator frame over his ears. He stared into the mirror, tilting his head in several direction, then a wide smile broke his tense face. He looked up at Kate, eyes gleaming behind the tinted lenses. "These are rad, Mom. I look like Tom Cruise. All the guys at school will want them."

"Yeah, they're rad, Tommy. Real rad," Kate said, heaving a sigh of relief. One obstacle overcome.

Tommy shot her a quizzical look at her choice of words, and Kate smiled weakly at his obvious double standard. She wished she had more enthusiasm, but the unproductiveness of her nightly vigil, the knowledge that her job was insecure and Jason's impending departure all caused her to feel heavy and dull. What was worse, Jason went out of his way to avoid her. Still coaching Tommy's team, he came and went with very few words. Even Tommy had noticed and had asked why Jason was acting that way.

"Can you read?" The clerk's question brought Kate's attention back to the present, and she watched as he handed Tommy a card with printing on it.

Tommy took the card apprehensively. He looked down and became very still. "B...Q...T...R." he spoke the letters slowly, then quickened his pace. "A,L,M,G." He stopped speaking, his eyes running down to the text. "When men come to that—no, this—place..."

Tommy looked at Kate, his face full of awe. "Mom," he said, his voice hushed, almost reverent, "the letters don't move anymore."

Tears of joy rushed to Kate's eyes, and she bent over and hugged Tommy tightly. "Oh, Tommy, I'm so glad."

"Aw, Mom, don't get mushy on me." Tommy squirmed out of her grasp, and despite her inner pain Kate smiled widely. It was a miracle.

Tommy avidly returned to reading the card while Kate went to the counter to pay the clerk. "This is so wonderful," she said, still blinking back tears of relief. "I thought he'd have to fight his disability his whole life."

"I did a research paper on dyslexia last year," the clerk said, writing up the invoice as he talked. "These glasses are a real breakthrough. They can't help everyone, but Tommy's one of the lucky kids."

"Thank God," Kate said.

"Do you have anything else to read?" Tommy called from the table.

"Sure do. Come on over here." The clerk smiled at Tommy, clearly enjoying his helping role.

Tommy bounded across the room as the clerk pulled out a cardboard-bound book with a picture of a horse on the cover.

"Oh, boy, horses. Someday Mom is going to buy me a horse, aren't you, Mom?" Tommy looked up at Kate with a mischievous grin as he took the volume from the clerk.

At Kate's skeptical expression Tommy laughed, then looked down at the colorful book. Kate felt lighthearted as she watched her son reading the cover.

"The Black Sta...Sta...Stalon. Is that it?"

"Close. *The Black Stallion*," the clerk corrected. "It's one of my favorite books. I think you'll like it. Take it."

"I can have it?"

"Sure can. It's yours."

"Gosh, thanks." Tommy looked in awe at the small, cheaply bound book in his hand, as though it were a precious gem. Kate hadn't seen Tommy look so delighted since he had received his Nintendo game. Slowly he opened the cover, then walked to a couch by the door. "I'll wait for you here, Mom," he called, immediately burying his face in the book.

Kate took her receipt from the clerk, then turned to get Tommy. Happiness swelled within her as she saw him concentrating intensely. Occasionally he mouthed the words as he read but, by God, he was reading and apparently enjoying every minute.

"Tommy, we have to go now."

"Oh, yeah." He closed the book with unmistakable reluctance.

"I can read, Mom. I can't wait to tell Jason. Are all books this good? It's a hot story. There's this beautiful black stallion and this kid, see. And they're on this ship..."

As they drove, Tommy told Kate everything he'd read in those few short minutes on the couch. And, Kate couldn't help but notice, even though the book was closed on his lap, Tommy wore the glasses all the way home. But his one simple statement had punctured her shaky happiness.

I can't wait to tell Jason. Tommy had gotten so attached, and Kate hadn't yet told him that Jason was leaving. It was premature. If her "stakeout" proved productive, then Jason wouldn't leave at all. But Kate's confidence was slipping. There were only four nights left.

As much as her own heart ached at the thought of losing Jason, the ache doubled when she considered Tommy's pain. The men he loved always seemed to leave him, and she didn't know how he would react at losing yet another.

She reached over and smoothed his hair. "I love you, kiddo," she said, realizing her throat was tight.

"I love you, too, Mom," Tommy replied, smiling brightly.

"ANOTHER RUN!" Jason glanced over his shoulder at Kate. "Did you get it?" he asked crisply, careful to remain businesslike. The flash of pain he saw in her eyes as she nodded hurt him, and he looked quickly away. How much pain he caused. Too much. She was going to be better off without him, he reminded himself.

Tommy was up next and hit a homer with bases loaded. The crowd of parents cheered outrageously, and Jason felt himself drawn into the excitement. The Indians were going to win this game and undoubtedly the season. It was too bad Jason wouldn't be around to see the final game.

It really didn't matter. Even if they lost that game, the Indians were far enough ahead that the championship was theirs. Jason wasn't needed, but right now his heart filled with pride at the team's home run—Tommy's home run.

He moved in front of the dugout opening and held out his hand as Tommy went in. "Atta boy," he said, receiving Tommy's energetic slap. "Outstanding hit."

Tommy smiled, then went up and down the line of seated boys, slapping each one's hand as he passed. Finished, he sat on the bench, but only for a moment. Getting up, he walked to the gate and stood beside Jason. "Did my mom tell you about my glasses?"

She hadn't, but Jason lied. "Yes, she did. But why don't you tell me, too."

"They're real neat. They have blue glass. But the best part is I can read. I'm reading the coolest book. *The Black Stallion*. Have you read it?"

Jason shook his head. He hadn't overcome his reading problem until he was a teenager, a little late for Walter

Farley's horse stories. "But I remember lots of my friends talking about it. Is it good?"

"Yeah!" Tommy's eyes lit up. "I didn't know reading could be fun." Then the boy's expression became serious. "I still read real slow, but the words don't look like ants anymore. You were right. I have a kind of dyslexia. They call it Soo...Scotop..."

"Scotopic Sensitivity Syndrome?" In his work with the literacy council Jason had heard about it.

"That's it. Grandpa has it, too, or at least he thinks he does."

"Your grandfather has dyslexia?" Tommy's words hit Jason with a wallop, bringing with them the answer to Sam's odd behavior the night Jason had talked with him about Tommy's reading problems. His mind became fuzzy as he went over all the ramifications of Tommy's announcement. "When did you find that out?"

"Last week. He told me how I had to cooperate with the testing people. He says he can't read because he tried to hide his problem all his life. He doesn't want that to happen to me." Tommy touched Jason's arm. "Thank you, Jason."

The touch brought Jason back into focus. "For what?" he asked.

"Grandpa said you talked to him and that's the reason he knew I needed to have the testing done." A wide smile crossed Tommy's face. "You know how Grandpa is about psychologists. But he was wrong. They aren't really that bad."

Jason wanted to say something but couldn't speak over the lump in his throat. For over a week he had been berating himself about his visit to Sam, thinking it had done nothing but make the situation worse. Now Tommy was telling him that it had helped, that it had changed his life.

The crowed roared, interrupting their conversation, and Jason looked away, grateful for the diversion.

"Joey Crogan hit a homer, too!" Tommy cheered along with the crowd and scrambled back into the dugout.

Jason turned toward the bleachers. Rhonda and Harry sat beside Kate, holding hands as they talked with her. They must have arrived while Jason was occupied with Tommy. During their mutual suspension, those two had revealed feelings for each other that they'd kept hidden for a long time and, according to the Channel Seven grapevine, were now openly dating. That was another thing that had turned out to be a cloud with a silver lining. Jason waved when Harry caught his eye, and Harry returned the wave enthusiastically. Even Rhonda mustered up a reserved little salute.

Something shifted in his mind—a new perspective emerged—and he realized how he'd been judging all his actions from a limited viewpoint. What seemed a disaster had turned into a triumph, and he'd been so busy flagellating himself that he hadn't even known about it.

True, he'd made some huge mistakes, and he'd live with the results of them for the rest of his life. But guilt and self-punishment weren't going to bring Stacey back, as much as he wished they could.

So what had he been doing? Why had he just given up? He wanted Kate to be his wife and he wanted Tommy as a son. He wanted his job in this small, backward town. It was about time he did something to make sure he got all those things.

But what?

KATE SHIFTED in her chair inside the stuffy previewing booth and looked at her watch. Only two o'clock. Discouragement weighed heavily on her, along with the fatigue that had become her constant companion these days. Split-shift sleeping wasn't getting the job done, and tonight was even worse because she'd skipped some sleep to go to Tommy's game.

She could bear her aching body, though, if only she felt she was making progress. The days were ticking off relentlessly. This was Tuesday, Jason's last day would be on Friday, and Chuck E. hadn't made an appearance since his resignation. Maybe she was wasting time and energy waiting every night for something that would never happen.

Her bladder was uncomfortably full, and she shifted again. She always hated to leave the booth in case someone showed up in her absence. But if nothing had happened during the past evenings, what made her think it would happen during the few moments she'd be gone?

Deciding nothing would, she got up and silently walked out of the studio to the nearest bathroom.

A few minutes later, feeling much relieved, she came out of the bathroom. But returning to the studio made her more uneasy than leaving. She had no way of knowing if someone had entered during her absence, and the glass windows on all the rooms made hiding impossible.

She moved slowly, peering through the windows as she approached each room. Nearly to the studio, she began relaxing. It looked as if this would be another uneventful night. The studio was coming up next, and she stopped to peer inside before moving in front of its window, fully expecting the room to be empty like all the others.

Her heart tripped when she saw Chuck E. Squirrel strutting across the animator's overhead monitor. The moment she'd prayed for was here! She edged forward expectantly to see who was sitting at the console, hoping that her suspicions were correct.

HE COULDN'T very well just walk in the front door. He might be seen. So Jason gingerly made his way through the darkness to the side door of the production wing. He had meant to arrive earlier but had fallen asleep on his couch, awakening only a little while ago and rushing over here. As he slipped on a rock, he questioned the wisdom of his decision to launch this investigation.

What made him think there would be anything to discover? After all, the culprit had asked for his head and gotten it. What would be gained by continuing the sabotage?

All he knew was that he had to do something, anything. He wasn't just going to leave everything he loved without putting up a fight.

But what if he failed? He had to consider that possibility. He couldn't just hang around Lakeview doing odd jobs and give up what he was trained to do. So where did that leave him and Kate?

Abandoning the question for another time, although not dismissing the idea that he could ask Kate to go with him, Jason pulled his keys from his pocket. The door was just a few feet away.

Once there he quickly unlocked it, went inside and pulled it shut behind him.

"WHAT ARE YOU DOING, Carlton?" Kate stood in the doorway of the studio, chest pounding in outrage. She wasn't surprised. Ever since Rhonda had admitted that Carlton had told her about Steve Karako, she'd suspected he was the culprit. Her only doubt had been that he lacked motive.

But motive was no longer necessary. His actions confirmed his guilt.

Carlton whirled toward the sound of her voice, and his mouth opened in shock. "Kate!" He whirled back, shut down the overhead monitor, then turned to look at her. "I was just catching up on some backlog."

"No, you weren't. I've been watching you for several minutes." His lies sickened her. "You're producing those Chuck E. Squirrel segments!"

"What are you doing here?" Carlton questioned arrogantly, narrowing his eyes into slits, apparently having decided to go on the offensive.

"Waiting for you to slip up."

"You almost caught me once before, you know," Carlton said with a sly grin. "That day you came looking for Amy. I was going to put Chuck into that wildlife program, but you were hunting for the tape, so I did something different. Did you like the AIDS special?" he asked with an ugly laugh.

"Did you steal the wisecracks from Harry?" Kate snapped through the tight fist of anger gripping her. Carlton had come close to shattering several lives, and Kate was appalled that he seemed proud of his handiwork.

"That dodo?" Carlton's sneer twisted his face into a hideous mask, suddenly revealing the anger he must have been covering for aeons. "I don't need him. I'm smart enough to come up with my own lines. Too smart for this place. But no one appreciates me, so I decided to show everyone just what I'm made of. They would never have caught me. When they started checking the tapes before airing, I just went off-line." He pointed to a VCR on the editing console. "I used that player right there."

Kate listened in horror, wondering why Carlton was telling her all this. It almost seemed as if he wanted to flaunt his cleverness.

"When they started printing out the switching programs, I beat them again. All that was needed was a command not to print. The instructions were there all along. They just couldn't see them."

"You were behind the damage done to the transformer, too, weren't you?" Kate asked. Although she was stunned by Carlton's admissions, another part of her was gratified to have these long-standing questions answered.

Carlton nodded smugly. "But the guy took off in the middle. Good help is so hard to find, isn't it?"

Kate ignored the question. "How did you get everyone's access codes?"

Carlton put his hands in his pockets, and the sound of keys jingling solved that puzzle. "I have keys to everything, Kate. Every time someone left keys lying around I had them copied. I even have a key to your house." He laughed again, and Kate felt a chill rush through her body. It suddenly occurred to her that he might be confessing only because he wasn't planning to give her the opportunity to tell anyone else. For the first time since entering the room she felt fear.

Apprehensively she crossed the room, heading for the telephone. "I'm calling Woody, Carlton. It's all over." She picked up the receiver.

"No, it isn't," Carlton replied calmly, adding fuel to Kate's suspicion. Her mouth went dry as he rose smoothly from his chair and was beside her in a shot. Grabbing her hand cruelly, he slammed it back into the phone cradle. The impact stung Kate's finger. With a yelp she loosened her grip on the receiver.

"Stop it!" she tried to yell, but her voice choked and the words came out in a feeble squeak. Little fingers of fear crept up her spine as she stared into Carlton's cold, purposeful eyes, now knowing full well he had no intentions of letting her get away alive. *That's ridiculous,* her mind insisted. *People didn't get murdered in Lakeview!* But her intuition knew she was wrong.

"I can't let you tell, Kate." Carlton smiled as he spoke—a twisted, angry smile, and Kate finally accepted that her intuition was right.

Tremors suddenly weakened her legs, but with an act of will she began inching away from him. She didn't move far. Carlton grabbed her wrists and pinned her against the table in front of the tape storage rack. For a moment terrible waves of terror froze her to the spot, rendering her unable to fight. *No!* her mind screamed, jolting her out of her trance, and she jerked her arms, trying to pull them from Carlton's painful grasp. Her elbow struck a cassette, and it fell with a clatter to the floor, the cacophony nearly unnerving her.

Still cruelly holding her wrists, Carlton arched her body over the table until her head was inches away from the cassette rack. Suddenly he released his grip, and with a rush of relief Kate raised her arms to push him away. But he already had his hands tightly around her throat, thumbs pushing against her windpipe.

Kate arched her body farther until her back screeched in protest. She pounded her fists against Carlton's shoulder as his thumbs continued to cut off her breath. She couldn't breathe... her lungs screamed for air... and Carlton's thumbs pressed harder... harder. Then her flailing arm struck a cassette. Instinctively her hand closed around it as though it were a lifeline. With all the force she had left, she swung her arm and slammed the tape against Carlton's head.

JASON MOVED CAREFULLY through the dim hallway, trying not to make any noise. His shoes seemed to leave thunderous footfalls on the linoleum surface. Getting ready to take yet another cautious step, he heard a clatter in the production studio.

Someone was in there! Jason moved more quickly, still trying not to cause any sound. Then he heard the scream and, throwing caution to the wind, he broke into a run.

Nearly skidding into the studio, he saw Carlton gripping Kate by the neck, shaking her viciously. Jason lunged forward and tore the man away, outraged that he even dared touch her. Kate staggered backward, nearly losing her balance before steadying herself against the table.

Carlton spun around to face Jason, fists up, ready to fight. Jason hoped he would use them. Nothing would feel better than smashing his fist against Carlton's nose despite the man's puny size. But, instead, Carlton lowered his fists, apparently realizing he was confronting a taller, more muscular person than the woman he'd just been terrorizing. He backed up warily until the very table over which he'd tried to choke Kate blocked his progress.

"Call the police, Kate," Jason said evenly, standing between Carlton and the door, legs spread, ready to leap if Carlton moved. His scar throbbed as a flush of anger flooded his face.

Kate picked up the phone. A few minutes later she walked to Jason's side. "The police are on their way. And so is Woody." She watched Carlton apprehensively, as if uncertain what he might do next.

"I've lost everything," Carlton mumbled. "Everything. Because of you!" He raised his head and glared at

Jason with such naked hate that Jason's blood chilled. How could anyone hate that much? "If you hadn't come, I would have been station manager by now."

"Woody's the manager, Carlton. You never stood a chance." Kate stared at the man in amazement. What delusions of grandeur went through that Machiavellian mind of his? "And what does this have to do with Jason?"

"Woody's job has been on the line for a long time." For a moment satisfaction replaced Carlton's angry expression, then vanished as the hate returned. "With him gone the job would've been mine. Then Jason came, bringing all these plans to turn the station around. They were working, too. Pretty soon Woody's job would have been secure. Where would I have been then?"

Jason gaped at Carlton in astonishment, relaxing his guarded stance. With the police on the way Jason was certain Carlton knew it was now futile to attempt escape. Besides, this incredible confession had Jason's mind reeling. How could anyone think that any job was worth such extreme actions? The man had almost committed murder!

"So I planned to get rid of you," Carlton continued, his eyes riveted on Jason. "You have a reputation for not tolerating carelessness, so I did the first squirrel episode to force you to fire someone, thinking the employees would get up in arms and demand that you go. When that didn't work, I told Rhonda how you had demanded we fire Steve, figuring she would pass the news around and bring about the same effect." Carlton pointed an accusing finger at Jason. "Why the hell didn't you stay where you came from?"

"But I was already leaving," Jason said in a choked whisper. "Why were you going to do another episode?"

"To make sure they canned Woody's hind end, too, that's why."

Kate looked over at Jason, who stared at Carlton in stunned confusion. Carlton's confession horrified her almost more than the close call she'd just escaped, and she wondered how he'd managed to deceive so many people for so long. Behind this natty fool everyone thought they knew had lain a cold, calculating man who would do anything to get what he wanted.

An inconsequential thought trailed through her hazy mind as she continued to stare at Carlton. It seemed to her that his appearance finally revealed his true self. His hair was in terrible disarray from their struggle, and one of the sleeves of his jacket hung from his shoulder, ripped at the seam.

Had she done that? She couldn't remember.

A siren wailed in the distance, and Carlton's eyes widened. "I'm not going with them!" he shouted, lurching forward and shoving Jason out of his path. As he passed, Jason's hand shot out and caught the torn sleeve. The cloth ripped with a raspy groan as Carlton jerked his arm away and bolted through the door, leaving Jason holding the empty sleeve.

Kate broke into a run, and Jason followed behind, trying to close Carlton's head start. He had headed for the front, and by the time Kate and Jason reached the lobby, the door was wide open, police swarming everywhere. Carlton gave up without a fight and was soon whisked away to a squad car. Woody was there also, having unlocked the door for the police.

For the following half hour the three of them waited around to give their statements. While Kate was being interviewed, Woody approached Jason. "Guess I can tear up that letter now?" he said.

"I'm not sure, Woody." Jason looked over at Kate. "I have some things to work out first."

He saw Woody's gaze follow his own, and when he looked back, the man was smiling. "Well, I think I'll just hold on to it. I have a feeling you'll be sticking around."

Jason wished he felt as confident, but right now he was struggling with his anger. Why had Kate endangered herself this way?

Seeing that the officer had concluded the interview, Jason walked over and took Kate's arm. She looked deathly tired, and he wondered how many nights she'd spent here. "I'll take you home," he said.

"I have to get my purse," she replied wearily. "It's still in the previewing booth."

Kate forced her feet to plod one after the other as she walked beside Jason down what now seemed the world's longest hallway. As much as she wanted to talk about what had happened, about Jason's plans for the future, she was so exhausted that she was fighting nausea. Her head spun and a dull throb behind her ears tormented her. Once inside the studio, she grabbed her purse and turned gratefully back to Jason. "I'm ready," she said wearily.

"Are you sure?" Jason asked coldly.

Kate's head shot up, and she looked into his eyes, totally unprepared for what she saw. They were slits of cold fury. Involuntarily she stepped back. She hadn't expected undying gratitude, but she'd never even imagined this icy rage.

"You could have been killed, Kate! Don't you know that?" Jason's voice began to rise, drowning out the hum of the computer. Kate flinched, more from the volume, than from the meaning of his words. "What the hell were you doing here in the middle of the night?" he roared.

She blinked rapidly as her throat began to thicken. "I...I was—" She couldn't speak. "I'm so tired," she said at last. "I've been here every night since you said you were leaving." The tears broke loose, streaming down her face. Kate gulped, determined to defend herself despite her sobs. "Now you don't have to go! I did it for us," she wailed. "To keep...keep you from leaving.

"I love you, Jason. I...could...couldn't let you go without doing anything about it." She brushed her tears from her face with the backs of her hands, angry now. Angry at Jason, angry at herself. She took a deep breath, only vaguely aware that Jason's expression had softened, that the ice in his eyes had melted. Sinking into a chair, she gave up. What was there left to fight for?

Jason knelt on the floor beside her. Gently he cupped her chin in one hand and brushed away her tears with the other. Her eyes were focused somewhere in the distance, not looking at him. Purposefully, he was certain. Feeling almost unworthy to touch her, he gazed at her streaked face, trying to express his love wordlessly. "You did this for me?"

She nodded, sniffling at the same time.

"Even though you knew you might catch one of your friends in here?"

"Yes." Her gaze flickered in his direction, then returned where it was.

"No one has ever done anything like that for me before," Jason said softly with wonder. He'd always known Kate was special, caring, but he'd never realized she was also courageous and loyal. To a fault, he thought ruefully, as his gaze drifted to the red marks on her throat. They were already starting to darken. He touched one of the marks, wishing he had the power to heal her pain instantly.

She could see him from the corner of her eye, and he was staring at her as if she were some kind of deity. But she was afraid to trust it. He hadn't said anything about staying in Lakeview, about his feelings for her. Maybe he wanted to go. Maybe he didn't love her anymore.

"I'm on my knees, Kate." Jason brushed back her hair.

"So I see," she replied, puzzled.

"Isn't this where I'm supposed to be when I ask you to be my wife?"

"What?" Kate's exhaustion vanished. A smile tugged at her lips, then spread wide. Tears returned, this time happy tears.

"Will you marry me, Kate?" He wasn't smiling. His golden eyes shone with unshed tears, and Kate realized he was afraid she would refuse.

"Yes. Oh, yes!" She saw the exalted smile cross his face as she threw her arms around him.

"I love you, Kate," he whispered against her hair, "and I want to take care of you and Tommy."

"You don't need to, Jason. I just need your love. I can take care of us myself."

"I know," he sighed. "And, actually, you do a pretty good job of taking care of me, too."

He tilted her chin and looked into those exquisite blue eyes, eyes shining with love for him, and realized what a gift she'd given him—to be loved for who he was, not what he did. It was a whole new idea to him. He felt the eternal shadow that had darkened his life lifting, and something cracked inside him with a sweet and tender ache.

When he lowered his head to kiss her, Jason wasn't smiling anymore.

Neither was Kate.

AUTHOR'S NOTE

The glasses prescribed for Tommy Gregory in WALK-
ING ON AIR were developed in 1981 by Helen Irlen of
the Irlen Institute for Perceptual and Learning Disabili-
ties, located in Long Beach, California.

An estimated fifty to sixty percent of all people experiencing dyslexia suffer from Scotopic Sensitivity Syndrome. Their brains have difficulty handling light, and
this difficulty is not detected by normal eye examina-
tions. These glasses, specifically tinted for the wearer,
have produced dramatic improvement. Irlen Clinics are
located throughout the United States.

Following the success of WITH THIS RING, Harlequin cordially invites you to enjoy the romance of the wedding season with

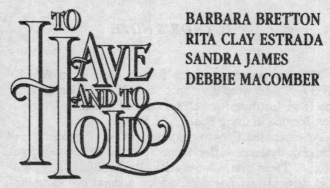

BARBARA BRETTON
RITA CLAY ESTRADA
SANDRA JAMES
DEBBIE MACOMBER

A collection of romantic stories that celebrate the joy, excitement, and mishaps of planning that special day by these four award-winning Harlequin authors.

Available in April at your favorite Harlequin retail outlets.

"GET AWAY FROM IT ALL" SWEEPSTAKES

HERE'S HOW THE SWEEPSTAKES WORKS

NO PURCHASE NECESSARY

To enter each drawing, complete the appropriate Official Entry Form or a 3" by 5" index card by hand-printing your name, address and phone number and the trip destination that the entry is being submitted for (i.e., Caneel Bay, Canyon Ranch or London and the English Countryside) and mailing it to: Get Away From It All Sweepstakes, P.O. Box 1397, Buffalo, New York 14269-1397.

No responsibility is assumed for lost, late or misdirected mail. Entries must be sent separately with first class postage affixed, and be received by: 4/15/92 for the Caneel Bay Vacation Drawing, 5/15/92 for the Canyon Ranch Vacation Drawing and 6/15/92 for the London and the English Countryside Vacation Drawing. Sweepstakes is open to residents of the U.S. (except Puerto Rico) and Canada, 21 years of age or older as of 5/31/92.

For complete rules send a self-addressed, stamped (WA residents need not affix return postage) envelope to: Get Away From It All Sweepstakes, P.O. Box 4892, Blair, NE 68009.

© 1992 HARLEQUIN ENTERPRISES LTD.   SWP-RLS

"GET AWAY FROM IT ALL" SWEEPSTAKES

HERE'S HOW THE SWEEPSTAKES WORKS

NO PURCHASE NECESSARY

To enter each drawing, complete the appropriate Official Entry Form or a 3" by 5" index card by hand-printing your name, address and phone number and the trip destination that the entry is being submitted for (i.e., Caneel Bay, Canyon Ranch or London and the English Countryside) and mailing it to: Get Away From It All Sweepstakes, P.O. Box 1397, Buffalo, New York 14269-1397.

No responsibility is assumed for lost, late or misdirected mail. Entries must be sent separately with first class postage affixed, and be received by: 4/15/92 for the Caneel Bay Vacation Drawing, 5/15/92 for the Canyon Ranch Vacation Drawing and 6/15/92 for the London and the English Countryside Vacation Drawing. Sweepstakes is open to residents of the U.S. (except Puerto Rico) and Canada, 21 years of age or older as of 5/31/92.

For complete rules send a self-addressed, stamped (WA residents need not affix return postage) envelope to: Get Away From It All Sweepstakes, P.O. Box 4892, Blair, NE 68009.

© 1992 HARLEQUIN ENTERPRISES LTD.   SWP-RLS

"GET AWAY FROM IT ALL"

Brand-new Subscribers-Only Sweepstakes

OFFICIAL ENTRY FORM

This entry must be received by: April 15, 1992
This month's winner will be notified by: April 30, 1992
Trip must be taken between: May 31, 1992—May 31, 1993

YES, I want to win the Caneel Bay Plantation vacation for two. I understand the prize includes round-trip airfare and the two additional prizes revealed in the BONUS PRIZES insert.

Name _____

Address _____

City _____

State/Prov._____ Zip/Postal Code_____

Daytime phone number _____
(Area Code)

Return entries with invoice in envelope provided. Each book in this shipment has two entry coupons — and the more coupons you enter, the better your chances of winning!
© 1992 HARLEQUIN ENTERPRISES LTD.   1M-CPN

"GET AWAY FROM IT ALL"

Brand-new Subscribers-Only Sweepstakes

OFFICIAL ENTRY FORM

This entry must be received by: April 15, 1992
This month's winner will be notified by: April 30, 1992
Trip must be taken between: May 31, 1992—May 31, 1993

YES, I want to win the Caneel Bay Plantation vacation for two. I understand the prize includes round-trip airfare and the two additional prizes revealed in the BONUS PRIZES insert.

Name _____

Address _____

City _____

State/Prov._____ Zip/Postal Code_____

Daytime phone number _____
(Area Code)

Return entries with invoice in envelope provided. Each book in this shipment has two entry coupons — and the more coupons you enter, the better your chances of winning!
© 1992 HARLEQUIN ENTERPRISES LTD.   1M-CPN